HALEY GALLANT

A VOW OF BLOOD AND SAP

WHISPERS OF THE FLORA: BOOK ONE

Hylosis Publishing LLC
hylosis.pub

ISBN eBook: 9798894030203
ISBN Paperback: 9798894030210
ISBN Hardcover: 9798894030227

To my husband.

Thank you for being my partner in everything.

ACKNOWLEDGMENTS

I want to offer a quick thank you to a few of the people who have helped make this book a reality. Thank you to my husband for always supporting my writing and all my dreams. Thank you to my parents for encouraging me to write since I was very young. Thank you to Jotan for giving me this amazing opportunity to bring A Vow of Blood and Sap to life. **And thank you to *you*, the reader: you're the reason any of this is possible.**

TABLE OF CONTENTS

"MISTAKES HAPPEN,
SOMETIMES FOR NO
FAULT OF YOUR OWN.

IT'S THE
INTENTION
IN YOUR HEART
WHICH TRULY MATTERS."

—PRINCESS VALIA MARTEV

A VOW OF BLOOD AND SAP

CHAPTER ONE
INTRUSION

alia stared out the window at the drizzling rain. The colors of the mountains and trees outside—usually a vibrant green—seemed muted, like someone had smudged a wet sponge across the landscape. The colorful buildings of Avania's capital were equally dimmed.

Valia couldn't blame the rain, though. Even the colors inside her chamber were faded. Ever since her mother and sisters had been killed, nothing had been the same. Not the bright tapestries in her chamber, nor the rich food the chefs prepared, nor even Valia's father.

"Princess?" One of Valia's handmaidens, a pretty girl of thirteen cycles, poked her head around the door. "The king summons you to dinner."

"Thank you, Kaleen. Tell him... I don't feel well." Valia pressed her forehead against the cool glass of the window and turned her gaze away. At first, Valia had hoped she and her father could take solace in each other as the last two surviving members of the Martev family, but that dream had quickly evaporated. All the king wanted to do now was talk about Valia's mother and sisters. He asked Valia to repeat the story of their deaths again and again and analyzed how, if she'd acted just a little quicker, they might have lived. He hardly seemed to care about Valia anymore.

It was too painful.

"Okay, Princess." Her handmaiden retreated, leaving Valia alone again. The wind from the closing door swept the flame away from Valia's candle. She sighed.

Normally, Valia would have pricked her finger and recited a seed spell, the kind of magic she'd been using since she was a child. The candle would have sputtered to life across the room without her getting to her feet.

Yet now, Valia's magic seemed to have deserted her too. She couldn't count the number of times she'd tried to use a spell, even a simple one, to no avail since her family's deaths.

Valia rose to her feet and pattered across the chamber. The flagstones stung with a bitter cold despite the fire in the hearth. She passed the looking glass on her wall, which reflected a woman more worn than she'd ever seen herself before. Her springy dark curls were flat and dull, her bright blue eyes were empty, and her pink cheeks were pale and drawn. Valia bent forward and lit the candle in the fire of the hearth, but it sputtered out with the breeze of the door opening again.

Valia whirled, slightly annoyed now, but it wasn't one of her handmaidens standing in the doorway this time. It was a man. A strange man.

Valia froze. The man looked ordinary enough. He was tall and muscular, with black clothes and short hair. He might have been a palace guard out of uniform, but the edges of his frame seemed blurred somehow.

"Princess?" The man's eyes widened, and he stepped closer. Instinctively, Valia took a large step back.

"Who are you?"

"Come, quickly." The man took another step and reached for Valia's wrist. She pulled away, but not fast enough. His long, strong fingers closed around her, sending a shiver up her arm. His hand was... warm? Solid?

"Let go of me!" Valia tried to yank her hand away, but his grip was firm. "Who are you?!"

"I'm here to bring you home." He pulled her toward the door. "Hurry. I'll explain everything, but first we have to get out of here."

Valia tried to yank her hand away again. She reached into her mind for a spell that would knock this intruder back, sound an alarm for help, *anything*. A spell like that might need more than a simple drop of blood, but Valia was ready to pay the price. Yet, her powers eluded her like slippery eels in the back of her mind.

"Stop fighting me. They'll be here any moment." The intruder sounded genuinely annoyed that Valia had a problem with a stranger dragging her out of her bedchamber. Speaking of which, where *were* her guards? The man was right that they should be here by now. "Princess, your father sent me."

Valia let out an unladylike snort. "My father is down the hall right this moment. He didn't send you."

"Your father isn't down the hall." The man tugged more forcefully on her arm. "Listen to me. We don't have much time. We have to—" The door flew open. Behind it stood one of Valia's guards, a drawn sword in his hand. *Finally.*

"Princess, get back!" Valia ducked as the guard lunged forward, sword extended. The man pivoted out of the way but was forced to release Valia's hand to do so. She tripped backward and made it to the safety of her windowsill as the guard turned toward the man again. From the safety of her windowsill, Valia watched as the intruder grasped a coiled whip that had been secured to his back.

The intruder pivoted away from another strike. He knocked the guard down with a swift kick behind the knee and quickly repositioned to the far side of Valia's sizable chamber. The whip flicked through the air and clipped the guard on the hand. Wincing, the guard lost his grip on his sword, and it clattered to the ground.

The man held firm and swung the whip again in a whistling arc, raking the guard's neck. Blood spurt out from the cut, though in the candlelight, it appeared to Valia as if it were dark blue, almost black. The guard stumbled back. The whip recoiled and struck again in an instant, this time wrapping around the guard's waist. The guard grabbed onto the whip in an attempt to stop its relentless strikes—a fatal mistake. The intruder yanked straight back, pulling the guard into him. In one smooth motion, he drew a dagger from his boot and lunged forward, plunging it upward through the opening beneath the guard's helmet. A bloom of dark blood spilled down the guard's chest plate as he collapsed, motionless.

Valia gasped as she backed further into the corner. She pricked her thumb, ready to fight with whatever magic she could muster. Before she could cast, three more guards poured into the room. Without hesitation, the intruder struck the closest guard. Dark blood leaked from a gash on the guard's face, which seemed to twist like melted candlewax. Valia stared, both horrified and confused. It must have been a trick of the light, as he looked normal just a moment later.

The three guards operated in unison, slowly circling the intruder while holding a defensive stance. As skilled as he seemed to be, he was no match for three royal guards. As he held two of them at a distance, the third burst forward and struck him on the back of the head with the hilt of his sword. The intruder went limp and slumped to the ground.

"Who *is* that?" Valia asked from the windowsill.

One of the guards raised his head. "Princess, this man... has murdered our king," he said. His eyes were like two dark pools, devoid of any emotion. "King Aran was asleep in his room when this man attacked. We can only assume he was trying to kill you next."

"M... my father?" Valia's heart began to race even faster. Even though they hadn't been on good terms recently, her father was the only remaining member of her family. He couldn't be dead. *He couldn't be.*

"It's alright, Princess." One of the guards crossed the room to her and gently placed his hand on her wrist. "We'll keep you safe. You're the last living member of the royal family, after all."

But Valia could hardly understand his words. She only felt his hand on her wrist, just where the intruder had touched her. Where the intruder's hand had been warm and solid, her guard's hand felt cold and insubstantial. There had been that fuzziness around the man's outline, too. And... where was the slain guard? Had two guards already carried him off while she was speaking with the one? Yet, when Valia looked at the spot where his body had been, there was no blood. There was nothing there at all.

Something wasn't right.

Valia watched in silence as the guards hauled the unconscious intruder out of the room. She walked over and inspected his weapons, still lying on the chamber floor. The dagger was ornate, with unfamiliar markings and a dark material embedded in the handle. For how solid it looked, it was light as a feather. And she'd never seen someone use a whip in combat. Unlike the dagger, it was heavier than it looked. Again, there was no blood.

Her mind returned from the mystery of the blood to what the guard had said. Was her father truly dead?

Her heart in her throat, Valia rushed down the hallway and up the stairs to King Aran's chambers. The further she ran from her room, the more her heart pounded and the colder the air grew. She flung open the doors to her father's rooms. She hesitated at the doorway as she looked at the neatly made bed. Her father wasn't in it, living or not. And... hadn't her handmaiden said he was waiting for her at dinner anyway?

CHAPTER TWO
DAYBREAK

he next morning, Avania fell into mourning for its lost king. A single, sad bell tolled across the capital city of Wyra, calling its citizens to the palace. When Valia awoke from the little sleep she managed to get, her handmaiden Kaleen dressed her in black and escorted her to the royal gardens where the ceremonies to mark the death of a monarch were traditionally held. As they walked, Valia's mind replayed the scenes from the night before over and over.

"Kaleen."

"Yes, Princess?"

"I went to find my father last night." Valia bit her lip. "I went to his bedchamber, where the guards said he'd been murdered. But... he wasn't there."

"Oh, Princess." Kaleen laid a cold hand on Valia's shoulder and brought her to a stop. "This kind of thing is normal after a tragedy. Your mind plays tricks on you. Your father was in the dining hall, not in his chambers."

"Oh." Valia shook her head slightly. "I... I must have misheard."

"Yes, Princess." Kaleen nodded in agreement. "Now, focus on the ceremonies today. As the last living member of the royal family, it's your duty to be strong for the whole of Avania."

"I... of course..."

In the gardens, a crowd of Avanian citizens gathered. Kaleen led Valia to the front, where her father lay in an ornate coffin surrounded by a ring of flowers and dancing fluttermoss. There, Valia stood in silence with the rest of the city as King Aran was returned to the Flora.

Valia's mind wandered. She knew she should be in mourning, focused on the tragedy of losing her father, but she couldn't shake the feeling that something was off. Perhaps she was still in shock and desperate to believe that her father might still be alive.

An *illusion*, the intruder had claimed. What if he'd been right? For how long had she been under? And how could it possibly be so detailed? That would take an enormous amount of power. Maybe her mother's and sisters' deaths could be part of it as well? *Wishful thinking.* She steeled herself, remembering her duty to project strength.

As Valia read her father's funeral rights, the man remained in the back of her mind. She needed to see him again. At the very least, she would conduct his interrogation herself and ask him why he had killed the king—*her father.*

"I want to see the man," Valia decided as her nighttime routine was almost concluded.

"A man?" Kaleen looked up from the brush she'd been running through Valia's hair.

"The man. The intruder."

"The man... Princess, surely you don't mean the man who killed our king?"

Valia nodded. "Yes. I need to see him again. I need to talk to him."

"Oh, no. Princess." Kaleen met her eyes in the looking glass with an expression of utmost sympathy. "For what purpose? I don't think that's a good idea. Especially since if you'd gone to dinner with your father, you might have been there to save him. If your powers were working, of course."

Valia's mouth fell open as the words hit her like a blow to the chest. Kaleen had always been kind to her, but now, at her weakest moment, she dares say this. "How can you say that to me?!"

"Princess." Kaleen smiled a little too wide. "I'm merely trying to warn you. He's dangerous. If your powers were working, maybe you'd be able to keep yourself safe. But, as things are..."

The young handmaiden's words only steeled Valia's determination. It was another thing which didn't add up. All Valia's handmaidens had always been friendly and deferential. Especially Kaleen, who had been in her service for several cycles. It didn't make sense that Kaleen spoke to her like this now. It was as if she was trying to make Valia feel worse about her father's death.

After Kaleen stoked the fire, helped Valia into her nightgown, and retired to her own chambers, Valia quietly got up again. She pulled on a fur-lined mantle over her nightdress and peeked out the door. To her surprise, the guard in the hallway was asleep. It was lucky for her in this moment, but such a dereliction of duty was unheard of among the palace guard. Is *this* how a man snuck into the palace?

The man. Valia needed to see him. She went back into her room and grabbed the man's dagger. Without her powers, she would need some protection against him should things go unfavorably. She left her slippers, ignoring the biting cold of the stone beneath her bare feet, and tiptoed silently down the hall.

As Valia slipped through the palace, every guard she came upon was sleeping. Her heart sank; she could no longer ignore something sinister was taking place in the palace.

Although she'd rarely been there before, Valia knew where the man would be held. The dungeons beneath the palace were bleak, inhabited only by the kingdom's worst criminals awaiting execution. Other criminals were generally exiled or, if a proper motivation could be exploited, conscripted by the crown for tasks no one else was willing to do.

Valia crept down the stairs and into the dungeons. The hallway was lit only by flickering candles in wall sconces. A chill radiated from the walls and seeped into Valia's bones.

"Finally, the real Princess Valia. I knew you'd come." The voice drew Valia's attention to a corner cell as she cautiously moved toward it. There he was. He'd been sitting in the corner of the cell, but as she approached, he leaped to his feet with the agility of a skysail sprite.

"You." Valia crossed her arms across her stomach and stepped closer. She *didn't* imagine it; the man's outline really was flickering. "Are you using a spell?"

"What do you mean?"

"It's like you aren't quite here." Valia approached until she stood just outside the bars.

"You see it now, don't you?" The man ran a hand through his tousled hair and stepped closer. Though separated by the bars, they were close enough that Valia could feel the heat radiating from his body. She had to tilt her head back to meet his piercing grey eyes. "But it's not me, it's—"

"Quiet. Did you kill my father?"

"No. Your father is alive and well, Princess. Well... he's alive."

"Don't lie to me. I saw him in his coffin myself."

"Not real. You'll have to keep up." The man ran a hand through his hair again until it stuck almost straight up. It was a striking juxtaposition to the rest of his hard, military appearance.

"An illusion?" Valia's voice sounded unsure to her own ears. "Who is doing it to me? How? Explain." Surely, the sacrifice needed to maintain a spell like this must be deadly to the caster.

"What do you remember about the last day you saw your mother and sisters?" the man asked. Valia was half offended he dare remind her of that awful day and half tired from recounting what had happened to her father, but she decided to indulge his question in light of her current situation. "We were... we were on a picnic." She closed her eyes and searched her mind for details.

Valia sat on a rock on the riverbank and squished wet sand with her toes—a pleasing contrast to the warm sun on her face.

Valia's mother had whisked all her girls away for a daytime retreat out of the blue. None of her girls had ever visited the Garden of Luma, and it was the perfect day to do so. It was a sprawling field of natural starflowers—a material used in floramancy for how it emits light when it blooms. Even during the daytime, the sheer number of them would brighten the area with a soothing glow.

Normally, after a starflower finished its three-day-long bloom, they would quickly wilt and crumble into dust, making way for other types of plants to grow in its place. Fields of them would appear all around Avania, seemingly at random, before completing their cycle and cropping up elsewhere. Except they'd always regrow at the Garden of Luma, too. A special permit was needed to enter the area for common folk, and it was generally reserved for those studying its mysteries.

While basking in the gentle beauty of the garden, they snacked on tomatoes brought from the palace garden and fresh flatbread from a local bakery. Valia's eldest sister sang along with the birds in the trees. The youngest threw rocks into the river. It was a much-needed peace amidst the recent chaos in the region, and the day seemed perfect.

A sudden boom pierced through the sky across the riverbank, followed by sharp sizzle. A man yelled out, and another sound followed. One of their royal escort came sprinting toward them from the direction of the sound. "We're under attack! Protect the—"

Another sound broke out, and cloud of black smoke burst forth from his armor as it collapsed into a pile on the ground. His helmet rolled into the river as Valia and her family looked on in terror.

Valia leaped to her feet, directing her family toward the nearby trees for cover. She readied protective spells, with incantations spilling over her lips as she pledged sacrifices to the Flora.

The rest of their escort closed in around them from every direction, attempting to mount some sort of defense, but one by one they disappeared into clouds of black smoke. Valia and her family stood there, desperately seeking to identify their attacker before they were next.

There was a short moment of silence before Valia heard the screams of her sisters behind her. She turned around and found herself completely alone, struggling to breathe from the black clouds which filled the air. Then, darkness. A moment later, she awoke in her bedchamber.

"I... don't really know what I saw..." Valia admitted. "They were just... gone. Disappeared into a puff of black smoke."

"That's new. Ever hear of the draevori?"

"Draevori..." Valia shook her head. "From the storybooks? Those are just a legend to frighten children into behaving."

"No." The man shook his head firmly. "*Real* draevori. This whole palace, your father dying, this very cell—it's their construct. The draevori feed on powers like yours. The greater the power of their captive, the more sustenance they gain from their pain. It was *you* they wanted. Your family was collateral damage."

"No..." Valia shook her head and took a step back. Something *was* off, but her mind rebelled against the idea of draevori. A draevor hadn't been seen in Avania for hundreds of cycles, if the texts were to be believed. It had been so long since anyone had encountered one that they were more legend than anything. "Even if that were the case, I've never heard a tale of a draevor doing anything like what happened to my family. Your lies are unconvincing. You *did* kill my father."

She took another step back, but the man's hand shot out between the bars and grabbed her wrist again. He pulled her closer until she was pressed against the bars. He flipped her hand, then ran his rough thumb over the inside of Valia's soft wrist. She shivered as warmth bloomed from his touch.

"Do you feel that?" The man asked, his voice low.

"What are you doing?" She attempted a righteously indignant tone, but her voice came out softer than she intended.

"Wake up. Break this illusion so we can get out of here. They'll kill me as soon as they find out I have no powers for them to drain."

The illusion. Valia thought back on the last few days. More than a few? She wasn't sure how long had passed.

There was the fact that the man's touch felt so different from everyone else's and that he didn't quite seem to belong to the world around him. Then there was everything else: the people who'd been unnecessarily mean, including her father when he'd blamed her for her mother and sisters' deaths. Things that didn't quite add up, from the faded colors and muted sounds to the way everything felt just a little bit foggy. There was the dark blood from the guard's wounds, the fact that no one seemed able to agree on where her father had died. And the suffering. *That* certainly matched the man's claims.

"Break the illusion..." Valia whispered. "How?"

"You've been here longer than I have. Focus. Use your powers to find a weakness." The man released her wrist and ran a hand through his hair. Valia felt the biting cold return to her arm.

Valia squeezed her eyes shut. She reached for the magic that had always come so easily to her but found only silence, as if it was afraid to be found.

"Well?" the man asked.

"My magic doesn't work here." Valia let out a puff of air and opened her eyes. The man was still close. "At least I'm trying something. How exactly are *you* helping?"

"I'm saving you."

"Right. Great job you're doing." Valia gestured at the cell. "Why are you trying to help me, anyway?"

"Like I said, your father sent me to find you. It's... something I'm good at." The man flashed a white-toothed smile so incongruous with the dark, dingy dungeon that Valia had to do a double-take.

"A mercenary. Fine. And why would the draevori kill you?" Valia asked. "You said they draw energy from suffering. Shouldn't they just make you suffer?"

"I have no powers." It was almost amusing to hear such a statement from a man who was so much stronger than her that he'd repeatedly been able to capture her by the wrist, but Valia knew what he meant. "They encourage you to use them so they can take it for themselves. They've nothing to gain by keeping me alive. And my being here is clearly making you suspicious."

"Suspicious is an understatement." Valia leaned against the bars again. "I see… flickers around you." She gestured to the edge of the man's arm, which blurred slightly against the dungeon wall behind him.

"So, you want me to, what? Wave my arms around?" The man raised his eyebrows as he lifted his arms in a half-hearted wave. Valia rolled her eyes. Even the feeling of annoyance was welcome. It was so different from the numbness she'd been feeling.

"No. Just be, I don't know… real?"

"Be real?" The man sighed in frustration and his hand raised as if to muss his hair again. This time, Valia grabbed his hand and threaded her fingers between his. His hand was warm, and his palm rough. It was the hand of a highly physical man. A warrior. Dense and strong for gripping a sword, with callouses suggesting skill with a bow. Playing along, the man skimmed his thumb over the side of her hand. The world around them flickered, as though it was illuminated by a single, weak candle.

"What does this place really look like?" she asked.

"A damp cave, I'd wager. That's where I was headed before entering this illusion."

"Why did they let me get down here to see you, anyway?" Valia mused. "They must know I was suspicious."

"Maybe they're growing weak. Or maybe it's their last effort to get your powers to show themselves. Could be another trick. Either way, this will be our only chance, and we must take it."

His words sent a shard of fear into Valia's heart. Fear, and resignation. There was a good chance she'd be stuck here until her magic and her life force were sapped and her body withered away.

As the dark thoughts rolled through Valia's mind like storm clouds, the palace walls around her solidified. She could make out a rat scuttling across the floor and cracks between the flagstones—details that had been fuzzy just a moment earlier.

"The illusion draws on our fears and sadness," Valia whispered. "*You* said that. When I worry, the illusion grows more real. I need a distraction."

"Sure. I have an idea."

"Good. Finally, you can be useful. What is it?"

"I'm not sure it's befitting such a prim and proper princess." The man's mouth twisted in a half smile.

Valia felt another rush of annoyance. "Are our lives not at stake, annoying man? Just do it."

The man reached between the bars with his free hand, thrust his fingers into Valia's hair, and pulled her in. Her cheeks pressed against the bars as he captured her mouth with his. Where his hand felt warm, his lips scorched hers, as if igniting her blood and bones. Her eyes slipped close as she lost herself in the feeling of his skin on hers, in the salty taste of his mouth, in how his hand tugged lightly downward on her hair to keep her chin tilted upward.

Then, just as quickly as the kiss had begun, the man released her. Valia stumbled backward as the walls around her flickered, morphed, then seemed to melt away. Valia's breath caught. She and the man were standing in some kind of cave. *He was right.* The walls were damp and covered in a soft green moss. The floor was streaked with soot and something red that must have been blood. Two torches lit the area from either side.

The cage holding the man was *real*, though. The bars were thicker than expected, and to Valia's horror, there was no visible door.

"Oh, Flora." Valia's knees were weak. She looked down to see that she was no longer in her pressed white nightgown and mantle, but in the same blue dress she'd worn to the river with her family, now dirty and thin. That explained why she'd never been able to get warm. "There's... no door."

"Run." The man wrapped his broad hands around the bars. "If you run now, you'll have a chance. There's no way out for me."

"But how did you even get in there?"

"Maybe I *do* have powers." The man snorted as though this were all some big joke, but his steely eyes gave away a flicker of fear.

Valia looked around the cave. They were alone, for now. "Hold on. With the illusion broken, my powers might work again."

"And you think you can bend metal? These bars are thicker than my wrist."

"Well, my rings appear to be real. Like you said, they wanted me equipped to use my powers. I have to try." Valia sank to her knees on the hard stone floor and folded her hands together. Trying to steady her breath, she flipped through the spells she knew in her mind, looking for something that could bend or break metal. One came to mind: an old spell she'd once used to make a small metal statue of an elephant for her youngest sister. On a much larger scale, it might just work...

"Princess." There was a warning in the man's voice. "Listen..." They paused in silence and looked in each other's eyes to acknowledge the unnatural sound bouncing off the cave's walls. "They're coming."

Valia pulled out the man's dagger she brought from her illusory chambers and pointed it at him. "It's going to be on *you* to get us out of here," she said. She gently tossed it through the bars onto the floor. She raised her eyes to the man's. "I'm going to have to sacrifice something big."

Her eyes slid shut again as she offered the Flora her sight for the next day. Valia pricked her thumb with the small silver ring on her index finger, then pressed the drop of blood back against her gale ring on the same finger. The words for the spell tripped merrily over her lips, as though her magic had been aching to be used.

Valia opened her eyes as the spell rushed out of her, warm and bright, and the bars began to bend. The man burst through the bent bars with his dagger raised as a dark, shadowy creature rushed into the cave, already bristling with magic. Exhaustion overtook Valia, and her world went dark.

"Get us out of here," Valia whispered. Then she tipped over, energy spent.

CHAPTER THREE
DISTANCE

alia awoke to the strange sensation of... *bouncing*? After a moment, her brain clicked into focus. She was on a horse. Behind her was a warm, strong torso with an arm around her waist that held her firmly in place. Her head rested against the shoulder behind it.

"You're awake," A low voice said in Valia's ear.

Valia took a sharp breath. "Did we make it? What happened?"

"Your spell worked. They were slow. After I get you back to Wyra, I'll come back for the rest of them."

"That doesn't sound like a good idea at all." Valia's tone was a bit too short to use with someone who had just saved her life, but she was scared and tired and couldn't see. "Why go back? They overpowered you once already."

"In the daytime, while I was trying to protect you. Next time will be different. And I want my whip back."

"Of course. Your whip. Couldn't you just get another one from Wyra? Or, you know, a proper sword for a proper mercenary?"

"I could."

"Then why not just leave it, and not risk yourself going to retrieve it?"

"Because it's mine."

Valia lifted her hands and rubbed her eyes as she rolled them at his answer, though she still couldn't see a thing. "Right. Where are we now? How long have we been riding?"

"Not long. I'm not sure precisely where we are, though it should be somewhere in the western part of the Blood Forest."

The tiny hairs on Valia's arms stood up. True to its name, the Blood Forest was home to many of Avania's more fearsome creatures, from manticores to multi-headed serpents and vicious mountain lions with backs spined like a porcupine's. It was also near the wild Lasin river, which bordered Tromin and the metems who lived there. Valia had never been this far east before, and she wasn't sure she wanted to be here now.

"The Blood Forest?" Valia bit her lip.

The man must have sensed her apprehension, because when he spoke again, his tone was gentler. "It's actually quite beautiful. Did you know it wasn't originally called the Blood Forest because of all the, well... all the people who've died here? Early explorers called it the Blood Forest because of a special kind of oak with bright red leaves that grows here. Sanguinoaks, they call them. We're riding through a grove now."

"I have a sanguinoak ring. My gale ring." Valia spun the ring around her finger, wondering if the wood inlaid into the metal band recognized that this was where it had grown. "I heard when it rains, the water that drips from the sanguinoaks is stained as red as blood."

"Yes, it's true."

"That's a terrifying thought. I don't think I'd want to see blood raining from the skies."

"It's not so bad." The man was quiet for a moment as the horse trotted on. "It smells nice. Like cinnamon. And the leaves are easy on the eyes."

"I wish I could see them."

"Hm." Another long pause. "Thank you for giving up your sight to free me."

"Thank *you* for getting me out after." They were both silent for a moment. Valia became very conscious of the man's hard chest behind her and his arm, firm and strong, around her. She'd never been this close to a strange man before. The princesses of Avania, even Valia as the second youngest and most free-spirited, were not encouraged to get friendly with men.

Yet instead of being uncomfortable, Valia found the man's warmth to be pleasant. The draevori illusion had been so cold and lonely.

"Do you need a break?" the man asked. As soon as he mentioned it, Valia realized her legs were slightly numb from riding and that she was terribly hungry and thirsty.

"Is it safe here?"

"Safe as anywhere."

Valia felt the horse slow beneath her, then come to a stop. The man pressed a pair of leather reins into Valia's hands.

"Hold here a moment."

Then he slipped off. Without his warmth, Valia's back rapidly cooled in the soft breeze. She realized all over again that she was dressed in a threadbare day gown, not traveling gear.

"Give me your hands."

Valia let the man take her hands, which he placed on his shoulders. He then took Valia around the waist and lifted her off the horse as if she weighed no more than a butterfly.

When he set her gently on the ground, Valia registered the crunch of leaves beneath her bare feet. The ground was cold, and she wished she'd at least worn her slippers. Provided the slippers had been *real*, of course.

"Is there anything sharp on the ground?" She wiggled a bare foot to emphasize her point.

"Just leaves and dirt. Wait here."

Valia heard the man's footsteps departing. She was alone and blind in the Blood Forest. Wonderful.

Valia forced herself to breathe deeply. As she did, she began to notice more of her surroundings. There was the sound of running water in the distance, probably a stream. She could hear birds singing and the soft whistle of wind blowing through leaves somewhere high above. The forest smelled fresh and natural. Valia took a cautious step forward with her hand outstretched and brushed against the rough bark of a tree trunk.

Valia's fear melted away, replaced by a deep peace. Yes, she'd just spent *who knew how long* captured by draevori of all things. Yes, her mother and sisters were gone. Yes, she was now temporarily blind and traveling with a strange, annoying man. A man she was completely dependent on. A man to whom she owed her life.

At the same time, she was in nature, in the fresh air. Valia always felt most alive when she was outside, surrounded by plants and animals. It tied into her magic, which worked best with the life around her.

Valia pricked her thumb. She felt a drop of blood well on her thumb—a small offering. She muttered the words to a spell of life discovery as she pressed the drop of blood to her sight ring. A wave of gentle energy swept from her in a circle and Valia knew she was in a clearing in the trees. The horse was behind her, the man was returning from the stream, and an owl nested in the tree far above her. Valia still couldn't see with her eyes, but she knew what was around her in the same way she knew the layout of her own chambers in the darkness. She could sense squirrels in the branches, fish in the stream, and bees somewhere in the distance. Valia's heart filled. She was surrounded by life again.

"Princess?"

The spell faded away like grains of sand scattered in the wind. Valia turned toward the man's voice, annoyed that he'd broken her concentration.

"Here." Valia felt a hand on her forearm, ever warm and solid.

"Come, this way. There's a log where we can sit and rest."

Valia let herself be led. As she went, though, she wished she'd given up something other than her sight. The sticks and pebbles beneath her bare feet were unpleasant. Yet the greater a sacrifice, the more likely the spell was to work, and Valia had needed that spell to work. It was worth this discomfort that they'd both escaped alive.

"I still don't know your name."

"Sit here." The hand moved to her other forearm and Valia carefully sat down.

"Are you going to tell me your name?"

"My name doesn't matter." Valia felt the log shift as he sat beside her. She could feel his warmth, but they weren't touching. "The day after tomorrow, we'll arrive in Wyra. You'll be back with your father in your palace, and we'll never see each other again."

"But you saved my life." Valia felt the ground with a bare toe. It was soft and mossy, so she slid off the log and onto the ground, where she could feel the bottoms of her feet to see if any pine needles had stuck in her skin.

"Yes, I've completed my task." The man's tone was a little strange, but Valia couldn't put her finger on it. She wished she could see his expression.

"You already know *my* name," she pointed out.

"I do. 'Princess.'"

His use of her title, rather than her name, stung worse than the rough forest floor against her bare feet. It was a clear sign that they weren't on the same level. Not in his opinion. It didn't matter that they'd saved each other or that they'd shared a fiery kiss. Valia was only a job to him, an objective to complete. Then again, she was the sole heir to an entire kingdom, and he was a mere sellsword.

"You're right. I don't need to know your name." Valia pushed herself abruptly to her feet. "Shall we keep going?"

"Rest first. Drink. You've been through an ordeal."

The man's tone was kinder now, but Valia wasn't interested in his kindness anymore. She *was* thirsty, though.

"Okay. Water, please."

A waterskin nudged Valia's hand and she took it. She drank long and deep from the cold water inside and, despite herself, felt a little better. It didn't matter if she knew the man's name. It didn't matter if this was just a job for him. Soon, she'd be home and this whole chapter of her life would be behind her.

"Thank you." Valia held out the half-empty waterskin. The man took it.

"Hungry? I've got some dried meat and traveler's bread in my bag."

Valia's nose wrinkled at the thought of the dry, old food. "Hold on, I can do better." She pricked her finger and cast the life discovery spell again. As always, it was a little harder the second time, like the magic had grown worn. This time, Valia focused on plants.

"There's an apple tree that way, near the stream." She pointed.

"Got it." Valia heard the man's footsteps disappearing in the direction of the tree. A few moments later, he crunched back toward her. Valia felt the cool, smooth sphere of an apple in her hand. It was heavier than she expected—or was it that her body was now weaker? She bit into it, savoring the crunch of the apple's flesh and the sweet juice spilling into her mouth.

"Thank you."

Valia ate her apple without further conversation, accepted another long drink of water, then let the man take her arm and lead her back to the horse. He helped her on, then climbed up behind her and wrapped an arm around her waist.

"I'm awake now," she pointed out. "And I'm a good rider. I'm not going to fall off."

The arm withdrew and Valia felt a stab of regret. It was nice to be held after the pain and loneliness of the draevori cave. The horse broke into a canter. Valia adjusted to the movement, grateful for her extensive experience with being on horseback.

"May I at least know the horse's name?" she asked.

"I don't know it." The man shifted behind her.

"Hm... Was it hard to find me?"

"Harder than usual, yes. Your father knew you were alive. He'd been told as much by a floramancer in his court. They were able to learn the area you were in, but not who or what had taken you. I rode there and... looked around. It's a dangerous area, with all kinds of creatures about. None had you, until the draevori."

It was the longest Valia had heard the man speak in one go, and she wanted to keep him talking.

"Draevori, though. I still hardly believe they actually exist. The most recent report of them was hundreds of cycles ago."

"Fallows too, right? I exterminated a pack on my way to you."

Valia shivered at the mention of fallows. They were another creature that, like a draevor, were more the stuff of legend than reality.

"Really? Do they really have thousands of teeth and move like shadows?"

"Two hundred at best. But they *are* fast, if you're unlucky enough to run into them at night. The men your father sent before me made that mistake."

"How many men did my father send for me?" Valia felt a longing to be home, knowing that her father *did* care about her.

"Based on his desperation in hiring me, plenty."

"Desperation?" Valia paused to let the man answer but moved on quickly when he returned her silence. She realized he must have meant her father was desperate to have her back. "My father used to tell me a story about fallows. He said some of them attacked the capital when he was just beginning his reign and that he had to send the entire Wyrian Lirrhguard to kill them."

"The pack I hunted had three. Farmers were losing their cattle and pigs. You wouldn't have still been alive if they had you, but they would have worked their way up to children, as they do."

Valia shivered again. That was another part of the legend of fallows: they ate babies and young children.

"How... honorable of you."

"I'm paid well for each head I return."

Valia stifled a sigh. "Well, whatever the reason, you saved the lives of the children who would have become victims of the fallows. That sounds good and honorable to me."

"Don't muddy it with honor and morals. I'm not a good man. Not here in Avania, nor anywhere else." A hint of emotion revealed itself through his words.

There was a long moment of silence in which Valia began to worry she'd somehow offended him with her attempt at a compliment. She didn't dare prod further. Whatever this man had done to see himself this way, she didn't need to know. They'd part ways soon enough.

He sighed softly in her ear. "I apologize, Princess. What I mean to say is... thank you for seeing me that way."

They rode on in silence. Valia tried several more times to start a conversation, but each time, she was met by a curt response or silence. Eventually, as tiredness set in, she leaned against the man's chest, listening to the sounds of the forest around them.

After the sun began to set, the man shifted behind Valia. "It's getting dark, and we're approaching a village. It's time to stop for the night."

"Okay."

"When we arrive, don't act like a princess," the man said. "It could be dangerous here."

"Does that mean you'll call me by my name?"

"No need."

"Have you been to this town before?"

"No."

"Do you think they'll have food and a warm bath?"

"Maybe."

"What a lovely conversation."

"It's not my job to entertain you."

The man was clearly done talking. It seemed the brief conversation they'd shared about how he'd found her was all she was going to get from him.

As they rode, Valia began to hear and smell civilization. Someone kept pigs nearby. She heard voices and the clatter of wheels on cobblestones.

A few moments later, the horse came to a stop in what smelled like a traveler's stable. The man leaped down, tied the horse in a stall, then lifted Valia off its back. Valia's legs seemed to have fallen asleep during the long ride and she almost collapsed to the ground. The man steadied her.

"All right, Princess?"

"I thought I wasn't supposed to be a princess here."

"It's an affectionate nickname I use for my wife. Come on. The inn's this way."

Did he really have a wife he called "princess?" Valia felt it was unlikely, but she couldn't help but wonder. More likely, he simply meant *wife* was the part she'd be playing in this village.

Valia felt his hand on her arm again as he gently led her. Through the pins and needles of circulation returning to her legs, she felt hard-packed dirt, then cobblestones that must have made up the walkway to the inn. The man's hand was firm and steady.

"Stairs."

She lifted her foot and climbed three stairs. The ground beneath her feet changed to hard planks and the air felt warmer. Valia heard plates scraping and quiet chatter. They must be inside now.

"Look at the size o' this one. How can I help ya, big man?" A gruff, unfamiliar voice called from across the room.

"My wife and I are looking for a room."

"Two rooms," Valia said softly.

"*One* room." His voice was quiet and firm. Valia was apprehensive about sharing a room with a strange man, but given the circumstances, she would allow it.

"Just the one night?" the innkeeper asked.

"One night." The man led her across the room. Valia kept wincing, worried she was about to run into a table or step on a nail, but he guided her well. Valia considered using another spell to get an idea of the room they were in but decided against it. If there were other floramancers—or perhaps even a metem—in the area, they could be drawn to her power.

"That'll be twelve florans."

There was the clink of coins, then the innkeeper spoke again.

"Alright. 'Ere's your key. Yer welcome to some food with it. Interested?"

Valia's stomach rumbled at the thought of food. Either the man heard it, or he was just as hungry, because he quickly said, "Yes, thank you. Can you bring it to the room?"

"Eager to get on with it, eh?" the keeper said, more than a hint of suggestion in his voice. Valia recoiled internally but kept a neutral expression.

"Something like that." There was a pause. "That your wife?"

"She is."

"Mine needs shoes, and they look to be about the same size. How much do you want for them?"

"Ain't fer sale."

"And now?" There was another clink of coins—far too many for a pair of shoes.

"Margery! Bring me your boots, the good ones!" In a quieter voice, he continued. "How'd ya lose yer shoes in the first place, miss?"

"We had to leave camp suddenly this morning and... I forgot them," Valia said. It was a near truth.

"Keep an eye on 'er," the innkeeper said, this time to the man. "Women, right?"

"Women," the man agreed. Valia bristled, but he continued. "My wife has saved my life. She may not be able to keep track of her footwear, but she's a force to be reckoned with when it matters. Thank you for the boots. We'll go upstairs."

The man guided Valia up the stairs and they reached their room without incident.

"Thank you."

"Your father will reimburse me." The man led her through a door, pushed her gently into a sitting position on what must have been a bed, and handed her something soft and worn that must have been the boots.

"Not for that. For standing up for me. For the boots. For saving my life." Maybe Valia should have said that last one sooner.

"As I said, the king will repay me for any expenses," the man said curtly. Valia set the boots on the floor and ran her hand over the worn bedspread.

"Is there anything soft for you to sleep on?"

"No."

"Do you want the blanket?"

"I'm fine."

"Are we ever going to have a conversation?"

"Probably not."

"Can you at least get me some water to wash up?"

"Yes. Stay there."

The man fetched a bucket of cold water, which Valia used to wash her face and her feet. She wished she could have a proper bath, but with the man somewhere in the room and only a small bucket of cold water, that was out of the question. A few moments later, their food arrived: two bowls of steaming soup filled with vegetables and a pair of fluffy bread rolls. Valia ate ravenously without assistance, then lay down on the bed.

"Good night, strange man."

"Good night, Princess."

She wanted to stay awake a little longer, at the very least to savor the feeling of a soft, warm bed, but exhaustion overtook her. She gladly fell into a different kind of darkness.

CHAPTER FOUR
SIGHT

alia was the first to wake. She opened her eyes and scanned the small room, grateful her vision was returned. It was sparse but clean, the wooden floor planks clearly scrubbed until they were nearly smooth. The wall planks were bare, and the ceiling was low. Above Valia's threadbare bed, there was one small window which let a beam of warm sunlight spill across her legs. On the pillow beside her rested a leaf, vibrant red and as broad as Valia's palm. At first, she wasn't certain where the leaf had come from, but she realized the man must have taken it from the Blood Forest so she could see it. It really was quite beautiful.

The man still slept on the floor. He wore dark trousers and a heavy cloak—the same clothes he'd appeared to have in the draevori cave—and slept on the hard floor absent any comforts. Valia felt a moment of sympathy, which she quickly quashed. It had been the man's choice to share her room instead of getting her own, so it was his own fault he'd spent an uncomfortable night on the floor.

Valia swung her legs out of bed and felt the smooth floor with her feet. Her eyes drifted to the man's face, which looked peaceful and relaxed in sleep. His eyelashes were surprisingly long for a man's, and his usually neat hair was mussed. Now that the illusion was gone, he looked *real* in a way Valia couldn't quite place. She felt her cheeks heat slightly at the memory of the kiss they'd shared in the draevori cave, and studied his lips.

Valia averted her eyes. The man had made it clear he didn't want any personal connection with her, and it didn't feel right to watch him sleep like this. Instead, she turned to kneel on the bed and looked out the small window.

The inn was right on the forest line. One glance at the tall trees outside and Valia knew a window wasn't enough. She had to go outside—*now*. For what felt like ages, she'd been deprived of the living world from which she drew so much of her power. No more.

Valia turned, grabbed her boots, and tiptoed across the floor. She unlocked the door slowly, wincing when the lock gave a loud click, and slipped into the hallway. There, she stopped to shove her feet into the boots before hurrying down the hallway and stairs. The next floor down had the room they must have come in through the night before. Now, in the early morning, there were a few people sitting around the large, round tables that filled the room.

Valia didn't stop to socialize. She went straight out the front door, down the steps, and into the forest. Immediately, she felt her shoulders relax and her breath deepen. Valia slowed her steps so she could skim her palms along the rough trunks of trees and smell the soft scent of flowers and pine. Sticks and dry leaves crunched beneath her boots and birds flitted between branches in the treetops.

Valia scooped a handful of dirt in one palm. A drop of blood on her surge ring was enough to coax a tiny seedling into a croton the size of her hand, with broad green and pink leaves and a twisting stem. This spell would require more from most floramancers, but for Valia, it was effortless. A smile spread across her face. Valia was *alive* again.

She gently lowered the dirt and seedling onto the ground. Now that she was in nature, rested and calm and free, her mental fog lifted. Hundreds of spells floated through her mind, ready to pluck like petals of a starflower should she need them.

Yet with this freedom came sadness. Valia's mother and sisters really were gone. Even if they had survived the initial attack, they would have been discarded quickly by the draevori. None of them had the connection with the Flora Valia did.

Valia slowed as memories came rushing back. Her mother, Ellara, had been a kind and thoughtful queen; the perfect balance to Valia's quick-to-act father. Her eldest sister, Samalia, had been regal, composed, and considered. She was a wise strategist, and the perfect heir to the throne. Avania would have thrived under her rule. Daria, Valia's second eldest sister, had been whip-smart and headstrong, always ready to rush into a fight, verbal or physical, to defend what she believed in. Litia, Valia's youngest sister at only fifteen cycles old, had been beautiful and shy, not yet ready to step into her power.

Now they were all gone. Valia's heart ached with the thought. She'd mourned them during her time as a prisoner of the draevori, but it had been hard to remember their faces. Now, the memories came flooding back like torrential rain.

In that moment, she wished she could turn back time. If she had another chance, she could act quicker. She could fight or run away and save her family. She could make things right again. She could make her family whole.

The croton, seeming to sense her pain, began to wilt. Valia pressed a bead of blood into her null ring, then her prism ring, to return the innocent croton to its unaltered form. She *could* heal this seedling, at least.

But... Valia still didn't know exactly what had happened with her family, even now that she was free. She hadn't actually seen them die. There must be a chance, however slim, that at least one of her family survived too. *She* did, after all.

Valia's heart fluttered with new hope. What if one of her sisters or her mother was alive somewhere? Her father would have searched, surely, but his connection with the Flora was weak at best. And his court floramancers' information wouldn't be as accurate as a blood relative's. Maybe, just maybe, someone was still alive. If anyone could find them, she could.

Valia hurried forward a few more steps into a mossy clearing. High oaks towered above her, casting dappled light on the clearing, but she barely saw them. She was completely consumed by the prospect that someone else might have survived.

Valia fell to her knees on the soft moss and searched for a spell that would help. Her mind landed on a simple spell, often taught to children, used to map family trees. It would create a constellation of tiny lights—one for each living member of a family.

She pricked her thumb and smeared a drop of blood onto her sight ring. As she gathered the magic from the sacrifice, she began to weave the family constellation spell. Another moment and...

"Princess!"

Valia's concentration was broken and the spell disintegrated in her hands like ancient parchment. Valia turned, irritated, only to feel a hand clasp around her upper arm and haul her to her feet.

"What are you doing?" she asked the man.

"I could ask you the same." He began to haul her back toward the inn, until Valia shook him off.

"I can walk on my own, thanks."

"Can you?" He glared at her. "I woke up and you were gone. For all I know, you could have been carried off by another draevor. You could have died."

"And then you wouldn't have gotten your reward, right?"

"I—" The man shook his head. "You just can't wander off like that."

"Nothing happened!" Valia protested. "I just wanted to go outside, now that my vision is back."

"You could have woken me." One of his hands shot out in Valia's path, trapping her between him and a tree. Valia's fury grew as she turned toward him. She was tempted to reach for magic, but the man wasn't actually touching her, and she could still walk away.

"What?" Her voice came out clipped, but when she raised her gaze to meet his eyes, she didn't see the anger she expected. His gaze was intense, but he looked almost... worried. It was strange to see concern on the man's handsome features after he'd barely blinked an eyelash in the draevori cave. Valia softened slightly against the tree behind her.

"I can't let anything happen to you. Give me your word you won't go off alone again."

"I—" Valia felt a little flustered with the man so close to her. The way it had felt to kiss him through the bars of the cage rushed back and she felt flushed, despite herself. They'd kissed to break the illusion. That was all. So why did her heart flutter?

"Swear it." His eyes bored down on her. He was close enough that Valia could see the growing stubble along his cheeks and a small crease near one of his ears—probably from sleeping on the floorboards.

"I swear..."

Just as quickly as he'd stopped her, the man pulled his hand back and turned to continue back to the inn. Valia grabbed his arm before he could go.

"But *you* must promise me we'll talk. Otherwise, I'll die of boredom. No reward for you then."

The man shook his head, but Valia was almost certain she saw a flicker of a smile. "I'm not going to promise that." He gently removed his arm from her hands and began to walk. Valia followed.

"Come on. You're a mercenary. You must have some great stories."

"Let's gather our belongings. The inn offers breakfast. We can take something for the road."

Valia rolled her eyes. The man might worry about her, or at least about the coin he'd get for returning her safely, but it was clear he was never going to have a real conversation with her. Fine.

Back inside, they went upstairs to gather the man's bag, then each took bread, cheese, and an apple from the innkeeper.

"Do you know of anyone selling a horse in town?" the man asked the innkeeper as they collected the food.

"For sale, no." The innkeeper shook his head. "Well, Niel has an old nag, but it's better off at the knacker's yard. 'Specially for the price he's asking."

"Thank you anyway." They left.

"It looks like we'll be riding doubles still," Valia said cheerfully. "That'll make it easier to talk."

"Lovely." The man rolled his eyes and Valia stifled a laugh at the dramatic gesture. It was something she'd expect to see from her sister Daria, not from such a serious man. "Can you climb up without help?"

"Yes." Valia used the low stone wall that bordered the inn to get a little height before swinging her leg over the horse's back. The horse shifted beneath her, and she patted the side of his neck. She couldn't wait to see her own horse, Star, back in Wyra.

A moment later, the man climbed up behind her. He reached around to take the reins, then clicked his tongue to encourage the horse into a light trot. The village was tiny; it wasn't long before they'd passed the last building. Soon, it looked like they were in the heart of the forest. The trees were tall and their trunks gnarled, as though they'd stood for a thousand cycles. Perhaps they had. Valia spotted squirrels and small birds flitting from branch to branch. A rustle in the distance alerted her to a bright-eyed doe, which looked at her for a long moment before darting into the underbrush.

"If we push hard, can we make it to Wyra tonight?" Valia was eager to be home.

"No." The man's voice was decisive. "Not with the two of us on one horse like this. We'll need to stop for one more night."

"Alright." Valia settled in for another long, silent day. At least today she could enjoy the sights of the forest around them, from babbling brooks to huge rock formations that looked like animals. They were out of the Blood Forest now, far from its red-leafed trees.

After a while, Valia's legs began to ache. She was used to long days of riding, but her captivity had left her weak. Just as she was building up the nerve to ask for a break, the trees opened into a small meadow of starflowers.

"Oh!" Valia smiled. "Can we stop here for a short break?"

The man didn't answer, but the horse slowed to a stop, and she was able to slide off. The man jumped down after her.

"Aren't they beautiful?" Valia knelt in the dirt and cupped her hands around one of the small flowers. In the darkness of her cupped hands, it shone with a small but bright white light.

"They're useful in the dark." The man shifted behind her. When Valia glanced back, she saw his eyes were on the horizon, scanning for danger. "I use them sometimes, when I travel at night."

Valia smiled down at the flower in her hands. When he didn't think about it, the man *did* talk. At least, sometimes.

"When we were young, my little sister was fearful of the dark. I gave her a pot of starflowers just about to bloom for her room, so that she wouldn't have to be afraid."

"Sometimes it's good to have a healthy fear of the dark."

Valia glanced back again to see that the man's face was clouded. "Are *you* scared of the dark?" Valia was incredulous. This man had fought a draevor, after all, without so much as a hint of fear.

"I respect the darkness. It can hide all kinds of horrors. Better to be wary than dead."

"Well..." Valia straightened and turned back to him, brushing the dirt from her worn dress as she stood. "You never have to be scared of the dark while *I'm* around." She put her left hand behind her back and pressed a bead of blood into her lumen ring. Immediately, the area around them was illuminated with a bright, shining light that sparkled and danced as it enveloped them. The starflowers began to glow brighter too, perhaps in response to magic drawn from one of their kind.

"Stop!" The man clasped Valia's arm. Surprised by the gesture and the urgency in his voice, Valia let the spell go and ordinary daylight returned.

"Come on." She crossed her arms and raised her eyebrows. "We're all alone out here. What's wrong with having a little fun?"

"Fun?" The man scoffed. "Magic isn't *fun*. I admit it can be useful, but you can't just throw around spells for no reason like that. What if someone saw us? What if you drained your power and couldn't fight if something attacked? What if the spell went wrong and killed us both?"

"First of all, my magic *never* goes wrong." Valia drew herself up to her full height, which was still a full head shorter than the man.

"Second, that was a tiny seed spell. I could do those all day without breaking a sweat. And third, magic *is* fun." She threw her arms out to her sides as if she could encompass the field of flowers, the faraway shadows of mountains, and the gush of a nearby stream. "Floramancy is natural, as much as anything else."

The man gave a frustrated sigh and ran his hand through his hair. "Just... don't do it again."

Valia had agreed to his request not to wander off alone, but this felt like too much. She wasn't going to put her magic—which was as much a part of her as her nose—to the side just because it made this stranger a little uncomfortable. Instead of acquiescing, Valia stood her ground.

"No."

"Typical bleeder. Zero self-control." The man turned away, but Valia grabbed his arm.

"*What* did you just call me?"

To his credit, the man looked a little sheepish.

"Princess..."

"I get that you won't call me by my name, but I didn't think we'd slipped into insults."

"I shouldn't have said that. But my point stands. It's foolish to use those powers while we're out in the open like this. Anything can happen. You need to be more careful." The man ran his hand through his hair again and looked away. His eyes narrowed.

"So now I'm a fool, too?"

"I didn't say that."

They glared at each other for a long moment. Valia's hands curled into fists. Part of her wanted to cast another spell. Nothing that would *hurt* the man, but an illusion perhaps. She could make the flowers grow into a wall around them or shake the ground beneath his feet. Valia held herself back. If she used magic now, it would only prove to this man she was every bit the impetuous floramancer he seemed to think she was.

Finally, the man sighed. "Look. I can see you're capable and intelligent. Except for when you ran off this morning. And this spell." He seemed to be reconsidering his compliment, so Valia jumped in quickly.

"Thank you. I won't do any flashy spells, alright? At least, not without warning."

"Good." The man hesitated. "How hard is it for you to maintain that spell?"

"Not hard. It's very minor." Valia tilted her head. "Why?"

"You wanted to get back to Wyra tonight. If you can light the path like that after dark, maybe we can. The light would have to be much, much smaller, though. And directed only forward."

"I can do that!" Valia's heart soared at the thought of being home, then sank again at the memory that her sisters and mother wouldn't be there. Part of her wanted to drag this journey out, so she wouldn't have to face the palace without them, but it was better to get back. She'd be happy to light the way.

"Good. Let's continue."

"I'm ready."

They returned to the horse. This time, there was no handy fencepost nearby. Valia stared up at the horse, wishing she was taller. A minor seed spell, perhaps with her surge ring, to boost her strength. Or her gale ring to push herself off the ground—that could do the trick.

"Would you like some help?"

Valia turned to the man, her cheeks reddening. Of course, using the man who'd been easily lifting her on and off the horse for the past couple days was a solution, too.

"Yes, please. Without something to stand on, I'm a bit too short to reach."

The man didn't wait for her to finish talking. He just placed his hands on her waist and lifted her onto the horse's back. He climbed on behind her and clicked to the horse.

"So," Valia said conversationally. "You don't like magic. Are you a nix?"

Coming from the northern country of Kanalear, nix eschewed magic altogether. Nixes weren't common in Avania. Almost everyone here used magic in one way or another, although most could only wield minor spells to help with everyday tasks.

"I don't have a problem with your powers," the man said. "I have a problem with people who wield it carelessly."

"And you think I'm careless."

"I said you were smart. I believe that."

"Smart and careless aren't mutually exclusive."

The man didn't respond. Valia sighed and decided to ignore him again. There was no point in arguing.

They rode, breaking only to attend to biological necessities. Umbra came and went, with the sun passing behind the moon, shrouding the land in darkness for a few moments. Valia held herself back from casting a spell for light, as she normally would have.

Eventually, after riding through the rest of the day, long shadows grew from the trees and the forest began to wake with the sounds of dusk. Deer flitted across their path, and in the distance, an owl hooted. Valia ran her fingers absently over her rings, ready to reach for a light spell when it grew too dark to see. They still had time, though. It was barely twilight.

"Princess. It's time for your light."

It wasn't completely dark yet, but Valia didn't argue. She pricked her finger and pressed a drop of blood to her lumen ring. Then, she pressed another drop to her prism ring to direct the spell forward. Valia felt the pull of the incantation on her energy. Over time, it would become taxing. For now, she was able to maintain a small ball of warm white light that floated a few feet in front of them, illuminating the path ahead and parts of the trees nearby.

She wondered if the man really was fearful of the dark. The thought made him more human, somehow. Perhaps he wasn't always the hard, somber mercenary he seemed to be.

After a while riding through the darkness, Valia felt herself begin to tire.

"Can we have a break?" she asked. The man immediately pulled the horse to a stop in a small clearing and slid off, then helped her down. Valia guided the ball of light into the clearing, then sank onto the hard dirt. The man stayed standing, always watchful.

"Dim your light while we're not moving."

An owl hooted and he reached for his dagger, then let his hand fall. Valia extended her legs and stretched. A corner of her mind was still on the light spell, but it was a relief to be off the horse.

There was a rustle in the bushes and the man stiffened behind her. In the light from the spell, Valia could make out the outline of a large, dark shape in the bushes. Instinctively, she pressed a drop of blood to her sight ring and a wave of awareness spread from her. At the same time, she rose to her feet as quietly as she could.

"It's a bear," she said softly. "Her cubs are on the other side of us." The man swore under his breath and stepped forward, putting himself between Valia and the bear. He silently drew his dagger.

Valia grabbed his right arm. "Don't."

"Let go."

"*Don't.*"

The bear stalked out of the bushes. It loomed above them, huge and hulking, and let out a soft growl that shook Valia's bones. The man shook his arm free of Valia's grip. Before he could attack, Valia stepped in front of him, turning her back to the bear. Her heart was racing, but she knew she couldn't let the mercenary kill an animal that was only trying to protect her offspring.

She held the man's gray eyes with her own as she pricked her thumb and pressed blood into her link ring. Valia wasn't as skilled with it as some floramancers; she couldn't compel anyone to do anything they didn't already want to. Hopefully, a nudge would be enough. She concentrated all her effort and sent a feeling of peace radiating through the clearing. The light spell dimmed as Valia's focus diverted to her quelling spell. The bear took a step back, seeming to shrink slightly, and the man lowered the dagger in his hand.

"She's only worried about her cubs," Valia said in a low voice. "We aren't going to kill her for that. We're going to quietly walk away."

"Princess—" The man's voice was a challenge and a warning. His eyes were fixed on the bear behind her. Yet when Valia reached for his arm, he dropped his eyes briefly to meet hers.

"*Trust me.*" Whether it was her words or the feeling of peace, Valia wasn't sure, but the man allowed her to lead him to the side. As soon as they were out of the way, the bear ambled across the clearing to join her cubs. The man stiffened as the bear passed, but it wasn't interested in them anymore.

They took a few more slow, painstaking steps before reaching their undisturbed horse. Without speaking, the man grabbed Valia and lifted her on, then swung up behind her. The path was dark now, as Valia was still recovering from the quelling spell, but there was faint light from the bright moon above and the horse seemed to know the way. The man pushed the horse straight into a full gallop, which they held for a short time in silence.

"You chose the bear?" The man's voice was low and wondering. He didn't sound angry. "It could have killed us, but you chose to risk our lives to protect it."

"I chose all our lives."

"I wouldn't have done that."

"But you did," Valia pointed out. "You chose to leave with me instead of attacking."

"I... suppose I did..."

Valia's heart was still racing. She was thankful for the clop of the horse's hooves against the hard-packed dirt. She didn't want the man to know how scared she'd been—or how possible it had been for things to go wrong. Everything had happened in a blur. She could still hear the growl of the bear behind her and the wild intensity in the man's eyes as he'd armed himself. If she'd hesitated for only a moment, if the man hadn't listened to her, if the bear had been just a little more defensive...

The forests away from the palace were dangerous.

They rode in the darkness for a while, until Valia could gather the energy to recast her light spell. It was hardly necessary, though. Soon after the orb of light flickered into life, they passed the first farmer's home. It belonged to some intrepid soul who didn't fear the forest or the animals that roamed there, and it marked the beginning of civilization. Soon, they passed several more farms, then a footbridge over a small river Valia remembered from her own rides. They were almost to Wyra.

Soon after, they passed the great wall encircling the city proper, and Valia let the orb of light dissipate. The streets here were illuminated by lanterns and the flickering lights from homes. Valia and the man rode through the city, passing sleepy bakers on their way to work and cleaning crews who maintained the streets.

As they approached the wide doors leading to the palace, which were closed against the night, Valia felt her heart pound again. She couldn't imagine being back home, in the palace that would look all too similar to the twisted draevori version. She couldn't imagine being here without her mother and sisters.

"You're home, Princess," the man said behind her, his voice low. "Shall we alert a guard?"

CHAPTER FIVE
HOME

alia glanced back at the man in hopes of comfort, but his face was as stony, as always. She wondered what this man's life was really like. Did he fight otherworldly creatures and rescue princesses often? His muscular physique and ease with weapons certainly suggested that as a possibility.

The man guided the horse up to the front gates of the palace, then swung off. Valia slid off after him, her legs buckling slightly as she hit the ground. The man steadied her, his hand on her elbow.

"Are you well?"

"Yes. My legs just feel a little weak from the journey." Valia smiled, but it was a little forced.

"You there! Stay where you are and state your business," a guard called from beside the gate. Valia stepped closer, into the circle of light cast by a lamp suspended from the palace wall. The light illuminated her face. The guard squinted. "Princess Valia? Is that you?"

"Yes." Valia took another step closer. The young guard widened his eyes.

"Princess Valia, m-my apologies, I didn't recognize you. It's just, well, we thought…" the guard trailed off with a horrified look, then turned to the gate and called up to another man on the wall. The gates creaked open to reveal the familiar courtyard of Palace Annulus that Valia had walked so many times before. The guard gestured for her to enter, seeming not to trust himself to speak.

Valia took a deep breath and stepped through the gates. The man followed her, as quietly as a shadow, and Valia was grateful for his presence. This was her home, but it felt strange to be back here now and she wasn't ready to be alone.

"By Flora, it *is* her. Wake the king. Wake the staff." Lord Captain Poriev, the top royal military advisor to the crown and captain of the palace guard, motioned to his younger subordinates. He hurried down the stairs from the wall and led the way into the courtyard. "Let's get you inside, Princess."

"Thank you, Lord Captain. It's nice to see you." Valia attempted a thin smile. She'd expected returning to the palace to feel like a homecoming, but it didn't.

The captain inspected Valia with a concerned look on his face.

"You." Poriev stopped and faced the man. His gaze swept over the mercenary, resting for a long moment on his dagger. Poriev's eyes narrowed, and his hand went to the hilt of his sword. The man didn't react.

"Yes?" The man's voice was neutral, as though he were chatting with an acquaintance about the weather.

"Why are you following?"

"I rescued the princess. As soon as I'm paid, I'll be on my way," the man told him calmly.

"Did you touch her?"

Valia's eyes widened as the guard drew an inch of steel from his scabbard. Poriev had always been a kind, almost fatherly figure in the guard, but now he was acting like a hotheaded recruit faced with his first conflict.

The man still didn't react. Despite his eagerness to fight when he'd seen the bear, he appeared calm now. Valia stepped between the two men and turned toward the captain.

"Captain Poriev," Valia said in her best quelling princess voice. "This man rescued me from draevori and escorted me safely back home. He will receive his reward."

The captain glanced down at Valia, his green eyes softening in his weathered face. "Draevori?... Did he hurt you, Princess?"

"What?" Valia shook her head. "No. He saved me."

"Princess?"

Valia looked to the sound of the voice and saw Kaleen—the *real* Kaleen—racing toward her from across the courtyard. Her hand-maiden was dressed in a nightgown and slippers, her hair loose around her shoulders, with little care for her appearance. She raced straight to Valia and dropped into a low curtsey, then lifted back up, her cheeks flushed and her eyes shining.

"Princess!"

"Kaleen." Valia's heart warmed. How could she ever have mixed this vibrant, lively girl up with the draevor imposter? "It's *so* lovely to see you again."

"Are you alright?" Kaleen swept her eyes over Valia.

"I am. I will be."

"Would you like a bath? A meal? Maybe... some new clothes?" Kaleen blushed at the last suggestion, but Valia nodded.

"Yes, to all three."

Kaleen nodded and hurried back into the palace.

Valia's attention was pulled again by another figure. This one moved slowly across the courtyard, flanked by several footmen. King Aran had always looked young and regal for his age, but the loss of his family seemed to have aged him prematurely. He walked slowly now, with a limp, and his back slightly hunched. Like Kaleen, he was dressed in his nightshirt and slippers.

In an instant, tears sprang to Valia's eyes. She took a step toward her father, then another. King Aran's eyes met hers as he stopped a few paces away.

"Valia," he said, his voice filled with disbelief. At the sound of her name, Valia finally felt the homecoming she'd wished for.

"Papa," she said, a name she hadn't called him since she was a young girl. She ran across the courtyard's flagstones and flung herself into her father's arms. He felt frail and bony—much less substantial than she remembered.

"Is it really you?" the king asked.

"It's me. I'm home."

Aran pulled back from the hug and swept his eyes up and down Valia. "You look well, my dear. Are you well?"

"Yes. All things considered, I am."

"I am so glad to have you home. Thank Flora."

"Thank Flora."

King Aran gently set Valia aside and turned to the mercenary. Immediately, his affectionate blue eyes morphed into the cold hardness of just-set ice.

"You brought my daughter home." It was a statement.

"Yes, Your Majesty." The man sank into a half bow, but there was something a little off about the gesture. It had none of his usual grace.

"Did you harm her?" King Aran asked coldly.

"Father!" Valia turned to him. "He rescued me." It was more than strange that the man had been met with such suspicion not only by the guard, but by the king as well.

King Aran swept his eyes over the man. "I suppose you'll be wanting your reward, then."

"Yes, Your Majesty." Was there a hint of mocking in the man's tone?

The king held out his hand and one of his footmen rushed forward with a round wooden chit. "Take it and go."

The man took the chit from the footman's hand, turned it over to inspect it, then nodded and placed it in a pouch hanging from his waist. Without another word, and without even looking at Valia, he turned and strode toward the gates. Valia shot her father an annoyed look. Even if the man was distant, frustrating, and not very talkative, he had singlehandedly rescued Valia. It seemed to her that he deserved a little recognition for that.

Valia hurried after the mercenary and caught him before he reached the gate, despite his effortlessly long strides. Slowly, the man spun back toward her.

"Yes?" His tone was even colder than before, but Valia didn't back down.

"Thank you." Her tone was firm. "I owe you my life. I won't forget that."

The man hesitated, and for a moment, Valia was sure he was going to walk away without saying anything. But then he bent closer, until his lips were only inches from her ear.

"My name's Kirin," he whispered. "If you're ever in danger again, find me." He pressed a small disk into the palm of Valia's hand. She slipped it into a pocket on the side of her dress meant for her rings.

Then, he was gone. He moved so quickly that Valia barely registered his absence until he was halfway across the courtyard.

She stared after him as he passed through the gates and disappeared into the dim city streets outside.

Kirin. She'd expected a different name, somehow, though she wasn't sure what.

"What did he say to you, dear?" Valia's father called to her.

"He just said goodbye," Valia lied. She didn't know why she hid the truth, but the strange reaction everyone had shown toward the man, toward *Kirin*, made her wary. It didn't matter. She would likely never see him again.

Valia shook her head to clear it and returned to her father, who looked at her suspiciously.

"Alright, my dear. What matters is you're home now, and you'll have no further cause to associate with men like him."

"Mercenaries?"

King Aran shook his head. "I wish that was all. Let's not speak on this any further. You must be exhausted. Let's get you inside."

Valia let herself be led toward the palace door. She spared only one glance back at the closing gates before entering the palace.

The halls were darkened, illuminated by a few flickering candles, but Valia was relieved to find that it lacked the bone-aching chill of the draevori illusion.

"How are you faring?" she asked her father as they passed the main hall and began the climb up to the royal towers. "How is Avania?"

"We'll talk more in the morning." King Aran squeezed her arm reassuringly.

"We can talk now." Valia bit her lip. "I'm not even sure how long I've been gone. I feel like I'm missing so much."

"I know, my dear. We'll talk in the morning. I promise, I'll tell you everything."

"Alright." Valia glanced at her father, but his face revealed nothing of what he was thinking. "And mother, my sisters…" She couldn't bring herself to finish the question, but her father understood.

"They're gone, my dear. It's just us now."

Valia tried to ignore the tears pricking at the backs of her eyes. The spell she'd wanted to cast earlier that day, when she'd hoped to find a sign of her living family, felt silly now—like a child's naive hope.

"I hope you understand, my darling girl, there's nothing you could have done." He squeezed Valia's arm again. "We found… traces of them by the river. Clothes half-burnt to ash. Your mother's necklace was there. I've never seen anything like it. There's nothing you could have done differently to save them." He repeated himself to ensure she understood.

His words, so different from what his draevori impostor had said to her so many times, sent the tears Valia had held back spilling down her cheeks.

"Thank you." She wiped her tears quickly with the torn, dirty sleeve of her dress.

They reached the top of the stairs and passed the rooms that had belonged to Valia's elder sisters. Valia's chamber was at the end of the hallway, across from her younger sister's rooms. Valia glanced at the closed doors, then looked away. She couldn't stand the thought of those rooms being empty, now and forever.

"Did you know it was draevori, father? Why would they do this? How?"

"Rest, my dear. In the morning, we'll talk." King Aran hesitated. "But before you go, you'd tell me if that man hurt you, wouldn't you? I sent others, more trustworthy men, but none returned."

"He didn't hurt me." Valia frowned. "Why are you so worried that he did?"

"Trust me, dear. It's better you stay away from him and men like him in the future."

"Alright, father." Valia nodded. She was home now, so it wasn't hard to agree. She couldn't imagine what need she'd have for a mercenary with a whole army at her father's command.

"Rest well, Valia. You're home now."

"Thank you, father." Valia gave her father another quick hug, then stepped into her chambers.

In the short time Valia had been downstairs, Kaleen had drawn a hot bath, which steamed enticingly from the open door of Valia's bathing chamber. The table in Valia's chamber had been laid with all manner of food, from fresh fruit to soft bread and pastries. Nearby, her bed looked so warm and familiar that Valia almost collapsed from weariness right then and there.

The room looked like the version in the draevori illusion, but it was different, too. The colors were brighter, and the smells were stronger. Some things also looked completely different. That window was on another wall, for one, and the room somehow seemed... not smaller, but *fuller*. Less empty. Perhaps there had been flaws with the draevorian power—or perhaps with Valia's memory in her weakened state—but either way, she was thankful.

"Princess!" Kaleen bounded out of the bathing chamber, a mound of fresh linens in her arms. "I wasn't sure what you'd want to do first, so I got everything ready. Sorry, the kitchens didn't have much in the way of fresh food at this time of night, but I got everything I could."

"Oh, Kaleen." Valia felt teary again. "It's all wonderful. I think I'll start with the bath."

"Excellent choice, Princess." Kaleen set the linens on the small chaise longue in the corner of Valia's room and led the way to the bath. Valia removed her boots and let Kaleen help her out of her dress.

"What would you like me to do with... this?" Kaleen held up the torn, dirtied, threadbare blue dress that Valia had worn since she'd disappeared.

"Burn it," Valia said decisively. "Oh, wait." She reached for the dress and fished the disk Kirin had given her out of the pocket. She turned it over in her hand. It was made of a hard material that felt smooth and almost cold beneath Valia's fingertips. On one side, *Olanthian Seeker* was written in a curving script, and on the other, Valia could make out *Kirin Adante*. She frowned. Olanthus was a city in a nearby country, but she couldn't place exactly where, and the material was strange. It didn't seem quite like any stone or metal she'd ever known. Valia also knew most types of wood that grew in Avania, and many that didn't, but she didn't recognize this as any of them.

"And the boots?"

Valia was startled out of her musings by Kaleen's question. She quickly set the disk on the edge of the sink and turned to her handmaiden.

"I'll keep those." They were solid riding boots, and Valia was thankful to Kirin for the effort he'd gone through to get them for her. There was no need to throw them away.

"Yes, Princess." Kaleen set the boots aside. "Are you ready for your bath?"

But Valia's attention was drawn to the looking glass above the bath. In it, an unfamiliar woman stared back at her. The woman's black hair was knotted and messy. Her blue eyes were puffy. She was thin and looked almost fragile. Her cheekbones were a little too visible and her skin was pale from lack of sunlight, streaked with dirt. Yet she still looked more like herself than she had in the draevori palace.

Logically, Valia knew that this woman was her, but she was having trouble coming to terms with the idea. Strangely, her first thought was that she wished she'd looked nicer for the journey with Kirin. She wasn't sure what he'd been thinking, kissing her after seeing her like this—though she knew it had been the only way to shock her out of the illusion. That was all.

"Princess?"

"Sorry." Valia turned to Kaleen with as bright a smile as she could muster. "I just look a little different. That's all."

"It's nothing a nice bath, some food, and a good night's sleep won't fix," Kaleen said kindly. Valia wasn't so sure, but she nodded anyway. Kaleen dipped her hand into the bath and frowned. "Oh, the water has cooled a bit. Just a moment."

Kaleen pricked her finger with a small metal ring and pressed the blood to a wooden flux ring on another finger, her lips moving in an unspoken spell. Like most people in Avania, Kaleen could cast some minor seed spells. However, a flux ring was a rare and expensive item, reserved only for those near royalty or those who could afford it.

"It's ready, Princess."

"Thank you."

Valia stepped into the water, which was a perfect temperature, and felt her muscles begin to unspool. Her stress and aches seemed to melt away in the water. Kaleen appeared with a comb and a block of lemon-scented soap and Valia almost moaned with the relief of being clean at last. Working together, she and Kaleen tamed her unruly curls, then Valia washed herself thoroughly several times. After another rinse, she stepped out of the bath and let Kaleen wrap her in a warm towel, heated through another seed spell. Once she was dry, Kaleen helped her into a soft, lavender-scented nightdress.

"Thank you, Kaleen."

"Of course, Princess. Now, would you like to eat something?"

Valia fell on the food with the enthusiasm of someone who'd been on the brink of starvation. Food had never tasted better—except perhaps for that apple Kirin had brought her after they'd escaped the cave.

Kirin. Did he have food tonight? Did he have a warm bath and a soft bed? Valia thought he'd probably ridden off into the night to sleep at some inn somewhere—on the hard floor by choice. Or maybe he'd gone home. Valia had no idea if he had a home, but he probably did. Even mercenaries must live somewhere.

"Kaleen," Valia said around a mouthful of bread. "How long was I gone?"

"You don't know?" Kaleen's brow wrinkled. "I'm not sure I should tell you..."

"It's fine."

"Nineteen days."

"Right." Valia nodded as though this were a perfectly normal thing to hear. "Nineteen days. Okay."

"I shouldn't have told you." Kaleen's brow wrinkled further.

"No, it's okay. I would have found out anyway."

"If it isn't too forward to ask..." Kaleen clasped her hands. "Where were you?"

"In a cave," Valia said. "Draevori took me."

"Draevori?" Kaleen's green eyes widened. "Those are... real?"

"Apparently so."

"I... what... that must have been awful."

"A little bit." Valia regretted having broached this topic. She popped an entire strawberry into her mouth to forestall further questions, and Kaleen seemed to take the hint.

A few moments later, clean and with her stomach full, Valia felt exhaustion threaten to overwhelm her. She barely made it to her bed before she was asleep.

CHAPTER SIX

HEIR

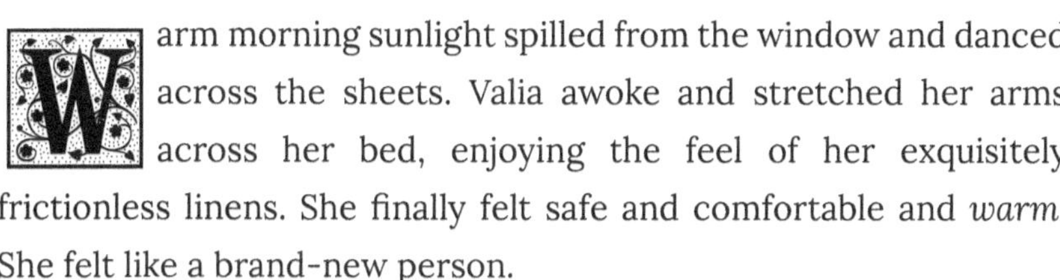

Warm morning sunlight spilled from the window and danced across the sheets. Valia awoke and stretched her arms across her bed, enjoying the feel of her exquisitely frictionless linens. She finally felt safe and comfortable and *warm.* She felt like a brand-new person.

Valia slowly pushed herself into a seated position. In the light of day, she realized just how different her real room looked from the one the draevori had conjured. Not only was the window on a different wall, but the bed was surrounded by gossamer curtains, the floor was covered in soft rugs instead of bare flagstones, and everything was full of color. Valia smiled and danced her thumbs across each of her rings in turn. She was *home.*

Valia slid out of bed and padded across the floor to her bathing chamber, where she washed her face with the bowl of water Kaleen had left out for her. The girl in the looking glass still looked a little too thin, but she ignored that. She wove her curls into a thick braid down her back, then returned to her bed.

A moment later, the door to her room opened and Kaleen entered, bearing a tray. She jumped when she caught sight of Valia, the tray rattling precariously, but was able to steady herself quickly.

"Oh, Princess, you're awake." Kaleen crossed the room on light feet, the tray now expertly balanced, and set it on Valia's side table. She wore the simple uniform of the palace staff: a green skirt with an apron and a pressed white blouse. Her blonde hair was gathered into a neat bun on her head. She looked older than Valia remembered. Her young handmaiden was growing up. "I've brought you chocolate."

"And breakfast?" Valia peered hopefully at the tray, but it bore only the mug of chocolate.

"King Aran has requested that you join him in the small dining hall for breakfast, when you're ready."

"Oh." Valia was taken aback. The princesses had usually eaten breakfast alone or with each other, all except for Samalia. As the heir to the throne, Samalia had joined their father for daily breakfasts to learn from him and share strategies. The only exception was formal breakfasts with dignitaries or to celebrate weddings, which were held in the main banquet hall and attended by all members of the royal family.

"Don't worry, I was told he wasn't in any hurry." Kaleen smiled reassuringly. "Enjoy your chocolate, then we'll get you dressed."

Valia took the mug of chocolate and sipped it. It was made just the way she remembered, sweet and with a sprinkle of cinnamon.

"Did you sleep well?" Kaleen hovered beside the bed, clasping and unclasping her hands.

"Yes, I slept well. Come, sit with me." Valia patted the side of the bed.

Kaleen perched on the edge of the bed. "I'm glad to hear it."

"How have you been?" Valia took another deep sip of chocolate.

"It's been... difficult." Kaleen looked away. "With you and the other princesses and the queen all... gone... and then everything that's happened..."

"What's happened?"

"Oh, nothing." Kaleen sat up a little straighter. "I just meant to say that we missed you."

Valia knew that there was something Kaleen wasn't telling her, but the handmaiden was clearly uncomfortable, so Valia didn't push.

"And how is your family?" she asked instead.

"My brother was accepted as a recruit into the Lirrhguard." Kaleen's pink cheeks glowed with pride. "My parents are well. I still visit them on my day off."

"Congratulations to your brother." Valia toasted Kaleen with her mug of chocolate, then drained the cup. Usually, she wasn't sure she'd have celebrated a boy barely eighteen joining the military during such uncertain times, but Kaleen had often told her this was her brother's dream, so it seemed like good news. "Well, I don't want to keep my father waiting. Let's get ready."

Kaleen got to her feet and hurried to Valia's wardrobe. Valia followed at a more sedate pace as Kaleen selected a deep blue gown with tiny silver stars.

"Isn't that a little too formal for breakfast with my father?" Valia asked.

Kaleen hesitated. "It's just that, since you're, well... your father will need you more, now."

Despite Kaleen's kind phrasing, the words hit Valia hard. With her older sisters gone, she was the heir now. The Martev legacy fell on her shoulders, and hers alone. Valia didn't want to think about that, now or ever, so she took the gown from Kaleen without protest.

Valia removed her nightdress, and Kaleen helped her step into the starry blue gown, then did up the laces in the back. At least this breakfast wasn't formal enough to require petticoats or, worst of all, a corset, Valia mused as Kaleen pulled the last of the laces snugly into place.

"Now, let me do your hair." Kaleen gestured for Valia to sit in front of the looking glass at her vanity. She expertly undid Valia's braid and began weaving her hair into a far more elaborate version. Luckily, it didn't take long, and soon Valia was slipping on a pair of black shoes and bidding Kaleen goodbye.

"Good luck! I'll press a circle for you!" Kaleen called as Valia left. It was unhelpful since Valia was already nervous and wanted to pretend everything was normal, but she smiled back at her hand-maiden and pressed a circle back by joining her thumb and pointer finger. It was a gesture often given for good luck, as it resembled a floramancer pricking their thumb for a spell.

Valia's father was waiting for her in the small dining hall when she came downstairs. *Small* may have been a misnomer; even though it was the smallest of the dining halls, the room still held four long tables down the length, with another widthwise across the back of the room, facing the others. Long, thin windows stretched from the floor to the gabled ceiling high above, letting shafts of warm morning light fall across the tables. The room was light, airy, and a little imposing.

"Good morning, Valia. Everyone, please leave us."

Valia refocused on her father, who sat at the head table. A single chair had been positioned across from him, and the table had been filled with delicious-smelling breakfast items. Valia crossed the room, her shoes echoing loudly on the flagstone floor, as servants left the room.

"Good morning, father."

King Aran gestured to the seat across from him. "Please, join me. It really is so wonderful to have you back, my dear."

"It's good to *be* back." Valia slid into the chair and surveyed the breakfast options. Her mouth began to water.

"Please, help yourself." King Aran gestured to the food. "I asked the kitchen to make all your favorites."

It was true. Everything from slivers of orelai fruit from the southern coast to tiny chocolate-studded pastries—Valia's favorite food as a child—was laid out on the table in front of them. Valia loaded her plate but, despite her hunger, she didn't eat.

"I feel like there's a lot I missed." She toyed with a piece of fruit, her eyes fixed on her plate. "What has happened while I was gone?"

King Aran sighed. "My dear. Avania has seen better days. With our family weakened and the threat of darkness seemingly at our doorstep, the population has been restless. We've had an increase in bandit activity, and even some reports of metemancy in our borders. On top of that, strange things have been happening around the country. Creatures unseen in ages have reappeared. Several floramancers have reported their powers seem weakened. There have been droughts and an increase in disease."

Valia leaned forward, her plate of food forgotten. "Do you know why?"

King Aran sighed, and, in that moment, he looked more like an old man than like Valia's vigorous father again. "Nothing has been confirmed yet. But there shall be answers soon, my dear. For everything. I promise you."

Valia examined her father. All her life, he'd seemed strong, undefeatable, capable of handling anything that happened—truly deserving of his kingly position. Even without any real floramantic abilities to speak of, King Aran had always been her hero. Yet now, with most of his family gone and his kingdom in disarray, Valia saw him for the person he was instead of the incomplete image she'd created in her mind.

"I can't imagine how hard that must have been." Valia reached for her father's hand in comfort, but he abruptly sat back in his chair and picked up a fork.

"Well." He ate a bite of pastry. "Yes. But you're back now, my dear, and that is a great comfort to me. I know this is a lot to handle all at once, but there is something else we need to discuss."

"I'm ready."

"With your sisters gone..." he trailed off, then began again. "Now that it's just the two of us, you are my heir, Valia. My only heir. You've always been given a lot of space to do what you pleased, but that means that you missed out on the training Samalia and Daria received." A lump grew in Valia's throat at the mention of her sisters, but she nodded. It was just as Kaleen had said that morning: Valia needed to be there for her father and kingdom. And she would be. "You've lived an easy, comfortable life as a younger princess. You haven't had to learn our history or study statecraft. And most of all, you've been granted a floramantic ring for each finger due to your gifted nature, yet little knowledge of how to use them. That changes now."

"I understand. What do you need me to do?"

"We'll start with the affairs of the people. Then, personal lessons. You must learn how to use your abilities more effectively. The events of the last few seasons have shown us Avania is balancing on a razor's edge. First and foremost, you must be ready lead the people. To make the hard decisions, in case something happens to me."

An image of the draevori version of her father in his coffin flashed through Valia's mind. Her stomach clenched at the thought, and she hated the draevori for having put that in her mind.

"Nothing will happen to you, father."

King Aran smiled, but it was worn and weary. "Take today to rest and recover. Tomorrow, we begin."

"I can start today." Valia sat up a little straighter. She was exhausted and sad, but she felt compelled by duty.

"That's my Vali." King Aran's smile brightened. "Then, we begin today."

CHAPTER SEVEN
STORIES

"And when I returned, my crops were gone. Destroyed! Nary a grain left. Just burnt, black stalks." The farmer twisted his straw hat in his hands. "Please, Your Majesty. The farm is all we have. My wife and sons will go hungry without our crops. And we fear the raiders may return."

Valia bit her lip and glanced at her father. King Aran sat on his throne, his hands clasped in his lap. Throughout the farmer's impassioned speech, the king's expression remained neutral, as though they were discussing what to have for breakfast or naming constellations in the sky, not talking about a man's entire livelihood.

"Princess Valia." King Aran turned to her. "What shall be done?"

Valia's stomach twisted. If this was what Samalia had been dealing with since she was a young girl, Valia was doubly thankful for her low place on the ascension order. She wasn't sure what to do.

Yet the farmer stared at her as though she held his future in the palm of her hand which, she realized, she did. Valia took a breath.

"First, I want to offer my sincere apologies for the state of your farm. Such things are unacceptable in Avania, and I wish your farm could be restored to you as it was. Since this is not possible, we will try to solve your problem another way." Valia took another breath.

Her thumb danced across her rings, and she wished, not for the first time, that magic could solve this issue. She could regrow the man's crops with her powers, although it would take a toll on her. Yet, it wasn't feasible, because if she offered to restore this man's farm with the help of Flora, every farmer who came here with a similar problem would expect the same. There was no way she'd be able to help everyone, not when half a dozen farmers had come to them with similar problems in one morning. Valia might not know a lot about politics, but she knew she couldn't promise more to one person than she could give to everyone.

"We can offer you enough novaroot seeds from our seedbank to replant your fields. The novaroot will grow through the dry seasons and grant a single harvest by the end of the cycle. In the meantime, we'll make sure you leave with enough florans to sustain your family until the harvest is ready. We'll also increase the posting of the watch in your area. Fath—Your Majesty?"

King Aran stepped in, "Cyrosa Cindermar and twelve watchmen will patrol the area for one season. If any more fires begin, she will snuff them out, along with any marauders foolish enough to ignore her banner."

"Thank you, Your Majesty. Thank you, Your Highness. Flora smile upon you." The man swept into a low bow. He seemed truly grateful, but Valia's heart ached that she couldn't undo all his hardships.

"We will take a short break, then return to hear more concerns," King Aran said. He stood slowly, then nodded to Valia to follow him. She did so gratefully. The entire morning after breakfast had been spent hearing grievances in the throne room, and Valia was exhausted.

King Aran led the way into a small sitting room, where he filled two glasses with water and handed one to Valia. She drank deeply.

"My dear," he said, his voice kind. "You did well. You displayed kindness, composure, and generosity without offering too much of yourself. Your mother would be proud."

"Thank you, father." Valia set her cup down and crossed to the window. Outside, Wyra was colored with the reds and golds of early autumn, but the skies were gray. "But... shouldn't we be able to do more for them?"

"It simply isn't possible." Valia heard her father's footsteps behind her. "We must ration our limited resources. As hard as it is, sometimes we must put the good of the kingdom over the good of any individual."

"I know." Valia sighed. "I just... is it always like this?"

"More or less." King Aran joined her at the windowsill. "Citizens come to us with life and death problems in hope of a solution, and that solution is never easy. The more we give to one, the less we have to give to another. But, the scale of problems has increased. I haven't seen this many people attacked by creatures or having their crops destroyed or losing touch with Flora in my lifetime."

Valia pressed her palms against the hard wood of the windowsill. "I just wish we could figure out why this is happening. There's a cause. We just have to find it."

"I know, my dear. It's not as simple as it may seem. The world is vast, and its mysteries aplenty. Your mother and I tried everything to protect Avania, to maintain order and peace. What good that's done us now..." He trailed off, thinking of his absent queen.

They stood, side by side, for a while. Then Valia glanced at her father.

"You offered that woman from Canin to put a bounty on the seamoth that attacked her husband. I was wondering if we should offer the bounty to the mercenary who rescued me."

"My dear. That would be a mistake. There are many reputable mercenaries who can hunt seamoths. In any case, I've received word the man left Wyra the same night he arrived with you and has not returned since."

Valia bit her lip. Kirin had told her he would return to finish off the draevori, but she imagined he'd rest for a night or two.

Valia reached into her pocket and ran her finger around the man's token. She'd taken to carrying it with her, although she couldn't quite explain why, even to herself.

"My dear, take a break for now. It's been a long morning for you. I'll handle the rest of today's grievances. After umbra, we have a briefing with the grand marshal regarding border skirmishes with Tromin. You have a few personal lessons after that. Then, dinner with the ambassador from Kanalear. For now, rest."

Valia felt she should protest and offer to stay, but she really did need a break. "Thank you, father."

Valia didn't go to her chambers, though. Instead, she charted a direct course to the palace library. She'd been itching to visit here to get a head start on her numerous tutoring sessions about Avanian politics and history, and to look for clues as to why Avania seemed to be coming apart at the seams. But for now, Valia had something else in mind.

She picked out a few tomes, then found a quiet corner with a large armchair and a window overlooking Wyra. She sat with her legs folded beneath her and withdrew the token from her pocket.

She looked up Olanthus and discovered it to be a remote coastal city in Tromin—one of Avania's bordering countries—and built directly underneath the ever-present moon. Previously, Avania and

Tromin had been at war. In recent times, tensions had cooled into active distrust, with occasional skirmishes between discontent civilians near the border.

So, it seemed Kirin was from Tromin. Apart from being a former enemy, Tromin was notable for being a primarily metemantic country. Although Kirin hadn't seemed to use magic at all, Valia didn't like the idea that his country's mages manipulated unliving materials. Something about it just wasn't right.

Valia spent some time combing through texts to find the origin of the token's material. To her surprise, she couldn't find anything, even in the relatively obscure books.

Maybe, Valia thought with a warm pulse of excitement, she didn't need the books to figure this out. When her blood came into contact with plant material, she could feel a hint of the kind of power it could offer. She'd first noticed this as a child when, shortly after her attunement ceremony, she'd accidentally pricked her finger with an embroidery needle and gotten blood on the oak headboard of her bed. Immediately, she'd gotten a feeling of movement and vertigo, which was how she'd learned that oak was a force material. Valia's own rings were inlaid with particularly rare and powerful materials, but in a pinch, she could use nearly any flower for simple tasks.

Valia pricked her thumb with her ring and, holding the token in her free hand, allowed a single drop of blood to fall onto its surface. She waited with bated breath. Nothing happened. Curious, Valia tried once more, but there was still no reaction from the object in her hand.

Alarmed, Valia wiped the blood from the token on her dress and shoved it back into her pocket. It was unusual to find a material that didn't conduct the Flora, even a little.

He's from Tromin. Maybe her father and Poriev had been just-ified when they said Kirin was dangerous. It was difficult to believe after he'd saved her from the draevori, but Valia couldn't dismiss the idea. Not when the token in her pocket was clearly metemantic.

If you're ever in danger, find me. Kirin's words to her replayed in her head and Valia shoved herself to her feet. She wasn't in danger. At least, not from the kinds of beasts Kirin would slay. The danger in Avania would be much more powerful, already capable of destroying the royal family. Her family. Valia wasn't sure she could believe it to be a random attack from a long-extinct creature.

Valia tracked down one of the books on Avanian history and sat back in her chair, halfway hoping to stumble upon a piece of the puzzle, but also eager for the distraction. She lost herself in the texts, reading about Avanian kings and queens from five hundred cycles ago, which was interesting if not particularly helpful. Then, the sky outside the window quickly darkened, and Valia realized she was about to be late for her next meeting. She shelved the book and hurried out of the library.

Days of petitions, meetings, and lessons flew by. Valia ran from meeting to lesson to dinner, her mind too full, her body aching for nothing more than the quiet of her bed. This night, though, when stillness fell over the palace, and Valia's final tasks of the day were completed, she didn't want to sleep. Instead, she put on a cloak against the early chill and left her room. She passed her sisters' rooms, the doors still unopened, and made her way to the door leading to the top of the tower. A guard stationed at the end of the corridor nodded to her, and Valia began the climb.

At the top of the tower stood a small balcony. It had a lovely view over the nighttime lights of Wyra and of the stars in the inky black sky above, but Valia didn't stop to enjoy it. She lifted her skirts and climbed a trellis at the top of the tower onto the roof. This was the highest point of the palace, where nothing stood between Valia and the sky. She laid back against the worn shingles and looked up.

Throughout her childhood, Valia had come here when she needed to be alone. Growing up as a princess with three sisters, she'd rarely had a moment to herself. Even though the forest was close, this rooftop was always where she'd been most at peace.

Valia wished she could summon that peace today. Today, she only felt powerless. She hadn't been able to save her sisters or her mother. She hadn't been able to escape the draevori on her own. And now, she felt she couldn't be the kind of ruler Avania needed. Tears formed in Valia's eyes and rolled slowly down her cheeks. She wiped them away with the sleeve of her cloak. If only she could turn back time and have one more chance to do things right.

CHAPTER EIGHT
STARS

alia opened her eyes to warm sunlight and the sound of Kaleen clinking cups and plates. As opposed to the last few mornings when she'd been desperate for more time in bed, Valia grinned and sat up, ready to begin the day. After almost a season of nonstop meetings and training, King Aran had finally given her a day to herself.

"Good morning, Princess."

"Good morning, Kaleen." Valia grinned at her handmaiden. "You look nice today."

"Me?" Kaleen looked down at her uniform dress, then smoothed a hand over her braid. "I look as I always do."

"No, you look *especially* nice." Valia crossed her legs and reached for the cup of chocolate that Kaleen handed her. "This smells great."

"You're in a good mood today, Princess."

"I am." Valia sipped her hot chocolate. "I'm going for a ride with Star later. I can't wait."

"A ride? Is that safe?" Kaleen had gone to tend the fire, but she turned back to Valia, her young face creased with worry.

"I won't go far." It was sweet of Kaleen to be worried, but Valia had ridden the route dozens of times before without incident. The most terrifying creature she'd ever spotted so close to the palace had been a lopen, a rabbit-sized animal with hooves and a long tail that had skittered away when Valia rode by. Lopens were rumored to lure travelers deep into the forest at night. The travelers would return the next morning as if they'd spent all night at a tavern during a festival. They weren't much of a threat, and some people intentionally sought them out for fun.

After finishing her chocolate, Kaleen brought Valia her riding clothes and helped her dress. Then she wound Valia's hair into a tight, utilitarian braid to keep her curls at bay while she rode. Valia found the boots Kirin had bought and put them on.

Before too long, Valia was at the stables. The stable hand brought out Star, and Valia's heart melted. The horse looked just the same as she remembered, with a white and gray hide and a contrasted white spot on her forehead resembling a starflower. When she saw Valia, Star neighed and broke free of the stable hand's grip. Valia reached for her horse and hugged her around the neck. She held out an apple she'd taken from breakfast on an open palm. Star crunched the apple happily. Then, Valia mounted with the aid of multi-step stirrups made to accommodate her small stature.

As Valia rode through the palace gates—not the ones that led into the city, but those bordering the forest—she felt her worries begin to fade. Her mind felt sharper again among the trees and plants and animals. Valia should have made time to come out sooner.

Star picked up her pace on the familiar path and the trees became a blur beside them. Valia held out her arms as though she was flying, her legs keeping her expertly braced on Star's back. For a while, Star seemed eager to go faster and faster, but when they reached a small incline where the path narrowed, the horse slowed. Valia rubbed her neck.

"Good girl."

At a slower pace, they continued up the hill. Dense forest gave way to a meadow dotted with late-season flowers in pinks and blues. A small stream burbled through the center of the meadow.

Valia pulled Star to a stop and dismounted. She'd come to this meadow often with her sisters when they were younger. They'd played games of hiding and chasing and had lain on the grass, hands clasped, giggling until their stomachs hurt. Tears pricked at Valia's eyes, but she didn't let them fall. This wasn't a sad day. It was a day to remember the people she loved.

Valia smiled at the meadow where she'd lain with her sisters, giggling, weaving the flowers into bracelets. She smiled at the river where they'd learned to swim under the watchful eye of their mother. She smiled at the large, hollow tree where Litia had once hidden all morning while they'd all searched for her.

If Litia had been able to hide that long in such a small clearing, surely she could have hidden during the draevori attack.

Valia had hoped before that one of her sisters or her mother might have survived, but her full schedule along with her father's certainty that they'd all been killed made her forget her hope. Now, though, in the fresh air, with the birds singing and so much life around her, Valia's hope sparked again. Even if there was only a slim chance one of her dearests was out there, she had to know for herself.

Valia knelt in the soft grass and danced her thumb across her rings. As she had in the clearing outside the inn, Valia pressed blood to her sight ring. If the spell worked, it would show a constellation of Valia's immediate family. Valia held her breath as the last vestiges of the spell's power seeped into the air in front of her.

For a long moment, it seemed nothing would happen. The clearing was still, with nothing more than a distant crunch in the forest and the trilling of birds to break the silence. Then, a soft white light rose from the ground and settled in the air just in front of Valia. Valia knew from casting this spell as a child that this light represented her.

Another light rose, this one slightly dimmer, and settled above the first. This was Valia's father. Since Valia had no living grandparents, if a third light appeared, it would mean that someone had survived.

Valia waited, her heart pounding, as the moment stretched. Only a short moment passed, but they felt like the longest of Valia's life. Just as she was about to give up hope, a third light rose and settled beside Valia's.

Valia's breath caught. She stared at the three lights as if hoping to burn their image into her eyelids. This could only mean one of her sisters was alive. Tears sprang to her eyes, but for a completely different reason from before. She lifted her hand to brush against the stars, but they flickered out at her touch. No matter. One of her sisters had survived. Valia let out a soft, disbelieving laugh.

Valia knew several spells for finding people. Usually, she needed something of the person's to make the spell work, but since she was looking for her sisters, she needed nothing more than her own blood. Valia conjured up memories of her oldest sister, Samalia.

"Flora, hear me," Valia whispered, pricking her thumb and pressing blood to her sight ring again. "I—"

Before she knew what happened, Valia was hurtling through the air.

Confusion met fear as she tumbled above the grass, then landed on the hard ground and rolled to a halt. She gasped for air as she blinked wide-eyed at the blue sky above. She shoved herself to her feet and spun to search for her attacker. The world blurred, and the trees turned to streaks of orange and green. Valia spotted a fuzzy shape and heard a low roar and crunch—the same noise she'd dismissed while casting her spell.

Valia pressed her surge ring against a bloody spot on her thigh and prayed to the Flora for sharpened vision. Within moments, her vision cleared. She rolled and made it back to her feet, her shoulder stinging from cuts and scrapes.

A *manticore*? It roared again with its rows of sharp teeth bared and took a step closer. Its massive, leathery wings curled into its body, but its pointed tail swept from side to side like an agitated snake, ready to strike. A sweep of that tail must have been what sent Valia flying moments ago. Both its legs were tipped with long, sharp claws that dug into the soft earth of the meadow as it stalked forward.

Valia slowly backed away. She couldn't defeat a manticore by herself. Valia knew basic defensive magic, but she wasn't trained for combat. Her heart pounded. She couldn't die, not now, not when she was the only one who knew one of her sisters had survived. Not when she was the only one her father had left.

It was beyond unexpected for there to be a manticore this close to Wyra, but Valia didn't have time to ponder its cause or meaning. The manticore lunged, its teeth snapping at Valia's left as its tail struck at her right. Valia had just enough time to activate her gale ring and push herself backward, but not enough time to aim; she struck a tree and collapsed to the ground. The manticore stalked closer and Valia ran her thumbs across her rings, desperate for a plan. Alone in the forest, she couldn't cast anything above a mid-level trunk spell without the sacrifice leaving her vulnerable. *Think.*

Valia used her gale ring to send a wave of energy at the manticore. The spell's force sent the manticore sliding back an insignificant distance before its claws dug into the soft ground and it came to a stop, roaring even louder now.

Flora, help me! Using the same spell she had in the meadow with Kirin, Valia summoned a ball of bright white light, then sent it directly into the manticore's eyes. It hissed, more angry than hurt, but it was distracted. Valia seized the moment and limped deeper into the tree line. She crouched behind a bush and pressed blood to her lumen ring once again. As the manticore stalked closer, hissing and flicking its tail, a shape that could have been Valia darted out from behind the bush and froze in terror in front of the manticore. Hissing, the manticore struck with its tail, piercing the figure though its chest. Blood gushed as the manticore tossed the shape into the air, then turned to chase it, looking for all the world like a violent, scaly cat tormenting a bird. The spell was fuzzy and weak, but the manticore was still half-blind from her first spell. It seemed to have worked.

Behind the bush, Valia's head began to ache, and she knew she needed to get somewhere safe, right now. She crept toward the path and spotted Star. The horse, trained for adverse situations, seemed relatively unfazed. Valia whistled for the horse and Star ran to her. Valia managed to drag herself onto the horse's back.

"Take us home," she whispered, draping herself over Star. "Hurry, girl."

Star took the command to heart. She galloped toward the palace so quickly that it took all Valia's energy to hold on with the stabbing pain of every bounce. The trees blurred on either side of the path and Valia rested her head on Star's strained neck, exhausted. Once they were within earshot of the outer gate, Valia lifted her head and shouted to the guards to open it. They did, and Star barely had to slow as she flew through the gates and into the courtyard.

"Princess Valia? Are you alright?" The stable hand hurried toward her, alarmed.

Valia pulled Star to a stop and slid to the ground, wincing as her feet made contact with the hard dirt. Valia saw that some of her blood had smeared onto Star's flank, but the horse seemed uninjured.

"Take Star," she instructed, gesturing to the reigns.

"Princess, are you alright?" the stable hand repeated. His tone was increasingly worried; he must have noticed the blood dripping down Valia's leg from where she'd skidded along the ground.

"Yes." She began limping toward the palace. "But I need to speak with the king. Now." *One of my sisters is alive*, she thought. The excitement Valia felt was enough to keep her going, despite her aching joints and fresh bruises.

She passed Poriev, who was walking briskly toward the training ground, and called out to him. He turned, his eyes widening as he took in Valia's torn and bloodied clothing.

"There's a manticore in the forest," she told him. "In a clearing down the main path."

Poriev hurried to her, arms outstretched as though to catch her if she fell. Valia stepped back.

"I need to see my father."

"I'll escort you there."

"No, I can walk." Valia shook her head. "You have a manticore to worry about."

She hurried into the palace as quickly as her aching legs would take her, past servants and guards as they stared at her and her many wounds in horror.

CHAPTER NINE
BLOCKED

"ather!" Valia pushed the heavy oak door to her father's chancery open. King Aran sat behind his desk, surrounded by several of his advisors. Behind him, a portrait of Valia's mother smiled down on them, dressed in a ceremonial gown and wearing her favorite necklace. Through her exhaustion, Valia stared into her mother's painted face, drawing comfort and reassurance that she was doing the right thing.

"Valia, I'm busy. Please come back later." He didn't look up from the papers spread on his desk.

"This is important." Valia stepped into the room and one of the advisors caught sight of her, then cleared his throat. King Aran looked up. His blue eyes, so like Valia's, widened in shock.

"Valia? Everyone out. Send in the healers."

"The healers can wait." Valia's knee threatened to collapse from pain as she crossed to her father's desk, belying her point, but it didn't matter. "I need to talk to you."

The last of the advisors filed out, exchanging worried glances all the way, and Valia rested her hands on her father's desk to steady herself.

"I cast a family-finding spell," she told him. "And it revealed that one of my sisters is *alive!*"

King Aran was already shaking his head, his worried expression deepening. "My dear, that isn't possible. They are gone."

"No." Valia shook her head, then wished she hadn't. She felt so dizzy, her eyesight blurred. "I thought so too, but I tried the spell today, and the results were clear. One of my sisters survived. She's out there somewhere, and we need to find her!"

"My dear—"

"No. Watch." There was no time for her father's doubt. Valia pricked her finger and drew on her magic to repeat the family-finding spell. Despite it being a minor root spell, it took all her remaining energy to summon the power of the Flora. Still, she was successful, and the same three stars appeared in the air above her father's desk. Her knees weakened with the effort, and Valia sank involuntarily into the chair behind her as the three stars appeared.

"Valia, no." Her father swiped the stars away with the back of his hand and they fizzled into nothingness. "You're injured. Your brain might well be loose. This doesn't mean what you think it does."

"You saw it!" Valia was incredulous. "Three stars. You, me, and one of my sisters." She counted each family member off on her fingers, as though math might be the problem.

"My dear sweet girl," Aran said, his voice carrying the gentle tone people usually used with spooked horses or young children. "First, tell me what happened to you. You came back from a simple ride bloody and bruised. I can't ignore your injuries."

"A manticore, father. I've already apprised Lord Captain Poriev. But that hardly matters here." Valia tried to stand, but her legs wobbled. "One of my sisters—"

"Enough!" King Aran slammed his hand down on the desk, startling them both. "No more talk of this, not until the healers have seen you."

As if on cue, there was a knock on the door and one of the three royal healers entered.

"What seems to have happened?" the healer asked.

"Attacked by a manticore, of all things, this close to Wyra. Where is Poriev?" The king stood. "See to her. I have important matters to attend to."

Then he swept out of the room, all swirling purple cloak and anger. Valia turned to watch him go, then winced as dizziness returned. How could he walk out on her right now? Was *she* not an important matter? He needed to be looking for her missing sister. He needed to muster the might of Avania to find her.

"Let's have a look at you," the healer said briskly. She knelt in front of Valia, and using a contraption permanently affixed to her body, extracted blood into a disk of what looked like afir wood that hung on a band around her waist. Valia felt a wave of warmth sweep through her, then the healer nodded.

"Nothing is broken, only a few sprains and bruises. I'll transport you to your chambers, then put you in a healing sleep that should take care of almost everything."

"No." Valia tried to push herself to her feet, but the healer pushed her back into the chair. "No, I can't sleep. I have things to do."

"You must, Princess. It'll only be half a day at most."

"No." Valia took care not to shake her head but hoped that her urgency would be conveyed in her tone. All she could think of was one of her sisters, alone and imprisoned or injured somewhere, wondering if anyone was coming for her. She couldn't possibly sleep now.

"So stubborn, just like your father. I'll have you know I'm one of three people in the palace with the power to overrule you on matters of health. You're going to sleep."

She called for a guard, who picked Valia up despite her protests and carried her to her chambers. Kaleen was out during the day, so the healer helped Valia remove her torn and bloodied dress and her boots, then climb into bed.

"I can't sleep," Valia repeated. The healer paid her no mind. She pressed two more of the disks around her waist, then laid her hands on the sides of Valia's head. Valia quickly drifted into sleep.

"I think she's waking up. Princess?"

"My dear?"

Valia moaned. Her head ached softly, and she felt stiff, but a quick wiggle of her toes and fingers confirmed that everything seemed to be in working order. She pried her eyes open with a great force of will. Kaleen was sitting by her bedside, as was Valia's father.

"Princess, how are you feeling?" Kaleen leaned forward and brushed some of Valia's hair away from her face.

"I'm okay." Valia pushed herself into a seated position. "Father, we need to—"

"I know, you want to talk about your sisters." King Aran shifted closer. "And we will. I'm sorry I was harsh with you yesterday. I was worried about you, all battered and bruised not long after I'd just gotten you back."

"I understand, father. It's okay. So... we'll talk now?"

"Let Kaleen get you cleaned up. Then, I have something to show you."

"Okay." Valia nodded, relieved the action didn't make her dizzy this time, and that her father sounded more reasonable now.

The king stepped out. Kaleen helped Valia out of bed and into a warm bath. Kaleen seemed to understand that Valia didn't want to talk, because she helped her clean off the dried blood without asking any questions. It was unusual for the talkative handmaiden, but Valia was glad for the peace while still regaining her bearings. Soon, Valia was dressed in a simple dark gown, her hair braided down her back, with comfortable slippers. She stepped into the hallway, where her father had been standing with two of his advisors.

"Come, my dear."

"Where are we going?"

"I should have taken you sooner. I wanted to spare you the pain." King Aran gave Valia a tight smile. "That was wrong of me."

"...*Where* are we going?" Valia repeated, now more worried by his cryptic reply.

"We're going to visit our family." Heavy realization sank into Valia's stomach as King Aran led her across the gardens, through a small stand of trees, past the brinwood tree, and into the family burial grounds. Valia had been here before to pay tribute to her grandparents alongside her family, but she didn't want to be here now.

The king led her to a row of fresh graves, all of which were lovingly decorated with fresh flowers.

"One of my sisters is alive," Valia said, her voice quivering.

"No." The king led her to the first grave. "You have powers beyond my own. I'm sure if you try, you can feel them here. Everything we found at the Garden of Luma was brought here."

Valia sank to her knees in the new grass and drew on her sight ring. Almost immediately, tears began to pour down her cheeks. She did feel her mother and sisters here. Not them, exactly, but some remnant of who they had been. Her mother's quiet cleverness. Samalia's nurturing spirit. Daria's sharp wit. Litia's never-ending positivity. The spell she'd cast had shown that one of her sisters was alive, but that didn't seem to be the case. She felt them here, in their graves.

Valia's father helped her to her feet. He put his arm around her shoulders—a rare display of physical affection from the stoic man.

"Do you understand now? There's no way that your sisters are alive. Please, my dear, don't push on this any further. You'll only cause yourself more pain."

"Yes, father. I understand." Valia nodded. She let her father lead her back toward the palace, her eyes still blurry with tears. Until now, she'd held out a glimmer of hope that someone else might have survived, but that was gone now. Her family, except her father, were there in that graveyard. She'd never see them again.

"Take some time." Valia looked up and saw her caring father who also mourned his lost family transition to King Aran. "We have a meeting with Ambassador Roales, but take as much time as you need."

"No, I can come." Valia straightened up. "It's my duty to attend these meetings too now, father. Do I have a moment to change?"

The rest of the day passed in a never-ending blur of meetings and engagements. Valia did her best to focus on the ins and outs of political discourse and the many difficulties facing Avania, but her thoughts kept drifting back to her family.

It felt impossible her family-finding spell had failed her—not once, but twice. Yet, there had been no mistaking the essence of her family in those graves. Perhaps, Valia reasoned, the stress and overwhelm of everything had affected her magic. It did happen, sometimes. Valia had read about even the most powerful of floramancers losing touch with reality after particularly traumatic events. They'd lose their senses, not temporarily, but permanently. Some particularly powerful ones even lost their minds and went missing or mad, sacrificing so many memories to the Flora that they lost all sense of themselves. She'd certainly been through more than a few tragic and frightening events lately, though the rest of her magic seemed fine.

That night, after a late meeting with her father and his advisors about Wyrian security, Valia slumped off to bed. Kaleen tried to engage her in conversation as she helped her into her bath, but Valia struggled to keep up even the slightest bit of chatter. As Kaleen reheated the bathwater after it had grown cool, an idea overtook Valia, and she sat up straight in the tub.

"Kaleen."

"Yes, Princess?" Kaleen sounded more than a little surprised at Valia suddenly speaking after an evening of near silence.

"Would you do something for me?"

"Of course, Princess. What do you need?"

Valia pointed to her rings, which she'd carefully removed and set on the windowsill before getting into the bath. "Would you bring me my sight ring? The one with the dark purple inset."

"Of course." Kaleen carried the ring to Valia, almost reverent in her touch. Rings as particular as Valia's, with materials sourced from all over the known world, were precious, and it was very rare that any floramancer allowed another to even touch their rings.

"Would you perform a family tracking spell?" Valia asked. "I can tell you the procedure—"

"I can do it. I've mastered the spell so I can keep track of my brother, now that he'll be in the infantry. Should I..."

"Use my ring."

Kaleen nervously pressed a drop of blood to Valia's sight ring and muttered an incantation. A moment later, stars appeared in the air in front of her.

"That's me," Kaleen said softly. "My older brother. My two younger brothers—the twins. My baby sister. My mom. My dad. My aunt and uncle and my cousins. My grandparents..." She trailed off. Her constellation was so large that the stars at the periphery faded into nothingness as the amount of blood shared diluted. Valia felt a momentary stab of envy toward her handmaiden who had such a large family, but she pushed it away.

"Thank you. Now, I'd like you to cast the spell again, but for *my* family."

"Princess, that may not work the same." Kaleen bit her lip. "I'm not that skilled..."

"We can use my blood, and you can draw on my power." Valia hesitated. "If you're uncomfortable, I won't force you."

"No, it's alright. I don't mind. Just, if I may ask, Princess, why won't you cast the spell yourself?"

"I have. I've had some conflicting evidence, and I worry that my magic is just showing me what I want to see. I'm trying to understand where it went wrong, and why."

"We can try." Kaleen held out the ring. Valia let a drop of her blood fall onto it, then took her handmaiden's hand. It was a strange feeling, having someone else use her power. Valia could only compare it to the time a now-disgraced palace healer had decided to use leeches to cure one of Valia's childhood illnesses. The leeches had pulled on her blood until Valia felt weak and lightheaded. This felt similar, like a pulling sensation somewhere deep inside.

Kaleen spoke the words to the spell softly. Just as when Valia had cast the spell, three stars appeared in front of them.

"How many do you see?" Valia asked.

"Three stars, Princess." They stood, hands clasped, staring at the three stars. "But... aren't they..."

"I know. That's the mystery. How is it that the spell shows me three living members of my family, when I know that my sisters and mother are dead?" The final word was hard to speak, but Valia couldn't shy away from the truth. She'd been to the burial grounds. She sensed them there without a doubt.

"Kaleen." Valia squeezed her handmaiden's hand, then released it. "Thank you for your help. Please, tell no one about this."

"Shouldn't you tell the king?"

"I already have." Valia's voice was grim. "Would you help me out of the bath? I have work to do."

Kaleen helped Valia up. Valia dried herself and dressed in the thin cotton gown she wore to sleep.

"Shall I stay?" Kaleen asked.

"No, thank you. You've been immensely helpful already. You may retire for the night."

"Goodnight, Princess." Kaleen disappeared, with only a single worried glance thrown back in Valia's direction. Valia took her rings from the windowsill and slipped them back onto her fingers, muttering their names as she did so.

"Link, sight, lumen, surge, gale, flux, null, prism." Valia flexed her fingers, feeling more confident now that she wore her rings again. Perhaps it was just her imagination, but the rings seemed to glow in the darkness of her room as she spoke their names. "With all this at my power, I will find the truth."

Valia sat cross-legged on her bed. The dark sky outside was already studded with a rich tapestry of stars, but it might as well have been the moments of umbra for all Valia noticed. Valia cast with a focus she'd rarely found before. As she pressed blood to the sight ring, power began to gather. Valia asked for a lot of information, so she readily offered her sight for a day. She spoke the words of the spell and felt the magic grow until it almost pulsated around her—ready, hungry.

"Find them," she whispered. The magic grew, then suddenly was sucked sideways with an audible pop. Darkness descended as Valia's vision disappeared, but she knew the spell had failed. Valia waited, sightless, drumming her fingers against her leg.

What was that? She had cast the spell correctly. She had enough power. Her sacrifice had been sufficient. And the disappearance of the power hadn't been the way spells normally failed: with a fizzle like a candle in the rain. It was as though something had sucked the magic out of the room.

A moment later, Valia's sight returned as the Flora acknowledged that the spell had been unsuccessful. Valia reached for a new spell, this one a simpler spell meant only to name the members of Valia's family. Once again, power gathered as she readied her sacrifice and spoke the words, and again dissipated as though pulled from the room.

Valia tried spell after spell, long into the night, but even the family-finding spell no longer worked. There was only one conclusion: something was interfering with her magic. Or *someone*.

Valia's first thought was the draevori. Perhaps Kirin had been unsuccessful in killing them. But did they really have the ability to do such a thing? Would they have the inclination?

Valia got up, willing her tiredness away, and slipped on a robe and slippers against the cold floor. After her experience in the draevori palace, Valia would never again sneak around at night with bare feet.

In the hallway outside, the guard posted to her door looked at her peculiarly.

"Is all well, Your Highness?"

"Yes, thank you. I simply couldn't sleep and would like to fetch a book from the library."

"I'll walk with you." The guard fell into step beside Valia.

"That's really unnecessary," Valia protested, but the guard came anyway. He followed her down the sleepy halls of the palace, into the library, and all the way to the shelf on creatures that Valia was looking for. There were no books on draevors, though. Eventually, Valia found what she was looking for in an old section on fairy tales and folklore. The guard gave her a strange look but didn't comment.

"Shall we return to your room now, Your Highness?"

"Yes, fine." Valia was a little annoyed; she would've liked to stay in the library in case she needed further books, but the guard was just providing her with extra security, unsure when or where danger could strike next. She smiled at him. "Thank you."

"Yes, Princess."

They walked in silence back to Valia's room, where she bid him a goodnight and sat on her windowsill. She flipped the book open with her candle close to make out the words.

Draevori are friendly creatures, the book stated. Valia snorted under her breath. *Friendly. Right.* They deal in illusions, often of a subject's deepest desires or dreams, to help people discover themselves. Draevori are often nomadic, traveling between villages in search of subjects, and thrive in warmth and sunlight. Their skin is painted with dark blue patterns that reflect a draevor's personality and talents—a draevor who specializes in dreams of military prowess might have patterns of weapons and battlefields. Draevori gain energy and power from the emotions of their subjects.

Draevori play an important role in society, both to help people fulfill dreams they might not otherwise reach and to provide an outlet for potentially dangerous desires. In this way, they are often considered the devourers of dreams, absorbing one's deepest wants and desires, and guiding them toward either release or action. They are known to be helpful to humans and generally peaceable.

Valia slammed the book closed, more confused than enlightened. It was all too clear that this was a book on fairy tales, not on reality. The draevori *she'd* encountered had been anything but friendly, and the world they'd created had been far more nightmare than dream. The idea that draevori were nomadic also didn't add up. They'd seemed quite settled in their dank cave, out of the sunlight the text claimed they enjoyed.

Maybe Kirin could help. Not for the first time, Valia considered reaching out to him. If he'd gone after the draevori, he might have more insight into their purpose. Even if he hadn't, he'd remember more about the final escape than she did, blind and unconscious as she was.

Valia glanced at the token, which rested on her side table beneath a treatise on Avanian trade exports. Her father had warned her Kirin was dangerous, and after inspecting the token, she might agree. Yet, if he could help her...

Valia shook her head. Kirin had told her himself he was not a good person to involve herself with. Trying to find him would only serve as a distraction. She needed to focus on the issue at hand.

By the time Valia finally lay down to sleep, the pink and orange of dawn had already broken across the sky, and she was no closer to a solution than she'd been before.

CHAPTER TEN
DOUBT

alia awoke to the sound of Kaleen stoking the fire. The light was too bright, and Valia's head ached from her lack of sleep.

"Did I oversleep?" she croaked.

"No," Kaleen said. "But your father is already waiting for you at breakfast. After that, you'll have a meeting with Advisor Mibley about the decrease in wheat exports this autumn, then—"

"Thank you, Kaleen." Valia held up a hand. "I appreciate it, but I think I need a little chocolate before I can cope with the details of my schedule."

"Sorry, Princess." Kaleen gestured to the tray of chocolate that already waited on Valia's bedside. She gave the fire one last poke, then crossed to Valia. She leaned closer and lowered her voice. "Did you find anything out last night?"

Valia hesitated. She wanted to confide in someone, and it was clear her father wasn't that person. However, Kaleen was young and neither a floramancer nor royal advisor.

"Not really," she said, truthfully. She picked up the cup of chocolate and sipped. "Something seems to be blocking my magic."

Kaleen's brows furrowed. "Do you know what?"

"No."

"And... the third star?"

"That's what I need to find out." Her exhaustion dissipating with the memory of her purpose—and with the sugary warmth of the chocolate—Valia pushed off her covers and got to her feet. Kaleen brought over a light gray dress with a deep purple bodice and Valia shrugged. "That one's fine."

Kaleen helped her dress, then wound Valia's hair into an elaborate braid threaded with a matching purple ribbon.

"Thank you again for your help last night," Valia said. "You have tomorrow free, don't you? To visit your brother?"

"Yes. The fifth to ninth days are my free days. I'll leave after breakfast."

"Take another two days. Spend time with your family while you have them."

"Thank you." Kaleen curtseyed, both grateful and empathetic toward Valia. "Will you be alright?"

"Of course. Thank you, Kaleen." Valia still had time before breakfast with her father, so she made a beeline for the guard station. Lord Captain Poriev leaned against the wall, sipping a cup of something darker and stronger smelling than chocolate and barking an occasional order at a group of young recruits performing calisthenics on the dew-laden grass.

"Princess." He looked surprised to see her and immediately straightened up. The recruits copied his movement and stood at attention.

"Captain." Valia inclined her head. "Do you have a moment?"

"I do. Keep going!" he added to the recruits, who resumed their calisthenics without a hint of complaint. He led her into a small room in the guard station filled with so many weapons that Valia had to move an unsheathed, curved blade off a chair before she could sit. The small arsenal reminded her of Kirin for some reason, even though she'd only seen him with his whip and dagger.

"We combed the area for any creatures, Princess. Wyra is secure. I've posted extra watchmen and increased patrols," Poriev reported.

"Thank you, Lord Captain. I actually wanted to ask you about a small mystery I'm facing. As the commander of the palace guard, I understand that you have a good overview of the comings and goings of the royal family."

Poriev's expression went from one of polite suspicion to one of shuttered distance in an instant. It was as though a set of heavy iron bars had clamped down over his features.

"Princess, if you're here to ask about your sisters and your mother, I'm afraid I'll have to disappoint you. The king mentioned you might be asking around, and unfortunately, I've no more information than you've already heard."

Valia tilted her head. "I must say, Captain, it sounds more as though you've been ordered not to speak to me than that you have no information."

Poriev spread his hands on the table. "Those come down to the same thing, really."

"If you know something..."

"I can assure you that I have no reason to believe your mother or sisters are alive. I went to the Garden of Luma. I led the search party. I attended their funeral. Flora be with them."

"I understand. But is there any other explanation for the Flora showing me a living sibling?"

"I'm no floramancer, so I truly couldn't speak to that."

Valia gave Poriev a hard look, which he returned in kind. Then she pushed back her chair, accidentally knocking over a pile of bladed disks, and got to her feet.

"Thank you for your time."

"Of course, Princess."

Valia nodded her goodbye and headed back toward the palace. It was fully light now, though the morning air still carried the crisp chill of early fall. The recruits paused in their drills to salute Valia. She dropped them a curtsey, then wondered if that had been appropriate. She really needed a few more etiquette lessons, now that she was the heir.

Inside, Valia hurried to reach breakfast with her father. King Aran was already seated with a bowl of porridge in front of him and a pile of documents spread on the table. He looked up when she entered.

"Valia. How are you feeling?"

"Better, thank you." Valia strode down the center of the hall, ignoring the tall windows and long tables. At least she'd gotten accustomed to having her breakfasts here. "Father, I wanted to ask you something." She took her seat and reached for her own bowl of porridge, which was studded with fruit. "Last night, I tried the family-finding spell again, as well as a few others, and—"

"*Stop!*" King Aran stood to his full height and slammed his palms down on the table. "*Enough*, Valia! I know you wish your mother and sisters lived. I do, too. But this search is pointless! We are the only ones left. I *will not* hear you speak of this again!"

In the face of his fury, Valia felt once again as the girl of six cycles who'd snuck a horse out of the stables and gone for a solo trot around the training grounds, leaving huge muddy hoofprints in her wake. She forced herself to breathe deeply, her fingers trailing over her rings. She wasn't a child anymore.

"Father. I understand that they are gone. I simply wonder if there's any other explanation. Is it possible that—"

"No!" King Aran shoved his bowl away. "Stop this. We have important work to do, and no time for these childish games." He stormed out of the hall. Valia stared after him. Her father had rarely yelled at her or her sisters, even when they were children. Apart from the horse incident, she'd only heard him raise his voice on a handful of occasions. Valia knew he was upset about her mother and sisters' deaths, but this was a bit out of character.

His actions fed a suspicion that had been growing in the back of Valia's mind. Perhaps she did have a living sibling—a half sibling, perhaps? It wasn't unheard of for kings, and even queens, to bear children out of wedlock. Valia could hardly imagine either of her parents being unfaithful, but such things did happen. Especially if the child had been her mother's, it might explain why any spells cast with her father's blood would have been unable to locate the missing sibling.

Valia drummed her fingers on the table. She was still a little shaky from her father's unexpected outburst, but she needed to focus. Another child would explain the third star, but it wouldn't explain why her spells had been stifled.

Valia spent the rest of the day attending meetings. She spent every free moment either trying spells or asking around the palace for information. No one answered her, and no one met her eyes. As night fell, her father pulled her aside and once again told her off soundly.

"Don't ask anything else of anyone else," he told her. The fury was gone, but he sounded beyond disappointed now. Tired, too. "You're a princess. It's uncomfortable for them not to be able to answer you."

"Then *you* answer me, father. Don't treat me like a child. Please. Is there any chance that I have a living sibling?"

He looked her straight in the eye. "No. Now let this go, Valia."

That night, after Kaleen helped her into bed, Valia lay awake for a long while. It was clear she was being lied to. And it was equally clear something was interfering with her attempts to inquire into the situation. Maybe, somehow, one of her sisters still lived, at least in some way. Maybe what she'd felt in the burial grounds had been a trick. Maybe there was a half-sibling out there. Either way, Valia knew there was only one person who could give her the answers she sought, if her father wouldn't.

The Savani was a woman, or perhaps a creature, or a spirit. It was hard to say for sure. She lived alone on an island off the rugged coast of Avania, and its location was a closely guarded secret by those who knew it. Some described her as an old woman, others as a young child, and by a few as a beast with curved horns in her golden hair. What everyone agreed on was that she could answer the kinds of questions no one else could. She knew everything that had been, was, or would be. And, for a price, she would tell you.

Visiting the Savani was outlawed. The price was too great, and her work was considered unnatural. Yet, people visited anyway: young couples hoping to be blessed with children, soldiers on their way to war, old men searching for lost loves, even kings and queens looking for some advantage at the beginning of their reign. If anyone knew who that third star was—or why it showed her one if they didn't exist—it was the Savani.

Valia turned onto her other side and squished her pillow. Perhaps her father was right, and she should let this go. The star might be a half-sibling who was better off without knowing they possessed royal blood. It might even be a design of the Flora, which didn't always answer exactly as the caster would like.

Yet Valia couldn't ignore it any longer. She'd heard stories this season of strange and unprecedented occurrences across Avania. There was a story from a border town about a young child, drowned the day before, coming home to bed as if nothing had happened. From the south, a story of a rabid bear able to withstand dozens of arrows without slowing. Even if Valia's sisters had died, even if a part of them was in the soil in their burial plots, there was a chance some other part of them lived.

If the third star was a half-sibling, perhaps he or she was someone who could help. Someone to stand beside her and share the burden of the crown would be a blessing from the Flora indeed. And if the star was just a mistake in Valia's magic, she should know about it. She'd need to make sure her powers were under control before another dangerous situation inevitably arose.

Valia sat up, pushing her covers away. She decided: she would seek the Savani. Her certainty was accompanied by a flicker of guilt; her father had asked her to drop this. She'd have to leave without his knowledge or permission. The stress of Valia disappearing again would surely age him even further. Yet, he was the one obscuring the truth from her.

Valia slid out of bed. With a bead of blood and a flick of her wrist, she lit a candle on her bedside table. In the flickering light, she began to gather her best travelling clothes.

The coast near the Savani's island was several days' ride at best. Even in the familiar, usually safe woods just beyond the palace, Valia had just been attacked by a manticore. The stories from the rest of the country were even worse. There was no way she could make the journey alone without being attacked again.

Valia shoved a few necessities into her bag, then straightened up and turned to her bedside table, hands on her hips. Beneath the treatise lay Kirin's token.

There was something strange about him. Strange, and potentially untrustworthy. Yet he *had* been unusually protective of her on the journey back to Wyra. He'd told her that if she was in danger, she could call on him. And there was something that drew her to him despite her doubts.

Valia crossed to the bedside table and found the token. It fit perfectly into her palm. She turned it over several times, then paused with Kirin's name at the top. This token was enough to find him. At the very least, she'd know if he was close enough to help. Valia hurried to her desk, where she found a map of Avania. She spread it on the floor, then knelt in front of it, hoping Kirin was at least still in the country. Carefully, she pressed blood to her sight ring, held the token to her heart, and whispered to the Flora. Then, she let another drop of blood fall onto the map.

The blood began to glide across the paper, as though it had a mind of its own. It wiggled through the outskirts of Wyra, then came to rest in a mountainous area just outside of a small town called Abynth. Valia waited for a beat to make sure the spot was final, then lifted the map. Abynth was, at most, half a day's ride away.

Her heart began to race. She could find Kirin—he was *close*. She could pay him to help her. With his help, she could make it to the coast, and to the Savani. She could find the answers she sought.

Traveling at night would be dangerous, and the palace guards would stop her if she tried to leave now. She could go out the window, but the walls were sheer, and it was a long way down. Even with magic, it would be dangerous. No, Valia would need to leave in the morning. It would be tricky, since she'd been ordered not to go for any more solo rides after the manticore fiasco, but it was doable.

A few moments later, Valia's satchel was packed and stowed beneath her bed. She slid between the sheets again, reaching for sleep, though she knew she might lay awake until morning. This time tomorrow, she'd be on the way to the coast with the Trominite sellsword, *Kirin Adante*, by her side.

If all went well, of course...

CHAPTER ELEVEN
UPHILL

rincess! You're awake." Kaleen sounded surprised, which was an apt commentary on how tired Valia had been lately. She set down the tray with Valia's chocolate, then went to the wardrobe to select a dress.

"I wasn't that tired," Valia said. "And I'm already dressed for today."

Kaleen turned and her eyes widened as she took in Valia's plain gray dress and simple braid. "Princess, forgive my frankness, but you look like a servant."

"Thank you." Valia stood and dropped a curtsey. "Kaleen, I need your help." She quickly explained her plan to seek the Savani, at which point Kaleen shook her head.

"Princess, I don't think you should leave the palace. Not on your own."

"I'll have help," Valia reminded her. "And this is the only way. You saw the star for my sibling. I must ask the Savani what it means. Imagine if it were one of your brothers or your sister!"

Kaleen sighed. "Yes... I understand. Alright, tell me how to help."

Valia used a bit of blood and her lumen ring to create a simple illusion: her eyes became a dark brown and her freckles disappeared. It wasn't much, but along with a hood over her distinctive raven hair, a long-sleeved cloak, and a spell from her null ring to reduce detection, it should be enough for her to look like an ordinary maid —perhaps a colleague of Kaleen's, instead of the crown princess.

After a short time strategizing, Valia and Kaleen left her chambers. They walked together through the palace grounds, Kaleen nodding to a few acquaintances while Valia kept her head down. The gates were open with the ebb and flow of daytime traffic.

Valia smiled at Kaleen. "We're almost there."

"Are you sure about this?" Kaleen asked, glancing back at the palace. "Don't you want to speak with the king? He could send guards with you... or *for* you."

Valia remembered the fury and pain in her father's eyes as he slammed his hands on the table. "No. This is better. This is the only way." She picked up her step as she made a beeline for a nearby stable.

Valia wanted to bring Star, but she knew her distinctive horse would certainly be noticed. As it was, they looked like a pair of palace servants going home, which *was* half-true. Instead, Valia waited outside a small stable near Kaleen's home while her handmaiden purchased a horse with florans Valia had given her.

Kaleen emerged, anxiously leading a brown mare. "The stable keeper said her name was Bird."

"Nice to meet you, Bird." Valia took the reins. "And thank you, Kaleen."

"Be safe, Princess," Kaleen said.

"I will. Remember, when you return, tell everyone that you served me chocolate as usual and didn't see me again. Tell them you had no idea that I left or where I'm going."

Kaleen nodded. "Yes, Princess."

"And say hello to your family for me." She smiled and Kaleen did too. "They aren't far from here, are they?"

"No, just a short walk. Flora watch over you." Kaleen pressed a circle, then turned toward her family's home, her skirts fanning around her legs.

Valia used a nearby fence to ease her climb onto Bird's back. She'd asked for a shorter horse than Star. While Bird certainly was dainty for a horse, she still struggled to mount without help.

Valia paused to give Kaleen one last wave before she turned, then urged Bird forward. They quickly left Wyra behind, the city walls fading into farmer's fields, orchards, and scattered cottages. Valia followed the main thoroughfare toward Abynth. She wasn't alone; numerous other travelers on foot or on horseback, along with farmers riding on carts of hay and produce, were on the road as well. Valia spotted a few large groups of people in ragged clothing, carrying bundles, and stopped near the first.

"Where are you going, pray tell?" she asked. A woman with sunken eyes looked up at her. She carried an infant in her arms, who looked up at her silently with equally tired eyes.

"To Wyra," she said.

"And where are you coming from?"

"Lirrhend."

Valia was surprised. Lirrhend was in the far north, near the Nelirrhi mountain ranges which teemed with mysterious creatures. If these people had come on foot, and from the long way around, they must have been walking for dozens of days through dangerous territory.

"Why did you leave?" Valia asked.

"We lost everything. Farrows." The woman held her child closer and kept walking. Valia wasn't sure exactly what a farrow was, but it sounded like regional slang for fallows. The way the woman had pulled her child close was further confirmation. Valia dug into her satchel and handed the woman several florans. The woman accepted them, though she still didn't smile.

"Flora watch over you," Valia said.

"Maybe not," the woman replied.

Valia kept riding. She wanted to stop by each group to ask their stories and offer some coin but held herself back after the first time. She needed her coin for the journey ahead—and to pay the mercenary man.

As Valia rode closer to Abynth, she saw more signs of a kingdom in distress. Apart from the groups of ragged travelers, she passed several armed groups that didn't wear the uniform of the military. She rode past quickly, hoping to avoid trouble. Several farms appeared to be abandoned, and one village had a fountain with strange, greenish water that didn't look right.

Yet it was still the Avania Valia loved. She observed children playing in a field of corn, their laughter loud and free. In one orchard, farmers sang back and forth to each other as they filled baskets with shiny red apples. Fields of grain glowed golden under the blue skies. Cows grazed lazily on grassy meadows. When umbra fell, the farmers paused their work to gaze at the sky, admiring the stars and swirling colors that appeared suddenly against the blue sky, and Valia slowed her pace to look up, too.

Valia stopped on the outskirts of Abynth to check the map. Last night, Kirin had been in the foothills of the mountains to the southwest of the town, but he might not be there now. He didn't seem the type to stay long anywhere, much less on a mountainside. She angled herself in the approximate direction, then cast another finding spell. Now that she was closer, the Flora gave her a subtle pull in the right direction instead of marking the map.

Valia rode until the track curved toward Abynth, then turned off the road. Bird slowed as she was forced to pick her way over rocks and around tree stumps, until Valia started to wonder if it would be faster to walk. When the ground began to slope sharply up, she dismounted and called to the Flora to mark the horse, so Bird would be easier to find or call later.

Valia shouldered her satchel and began to climb. The forest began to thin, and the ground grew increasingly steep, until Valia had to use her hands to scramble up a patch of rocks. At the top of the rocky patch, she cast another finding spell. The tug toward Kirin was stronger. He was close.

Valia continued up. At this point, the trees were completely gone, replaced by an inclined field of thin mountainous grass and rocks. There were caves here, too, with huge and unsettling dark entrances. She considered casting a spell to find life nearby but decided against the waste of her energy. Valia cast the tracking spell again, wincing as her head pulsed a dull pain and she grew weary. She was tugged so hard by the spell that she almost fell over.

Valia scanned the area. To her right, the rocky expanse dropped off toward the forest below. In front of her was the narrow deer path she'd been following. To her left, where the tug had come from, was the foreboding mouth of a cave. The Flora seemed to be implying Kirin was in there—although, perhaps, he was beyond it. She couldn't be sure. What she was sure of was that she did not want to go inside any more caves.

Valia bit her lip, then called on the Flora for light—the same kind she'd used to navigate with Kirin on their way to Wyra. The ball gathered in Valia's hands, and she gently pushed it into the cave. It traveled a few feet, then...

"What in the—" The voice was masculine, annoyed, and comfortingly familiar. Valia's spirits rose as Kirin's face appeared in the light from the spell. He batted the ball of light away, glared at it as though it were personally responsible for all his woes, then scanned the area outside the cave. His sharp gray eyes met Valia's, and he squinted. "Ah, the bleeding Princess. I should have known. Who else would throw a ball of light at me?" He emerged from the cave into the sunlight and Valia stumbled back. Despite his comment about her floramancy, *he* was the one covered in blood, from his boots to his shirt to the tip of the whip he held in his hands.

"And a bloody mercenary. Is that yours?" She crinkled her nose at the sight.

"What?" Kirin glanced down and looked faintly surprised, then pursed his lips and nodded in silent self-approval. "Manticore blood. Seems they've become a problem in the area."

"Yes, I've noticed. It seems they'll be less of one with you here."

Kirin coiled his whip and set it on his back, then came closer. As he approached, he ran one hand through his hair, carelessly streaking half-coagulated blood into it.

"What are you doing here? Out touring Avania's caves again?"

"Funny," she said with a sarcastic chuckle. "You said I could find you if I was in danger."

He leaned and looked over her shoulder, then slowly scanned their surroundings. "What kind of danger?"

"Well, not exactly... yet? Um, I need your help. Here." Valia reached into her satchel and withdrew a heavy purse of coins, which she jingled. "I can pay. It's a job."

"I'm listening." Kirin leaned against a boulder and began cleaning his whip with a relatively clean patch of his shirt. "But I still don't know why you're out here alone. I expected you'd summon me with one of your servants."

"I need to get to the Savani."

"Which is..."

"The Savani." Valia raised her eyebrows. "You know, the all-knowing seer who lives off the coast?"

"A seer?" Kirin raised his eyebrows back at her. "Aren't your floramantic powers adequate?"

"No. I mean, yes, I'm a very capable floramancer," Valia snapped. "But the Savani is different. You just have to make sure I get there safely, in return for which I will give you a generous fee." She jingled the purse of coins again. "So, are you interested or not?"

Kirin didn't seem fazed by her outburst. He still leaned against the rock, wiping his whip.

"What's to stop me from just taking the coin from you now?" he asked. Valia felt a wave of nervous iciness flood her veins but forced herself to be calm.

"What makes you think you could?" She lazily lifted her sleeves and waved her fingers to show off her rings. In truth, she wasn't confident in her abilities when it came to combat, but there was no point in being that honest about her abilities right now.

"Right. Very capable floramancer." Kirin pushed off from the rock and strode toward her. For a moment, Valia thought he was coming to attack and lifted her hands into her idea of a threatening combat stance, but he brushed right past her.

"Where are you going?"

"To the coast, to see a very trustworthy seer. Are you coming or not?" he called over his shoulder. More exasperated than ever, Valia hurried after him.

"Don't you want to know why I'm going?"

"It's not in the job description." He descended the field of rocks and grass at a breakneck pace that left Valia scrambling to keep up. "I need to clean up and gather supplies. We can meet tomorrow evening in Wyra to set off."

"I'm coming with you," Valia countered. Kirin leaped athletically over a small boulder and Valia skirted it to keep up. Was he just showing off now, or intentionally trying to lose her?

"There's no need."

"There's some need. It's dangerous here, more than it used to be, and I don't think I'm exactly welcome back at the palace."

That made Kirin stop and turn slowly back to her. "You aren't?"

"Okay... I suppose I am, but there'll definitely be trouble. I saw the way they looked at you. Do you seriously think I came to you of all people on a crown-sanctioned expedition?"

Kirin's gaze swept over Valia. "I see. Outlaw princess. I like it." He continued his descent.

"You can call me Valia now."

"I could."

"Yes, you will, *Kirin*. It's a stipulation of the job."

He flinched a little at the sound of his name but didn't slow or reply. Valia continued to the next of her questions.

"Did you return to kill the draevori?"

"How do you think I got my whip back?" They were reentering the tree line now. Valia quietly reached out to the Flora with her link ring to call her horse. "But killing them wasn't necessary."

"Because...?" Valia had forgotten how annoying Kirin's reticence really was.

"Because they were already dead." Kirin glanced back at her. "When I returned to the cave, they were lying on the ground. It looked like they'd been dead a while."

"Someone else killed them?"

"Maybe, but it looked as if they'd been dead a hundred cycles. Little more than bones and dust. The work of a floramancer, maybe?"

"Possible, I suppose, but the power needed to turn several draevor to dust would require immense power." Valia bit her lip. "I saw something strange in the palace libraries about draevori. Apparently, they used to be friendly, cooperative, even helpful. I didn't believe it, but now I wonder..."

"You wonder?" Kirin prompted.

"Maybe magic wasn't what killed them. Maybe magic was what gave them life in the first place." Valia came to a stop, her mind swirling. Kirin kept walking for a few paces, then returned. "There have been reports of animals coming back to life recently. Birds and deer, even a bear. Maybe someone—or some*thing*—was keeping the draevori alive too. Maybe it's how they came back after ages of seeming extinction."

"Is that something floramancers can do?"

"No..." Valia looked up at Kirin. "Certainly not. Floramancy only works through what is already alive."

"Is this what you wanted to ask the seer about?"

"No." Valia pulled her hair back. "I thought knowing that wasn't in the job description."

"It's not." Kirin pivoted and began walking again, but Valia hurried after him and grabbed his arm.

"I'll tell you. Flora knows I need to tell *someone*. I cast a spell to show me my family, and the spell showed three living members: me, my father, and a sibling. I tried to find out who the sibling is. Maybe one of my sisters is alive somewhere, or maybe it's a half sibling born out of wedlock. I don't know. But I couldn't find answers anywhere. It was like something was blocking my magic."

"And this seer will be able to tell you who your sibling is?"

Valia nodded. "Who they are, where they are, what happened to them. Anything."

"I see." Kirin looked down at her, his gray eyes unreadable as always. "Valia—"

Just then, a nearby rustle revealed Bird. Kirin raised his hand to his whip, then relaxed once he saw it was only a horse.

"This is Bird," Valia told Kirin. "I borrowed her from Wyra. Do you have a horse?"

"The same one. But I left my horse along the trail like a sensible person, since horses don't generally enjoy climbing rocky slopes or coming face to face with manticores."

"Hey, I didn't know you were going to be in the mountains."

Kirin's brow furrowed. "And how exactly did you find me? Wait, did you bleed on my token?"

"Don't worry, it's not nearly as bloody as you are." Valia winked at him. "Now, we have a long way to go. Shall we get moving?"

Kirin sighed and fell into step with her as they continued their descent down the slope.

CHAPTER TWELVE
GLIMPSE

t the bottom of the slope, Kirin untied his horse from a tree and they both mounted. As Kirin led the way down a narrow country lane that curved through the forest in the general direction of Abynth, Valia couldn't help remembering the last time they'd ridden together. That time, they'd sat on the same horse, and she'd felt the warmth of Kirin's torso, the firm contours of his muscles behind her.

Valia focused on the path ahead. This was a professional arrangement, nothing more. The important thing was finding her missing sibling—not wondering why she half-wished she hadn't brought a horse so that they could ride together again.

"So, where do you live?" Valia asked as they crossed a small, clear stream and continued up the bank on the other side.

"Here and there. But, I do have a place near *here* where I keep things," Kirin told her. The path was broad enough for them to ride side by side, so Valia kept pace with him to make sure they could talk. "It's on the way to the coast. We'll stop there for a few things. You'll need different clothes too."

"What's wrong with my clothes?" Valia looked down at her gray dress, which was now muddy at the hem.

"Your dress may be plain up in that fancy palace of yours, but a commoner would never be able to afford such fine silks. Nice boots, though."

Valia glanced down at her shoes, which were the ones Kirin had bought for her at the inn. Did he remember that? Was his comment a reference to his previous wardrobe assistance? Or was he simply remarking how they looked like boots a commoner might wear?

"Thank you," she replied, a little primly. "So, we'll need some other dresses."

"Trousers and shirts," Kirin said. "We'll be riding most the time. Maybe running, too. Dodging bandits and wild creatures. I don't want you tripping over your skirts."

"I can run and ride in skirts just as well as you can in trousers."

"But could you run and ride even *better* in trousers?"

"You have a point. I'm happy to wear trousers." Valia smoothed her braid. "Happier than you would be to wear a skirt, I imagine."

A sound emerged from Kirin, a sound so foreign that Valia had to do a double take.

"Was that a laugh?"

"No." Kirin clicked to his horse, who picked up pace into a trot. Valia, grinning to herself, urged Bird to keep up.

For a while, they rode without speaking. The lane joined with the main thoroughfare Valia had taken on the way to Abynth, though they continued southwest instead of backtracking. It was after-umbra now, and the road was less crowded than it had been in the morning. They wound through farms and fields which soon gave way to a forest stained with the colors of autumn.

"Is this how the Blood Forest looked?" Valia asked, nodding to the gold and red leaves.

"No."

"Right. I forgot that you don't talk. This is going to be a fun journey."

"I talk."

"That was a great example right there. Can we take a short rest? I'm famished. Plus, I think you'd be well-served by a quick wash in that stream."

"I don't look sufficiently dashing to be a princess's bodyguard?" Kirin slowed his horse then dismounted gracefully. Valia pulled Bird up and hopped off.

"I would say you look a little too bloody to show your face in civil society," Valia countered. "We did get a few stares before, too."

"Maybe because a princess was journeying through the fields."

"Come on. I'm not that conspicuous. At least, not compared to a man literally covered in blood." Valia sat on a rock and unrolled a bundle of food Kaleen prepared. There were two bread rolls, several apples, a wedge of cheese, and a slice of sponge cake wrapped in waxy paper. Valia looked up from the bundle, intending to ask Kirin if he wanted to share.

Kirin had descended into the water, where he'd removed his shirt and was using cupped handfuls of water to wash his face, arms, and torso. A few scars, including what looked like a large burn, marred his tanned back. Valia quickly looked down, her cheeks heating, and tried to pretend she was deeply interested in inspecting the apples for ripeness.

She was the one who had suggested Kirin clean himself in the river. It shouldn't have taken her so off guard that he'd removed his shirt to do so.

A short while later, Kirin returned. His pants were still stained, but he'd thoroughly washed his shirt in the water. It now clung to him and Valia looked away again. He sat on the rock beside her and took an apple from her bundle.

"Fruit thief," Valia muttered.

"Consider it an advance on my payment." He crunched into the apple. Valia took another and tossed it from hand to hand.

"How long will it take us to get to the coast?"

"A few days, depending on which route we take. And if we run into any trouble."

"Have you been there before?"

"I have."

"What were you doing there?"

"I came to Avania for the first time by sea."

Valia paused with the apple in one hand. "So, you're not from Avania?"

"You didn't know that?" Kirin raised his eyebrows at her.

"I mean, I wanted to know it from *you*. Your token says you're from Olanthus. In Tromin, right? And it says you're a *Seeker*?" Valia took a deep breath. "I wanted to ask you about that."

"And I'm sure you will. We should get moving." Kirin took the last bite of his apple, tossed the core into the bushes, and stood. As he walked back toward the horses, he ran his hand through his hair. Valia rolled her eyes but got to her feet and followed. She still hadn't eaten any of her apple. Maybe Kirin's lack of chattiness was just a way to make sure he got to eat.

It wasn't lost on Valia that he hadn't told her anything about his origins. He clearly wasn't planning to, either.

As they rode on, Valia made a few more attempts to start a conversation, but Kirin was evasive as usual, and she soon gave up. A short while after their break, they arrived in a town where Kirin exited the main road. Just outside of town, they came to a small but well-maintained stone hut.

"Wait here," Kirin said gruffly as he made another acrobatic dismount from his horse.

"I'd rather not." Valia slid off Bird, patted the horse's neck, and followed Kirin to the door.

"It wasn't a suggestion."

"I don't take orders from you. Come now, I'd just like a bit of a break whilst you gather your things." *And I'd like to get a quick look at your home*, she thought.

"Fine." Kirin nudged open the door. Inside, the hut was even more bare than Valia had imagined. The main piece of furniture was a single bed, which looked to be a straw mattress on an old wooden frame. A worn wooden cupboard stood beside the bed. On the far side of the room was a makeshift kitchen. To Valia's surprise, there were no weapons beyond a bow on a hook beside the door.

"Stay in this room." Kirin swung his pack onto the floor and continued across the room to a narrow door that must lead to a washroom of sorts. "Just don't..." He trailed off, waved a hand vaguely at the room, then disappeared through the door. Valia stood in the center of the floor, suddenly feeling very much like an intruder. Perhaps she *should* have waited outside.

After a moment, though, her curiosity got the better of her. She slowly circled the room. From the basic room and rough furnishings, she'd have imagined Kirin was quite poor. Yet she knew from his extraordinary weapons and the way he freely spent florans that he had more than enough. So, why did he choose to live like this?

On the cupboard beside the bed, Valia spotted something that made her stop in her tracks. There was a small painting, the hyper-realistic kind usually made with magic. It depicted a young boy with dark hair and slate gray eyes—presumably Kirin—standing in front of a man and a woman. Both adults had their hands on the boy's shoulders, and all three were smiling. Valia leaned closer. The woman shared his gray eyes and the man his athletic build. She could be mistaken, but this seemed to be his family.

"What are you doing?" Kirin's voice behind her was colder than usual, with a certain bite to it. Valia quickly stepped away from the painting.

"Nothing, I just—"

His eyes flitted between her and the painting. In a quick stride, he brushed past her and turned the painting face down on the cupboard. "Enough snooping. Wait outside."

Valia was embarrassed enough to have been caught that she didn't argue. She exited the hut and stood for a long moment outside in the bright sunshine. Of course Kirin had a family; everyone came from somewhere. Yet it was strange to imagine him as a smiling child instead of the unreadable, potentially dangerous man he now was.

Where were his parents now? Did they approve of him being a mercenary? Were they still back in Tromin? Did he see them much? Valia knew she'd never ask any of this. Even if she did, Kirin wouldn't be likely to answer. Still, curiosity pressed at the back of Valia's mind.

Bird and Kirin's nameless horse picked at the grass around the hut. Valia went to them and offered them each an apple wedge, cut with the small knife she'd brought. Both horses crunched happily on the morsels of fruit while Valia cut the rest of the apple into pieces and ate it herself.

Soon, Kirin emerged from the hut, his hair sticking up as though he'd run his hand through it more than a few times, as he seemed to do. He'd changed his clothes—or she was fairly certain he had, since his shirt was now dry, and his trousers were no longer bloodstained. Otherwise, the clothes he wore now were indistinguishable from what he'd worn before.

"Do you own anything that isn't black or grey?" Valia asked.

"My bed linens are white. Time to go. We'll stop in town to buy something else for you to wear, then we continue south. We should be able to make good progress before nightfall."

It was a clear dismissal. Their playful teasing back and forth was gone now.

"I'm sorry I looked at your painting."

"Forget it." Kirin turned away from her, his face closed.

Valia wasn't sure if he meant that she should forget the indiscretion or that she should forget having seen the painting. Whether that painting was his family or not, it had clearly struck a nerve.

They both remounted their horses and headed into town, where Valia bought two pairs of trousers and three shirts: one green, one blue, and one purple. At least *one* of them should wear a little color.

Valia changed in a copse of trees outside Hani. She left the old dress neatly folded beneath an old elm tree before she returned to Kirin. Some lucky passerby would be its new owner.

"How do I look?" She twirled.

"Like a princess, still. I think it's something about the way you stand." Kirin was leaning against a tree eating the cake Valia had taken from the palace. She didn't mention she'd been looking forward to that cake. Instead, she gave an exaggerated slouch.

"Better?"

"Strangely, no. Let's continue. We need to make the most of the daylight."

"Okay, Kirin." Valia smiled sweetly and used a stump as leverage to mount Bird. Kirin didn't acknowledge her use of his name.

This was going to be a *long* journey.

CHAPTER THIRTEEN
BOUNTY

ith the lack of conversation as they rode, Valia became trapped in her thoughts. Her anxiety about the journey ahead began to sink in. They were not even half a day from Wyra, as their progress had been impeded by the need to gather supplies. Her father had surely noticed her disappearance by now. After everything that's happened, she may have given him a heart attack. Perhaps he sent more men after her. Perhaps men less kind than Kirin, who may consider him her new captor.

Valia, having barely slept the last two nights, grew so tired she worried she'd keel right off Bird and onto the ground below. Kirin, despite having apparently spent the night in an inhospitable cave, seemed active as ever. Valia couldn't help but find it annoying.

As dusk descended on the forest, strange sounds came from the trees. A low hiss, occasionally accompanied by a high squawk. It was probably nothing more than diurnal forest creatures, but Valia still ran her fingers back and forth over her rings, ready to call on her power if needed.

The hissing grew louder as the road curved sharply up a hillside.

"Kirin…" Valia said in a low voice.

"Keep moving." Kirin sounded as in control as he always did. Valia kept her eyes on the fading light and tried to ignore the noise. Just as she grew certain that some enormous serpent was about to come flying out of the trees, the path opened into a small village. The streets were lit by lamps, and the road was paved with flat, rectangular stones. As soon as the path changed, the hissing faded away.

"What was that?" Valia asked as they brought their horses to a halt beside the town's modest inn.

"Not sure," Kirin admitted. "But we're safe in town."

Valia slid off Bird's back and patted the horse's neck reassuringly. She wasn't sure if she was trying to reassure Bird or herself. Valia also wasn't sure they were all that much safer in town. What was to stop a draevor or manticore or any manner of other creature from wandering into the modest collection of buildings that constituted a village in this part of the country?

"Safe sounds good," she said instead. "I'll take the horses to the stables."

"I'll see about a room."

"*Rooms*," Valia corrected. "I know we needed to share a room when I was blind, but we can certainly have our own spaces now."

Kirin grumbled. "That'll make it harder to protect you. Which, if I remember correctly, is what I'm being paid for."

"The town is safe, isn't it?" She raised her eyebrows in challenge, and Kirin gave another grumbly sound, smoothed his hand through his hair, and headed for the inn. Valia led the horses to the inn's small stable, where she rubbed them down, then fetched water and hay from the stable's supply. It was uncommon for a princess to know how to take care of horses, but her mother had insisted from a young age that if any of the princesses were going to ride, they should know how to care for their own horses. She had wanted to teach them responsibility.

Valia certainly felt responsible now. She felt like the only person who knew about her sibling—or the only one who really believed one was out there, anyway. Now, she was taking two innocent horses and one not-so-innocent mercenary on a dangerous journey. A journey through a kingdom that was as unstable as a counterfeit surge ring made of dried grass and peddled to unsuspecting tourists.

Valia sighed, gave Bird and the nameless horse each a quick pat, and headed into the inn with her satchel on her shoulder. Kirin was seated at a long wooden table along with two other guests. Valia crossed to him and took a seat.

"Two rooms," he told her in a low voice. "Dinner and breakfast included. I'll be charging you."

"I wouldn't expect anything less." Valia took the bowl of watery soup and a hunk of crusty bread that Kirin slid to her. They ate in silence until one of the other guests leaned across the table.

"Where might the two of yous be coming from?" he asked in a regional drawl.

"Nowhere in particular," Kirin answered brusquely before Valia had a chance to say anything.

"And how did the two of yous come to be traveling together? Are yous married?"

Valia shifted in her seat and quickly ate the last piece of her bread. Something about this man's questioning made her a little uncomfortable, though she wasn't sure if her discomfort came from the way the man's beady eyes were trained on her or the scar down the right side of his face that looked fresh and puckered. He kept glancing at her rings until Valia curled her hands beneath the table.

"Yes. This is my wife." Kirin gestured to Valia with his head. "And she looks tired. Shall we go to bed, darling?"

The endearment from Kirin sounded as foreign as if he'd burst into song, but Valia recovered quickly.

"Yes husband, let's."

As they climbed the stairs, though, she heard the man whisper to his companion, "What kind of married couple books two rooms?"

"Kirin," she said as they reached the top of the stairs. "Maybe we *should* share a room."

"I thought you'd be perfectly safe."

"I will be." She thought of the men downstairs and felt her stomach turn. "I just thought it might make *you* feel more comfortable."

Kirin glanced at her sternly. His eyes held hers for a long moment, then he abruptly pushed open the door to the room in front of them and gestured for her to enter. He then walked loudly to his own room, opened the door, and slammed it shut. Valia felt confused, then relieved and grateful as he silently reappeared. He entered her room and locked the door behind them. She felt simultaneously safer and much more in danger because of his precautions.

"Take the bed," he said.

"I can take the floor this time."

"Oh no. We can't have a royal princess sleep on a wooden floor. That wouldn't be civilized." Kirin made playfully horrified eyes at her. "Take the bed. I'll sleep the same on either surface."

Valia conceded. She sat on the bed and removed her boots. She took her hair out of its braid and used her fingers to comb through it. She hadn't brought a hairbrush—a sore regret as she came across tangles too knotted to work out with her fingers. Kirin quietly removed his boots, then took one of the two blankets from the bed and lay on the floor.

"Shall I blow out the candle? Or will the dark frighten you?" Valia teased, remembering their conversation in the field of starflowers.

Kirin let out a sound somewhere between a chuckle and a sigh. "Whenever you're ready."

Valia used a seed spell to extinguish the candle across the room. She heard Kirin scoff in the darkness.

"Something you'd like to say?"

"No, Princess-Floramancer. Go to sleep."

"You can call me Valia."

"I could. Good night, Princess."

Valia was so exhausted she didn't even try to respond. She quickly found herself floating into a dream in which she and her sisters were children playing at the riverbank. She jumped into the river and felt the cool water close above her head. For a moment, she was weightless. Then Kirin was in the water with her, his dagger in hand, swimming smoothly past her.

A crash sounded. Had something fallen into the river? Valia's eyes flew open, and she saw light pouring in from the hallway. A dark figure stood over her and, instinctively, Valia lashed out. The figure went flying backward into the wall. Pain split Valia's head as her throat began to burn. For a moment, she thought she'd been hit, but no—this was the Flora's response to Valia's unplanned, unsacrificed spell. She managed to prick her finger and light the candle in time to see the man stagger upright again and Kirin leap across the room and sink his dagger into the man's throat. In the candlelight, she saw he was the man from the dining room whose beady eyes had made her so uncomfortable.

The man gurgled, blood pouring from his mouth in a macabre wave, then he slumped to the floor. Valia choked back a cry of fear as Kirin closed the door to the room and moved to her. His hands were red with the man's blood.

"Valia? Are you alright? Did he hurt you?" He reached for Valia as if he needed to touch her to make sure that she was really there but pulled back at the last moment. Instead, he swept his intense gaze over her.

Through the pain of her headache and burning in her throat, Valia recognized that he'd called her by name. She realized something else, too: as much as Kirin seemed compelled to put on a show of being uncaring and merciless, he had a caring heart.

"I'm okay. I used the Flora to push him away and my head aches, but I'm fine. He's not fine.... He's dead. You killed him." Valia began to feel shaky, both from the exertion of the unplanned spell and from the fact that she'd just witnessed a man die.

"He was going to kill you." Kirin tore his gaze from Valia and returned to the man's body. He held up a small blade that gleamed in the candlelight. He set the blade on the ground and rifled through the man's clothing. Valia put a hand to her mouth. A moment later, Kirin pulled out a piece of parchment, which he looked over, then handed to Valia. She took it, angled it toward the candlelight so she could read, and let out a small gasp.

The paper outlined a high bounty on floramantic rings. Just one of Valia's rings could have earned this man more than some farmers made in a lifetime. Valia curled her hands together in her lap.

"See?" Kirin left the man's slumped body on the floor and began to put his boots on. "He was going to kill you."

"I know, I know." Valia still felt shaky. "What are you doing?"

"We're leaving, now. If this man had this poster, anyone might. Inns like this aren't safe for you anymore." Kirin saw Valia was still sitting motionless on the bed and crossed to her with a few brisk strides. "It's going to be alright, but we need to leave. Come on."

Valia couldn't bring herself to move. Kirin grabbed her hand and gently pulled her to her feet.

"Come on, Valia. Let's go." Some of the man's blood smeared onto her palm from Kirin's. She wiped it against her trousers.

Valia took a deep breath and reached for her boots. After she had them on, Kirin blew out the candle and the two of them crept downstairs, through the dining room, and out into the night. To Valia's surprise, the sky had the cold blue tint of predawn light and birds were chirping with their early morning songs. It was later than she'd thought. Colder, too. Valia followed Kirin at a brisk pace to the stables, where he freed their horses. Wordlessly, he grabbed Valia around the waist and lifted her onto Bird, then jumped on the nameless horse's back. They rode out of the village as the first roosters were crowing good mornings.

Valia was so shaken and in so much pain from her splitting headache that it took her a while to notice they were going the wrong way.

"Isn't this the way we came?" she called to Kirin, who was slightly ahead of her.

"Yes. I'm taking you home."

Valia pulled on the reins to bring Bird to a standstill. When Kirin doubled back, she glared at him.

"You're not taking me home. I have a sibling out there who needs me. Maybe one of my sisters, maybe someone else, but whoever it is, I'm the only one who will help them."

Kirin glared back. "How will you help if you're dead? We're barely out of the capital and men are already trying to slit your throat while you sleep. And just how accurate is your little star spell? You can't risk your life when you don't even know for sure they exist. This journey is not safe for you."

"Kirin, I have to do this. I feel it in my bones. I'm still going, with or without you." She paused. "It would be much more dangerous without you."

Kirin sighed in exasperation, then brought his horse closer to Valia's until their knees brushed. He leaned toward her; his eyes narrowed.

"If we continue, you have to listen to me." His voice was cold and firm. "Every moment. No more arguing about separate rooms. No more rooms at all. We'll sleep in the forest. At least I know the dangers there. This won't be easy, and it won't be comfortable. If we continue, you have to do as I say."

Valia tried to make her eyes as hard as his. She leaned closer. "Fine. I'll do whatever it takes."

"Then take off your rings."

"What? No." Valia's thumb skimmed along her rings. "Without these, I'm powerless. You said it yourself, it's dangerous in Avania now. I can't leave myself vulnerable."

"Those rings of yours are more of a liability now with those bounty posters. You said you'd do whatever it takes."

"I will. But not that. It will take too long to put them back on if I need them… *when* I need them."

"You understand how important it is no one sees your rings now, don't you?"

"I do. And I'll keep my hands out of sight. Do you understand what it feels like to be completely powerless?"

"More than you'd know," Kirin muttered. "Fine, keep them, but keep them hidden. We'll revisit this later when I have a better solution."

Kirin muttered something under his breath in a language Valia didn't understand, though she imagined he was swearing. "Come, then. We have a lot of ground to cover."

He began riding back toward the village they'd just left. Valia turned Bird and followed. Her head throbbed with every fall of the horse's hooves, but she was still determined to reach the Savani.

Valia tried not to think about the fact a man was dead because of her. A bad man, probably, but there was no way of knowing for sure. She tried not to think about how effortlessly Kirin had killed him. There hadn't even been a struggle. No questions posed. Just because this man had been armed didn't necessarily mean that he wanted to kill her. Maybe he'd just wanted to slip off her rings, though that prospect was almost as terrifying. She tried not to think about how far they had to go and how many more dangers might await them.

She just rode on, following Kirin, as the dawn slowly lightened into another crisp autumn morning, and the night fell away behind them.

he area around Wyra was mostly farmland, but the further they got from the capital, the more they passed groves of leafy trees and small streams. Now, almost a full day's ride from the city where Valia had grown up, the scenery looked less familiar than before. Even the farms were different. Instead of the ones near Wyra where farmers mostly grew large quantities of one crop, the farms here seemed diversified, with small vegetable patches and livestock.

Valia couldn't enjoy the scenery as much as she would have liked, though, as her headache intensified throughout the ride. If it weren't itself spawned by the use of her powers, she might have called on the Flora to ease her pain. That would be of no use now.

Soon, her head ached so badly that she had to ask Kirin to stop so she could rest. As he cared for the horses, Valia circled the clearing, her vision blurry, until she found a maple tree. Pressing her fingers to it, she let a drop of her blood soak into the bark. The tree responded by releasing a small waterfall of sap water into Valia's waiting palm. She drank deeply, then lay down on the tree's mossy roots and let herself drift into sleep.

When she awoke a while later, she was covered with a blanket, and the pain in her head and throat had lessened.

"So, this is what happens when you anger the almighty Flora," Kirin said. He'd been sitting beside her, sharpening his dagger on a whetstone and keeping an eye on the horses and the road, while Valia slept.

"What?" Valia pushed herself upright and accepted a waterskin for a drink.

"Your headache." He gestured with his dagger. "It happened because you used your powers without paying in blood."

"Flora was hardly angered. There are worse consequences than a headache." She took another drink of water.

"Yet you still worship it? How sensible." Kirin ran his blade over the whetstone once more, then returned it to the sheath on his ankle and put the whetstone back in his pack.

"Worship? We coexist with the Flora. It gives us powers which benefit us greatly."

"And how exactly does the Flora benefit from you?"

"I... Does it matter? Avania has always prospered thanks to the Flora." She hesitated to comment further, thinking of Avania's current state of affairs. "Anyway, I feel better now." To prove her point, she got back to her feet, ignoring the way her head throbbed at the sudden motion.

"Do you feel better because of what you drank from the tree?"

"Partially." Valia leaned against the maple's trunk, trying to look casual instead of tired. "That was sap water. Maple water, in this case. It's what people use to make syrup, and it often helps floramancers regain power after being exhausted like this."

"I'm familiar with maple water, but I thought you could only get it in the spring."

"Usually, yes, but..." Valia held up her hands and wiggled her fingers, her rings glinting in the sunlight.

"Silly me. I would have thought it was because you're a princess and you asked so nicely."

Valia rolled her eyes, pleased the gesture didn't intensify the remnants of her headache.

Kirin was already swinging back onto his horse. Rejuvenated by the short break, she mounted Bird and eagerly followed.

The forest gave way to fields of vegetables and wheat on both sides. Unlike in the places they'd passed before, the crops here appeared to be thriving. The wheat was as golden as if it had been painted, the apple trees were heavy with bright, round fruit, and the vegetable patches were plump with cabbage and lettuce. The area was almost *too* colorful.

"These are gorgeous. Should we stop and get something to eat?" Valia asked. She'd spotted a collection of houses in the distance that looked like a village, and all the beautiful food growing just off the side of the road was making her hungry. The provisions she'd brought from the palace were already almost gone.

"Not here." Kirin swept his gaze over the fields and the road ahead as though monsters and militias might linger just around the next corner. He was always watchful, even when Valia felt comfortable and safe.

"Why not?"

"Look around." He glanced at her. "This place doesn't add up." When they approached an intersection, he chose the path that led away from the village. Valia glanced back at it, longing for the comforts of civilization, but didn't complain. She'd agreed to follow Kirin's instructions, and she would—at least, for now.

A little further on, Kirin slowed his horse to a walk, then came to a stop once a hissing sound cut through the fields. Valia paused beside him.

"What's going on? What is that?"

"Listen... There's something else. Beyond the hissing noise."

Valia held her breath and listened. Faintly, in the distance, she heard something, but she couldn't quite place the sound. It might have been an animal mewling, or a child crying. Valia pressed a drop of blood to her surge ring and prayed to the Flora to enhance her hearing. The sound of sobbing lifted from the air around her, as clearly as if coming from right beside her. Somehow, she still couldn't place the hissing.

"I hear it," Valia said. "It's coming from over there." As one, she and Kirin turned to the orchard on their left. The trees were studded with bright red cherries—even now, long after their season had passed—and the air smelled sweet and perfumed.

"Watch the horses." Kirin swung down from his horse and Valia followed.

"Right, because historically, I've been much safer alone." She fidgeted with her rings.

"Point taken. Stay behind me. Leave the horses free." Kirin drew the whip from his back, still coiled in one hand, then led the way into the orchard. Valia followed, her boots crunching lightly over the dead leaves and sticks on the ground. The sound of sobbing grew louder until Valia caught sight of a child. She was maybe three cycles old and dressed in a white gown several sizes too big for her. Her hair was fiery red and curly, and her face was just as red with her furious sobs. Her chubby hands were tied to the tree behind her.

"Flora..." Valia whispered.

"Stay back," Kirin warned. "I've seen this before." He looked up in the sky, squinting at the sun as if expecting something to fly down onto them from above.

Valia ached to run to the child, but she held back. Kirin crept closer, the whip unfurled and ready to strike. When he was no more than ten paces from the child, the hissing abruptly stopped, leaving them in the stillest of silences. Then, Valia heard a faint rustling behind her and turned to look.

The creature standing behind her was unlike anything she'd seen before. It was as though someone had taken a human and stretched until it was nearly twice as tall and deathly thin. Its skin was a sickly pale gray, and its hands ended in long, sharp claws. Its teeth were bared in a perpetual grimace. Worst of all, it had silently gotten close enough to Valia that it could have reached out and rake her stomach.

Valia gasped and stumbled back, but the creature ignored her. Instead, it continued its slow, shuffling walk toward the bound child.

"Kirin," Valia hissed. Kirin spun, caught sight of the creature, then turned to Valia as he readied his whip. In an instant, she saw him transform, his features hardening and his stance shifting. Kirin no longer looked like the man who joked with her about her princess clothes or held her gently while riding horseback together. Instead, he looked every bit the ruthless, fearsome man her father had warned her about.

"Get the child," he said, his voice low and commanding. "Run."

Valia sprinted past the creature, grateful now for her trousers instead of skirts, and fell to her knees in front of the child. Behind her, she heard the crack of Kirin's whip and a loud, angry screech.

"Hi," Valia said to the child, who had stopped crying and looked up at her with wide, fearful eyes. "It's okay." She pulled her knife from her satchel, flicked it open, and cut through the bonds that held the child's hands. In one motion, she scooped the girl into her arms and turned toward the creature.

Kirin had caught it around the wrist with the tail of his whip. The creature lunged at him with its free hand outstretched, its claws whistling through the air, and Kirin expertly rolled out of the way. He came up with his knife in hand and slashed at the creature as he tugged it sharply forward with the whip. Oily blue blood spilled from its stomach and the creature screeched again as it dove toward him.

This time, Kirin released the whip from around the creature's wrist and struck with it again as he spun out of the way. The whip caught the creature across its face. As he spun, he saw Valia with the child in her arms.

"I said run! Find the horses," he called. Despite the danger, his voice was calm and commanding. Valia hesitated. She needed to save the child, but she didn't want to leave Kirin in the middle of a fight.

"Go!" he shouted. He slashed with his dagger again and connected with one of the creature's claws. There was a ring of metal before Kirin rolled again and stabbed at the creature's leg. It screeched and fell to one knee.

Valia hugged the child to her chest and ran to the horses. Kirin was right; she needed to get the child somewhere safe, and he seemed to be winning. If anything, she was only distracting him. She ran as fast as she could with the child in her arms, dodging those too-ripe cherry trees and trying to ignore the creature's nightmarish screeches behind them.

As Valia and the child emerged onto the road, she realized what Kirin must be fighting. The too-perfect crops, the bound child, the tall, thin creature—this was a fallow. And worse, this child seemed to have been left there intentionally.

Valia ignored her revelation, focusing instead on the girl in her arms.

"Hi, sweetheart." She patted the child's back and, slowly, the girl lifted her head. Her bright green eyes, full of tears, met Valia's. "Everything's okay."

"Where's mama?" The child's voice was high and worried.

"I'm not sure." Valia stroked the child's back again. "What happened?"

"The men taked me in the night," the child said. "I'm hungey!"

"I'm sure you are. Don't worry, we'll sort this out. What's your name, dear?"

"Alie."

"Nice to meet you, Alie. Look there, our horses! Have you ever ridden on a horse before?"

Just as Valia approached the horses, a hand shot out from behind a tree and grabbed Valia by the wrist, yanking her to the side. Another man appeared in front and wrestled Alie away from her. A third man stepped out behind him.

"No! Let go of her!" Valia screamed. She wanted to use her gale ring to push them away, but her hands were firmly detained behind her.

"This child belongs to us, little miss. We'll be takin' her back, along with these fine horses for the troubles. Don't worry, your friend over there won't be needin' them no more."

"Kirin! Help me!" Valia called out. The men snickered at her unanswered cry for help.

"Kirin, eh? He'll be fallow-feed soon enough. My boys over there'll see to that. You just wait patiently right here, pretty lass, and we'll find a use for ya. There's benefits to livin' here in Meadowstead, can't ye see? We's ain't starvin' like the rest of this rotten country."

The man behind her lifted her sleeves to inspect the rings he felt on her hands. "Oi, boss, look at these fancy rings she's got on. She ain't starvin' either by the looks of these!" He yanked her rings off one by one and threw one to the man holding Alie.

Valia winced in pain through the rough treatment, and tears welled in her eyes with the feeling of complete helplessness. From what these men said, Kirin had just been ambushed after—or while—fighting that horrifying creature.

The leader inspected the ring. "Are these real, miss? Wow, fantastic. There's a big bounty on these."

"Flora, help me," Valia whispered. An ineffective push landed on the man, causing him to briefly lose his balance and roughly set down Alie.

"Whoa now. A real, live floramancer? Careful, bleeder, don't be making me drop this child. The fallow prefer—"

A whistling sound shot by Valia's ear, followed immediately by another one ending in an impact behind her. The hold on her hands released, and the man behind her fell stiff to the ground. The far man gripped his throat, making gurgling noises as he dropped to his knees. Kirin threw the bow taken from his attackers onto the ground and advanced briskly from the field.

The leader reached for his sword but was too slow. Kirin's whip wrapped around the man, pinning his arms to his side. Kirin yanked the man down to the ground and stopped with his boot on the man's face.

"Kirin..." Valia whimpered, breaking out in a cathartic cry. She dropped to her knees and held Alie, shielding her innocent eyes from the dead and dying men.

"How many?!" Kirin yelled at the man.

"How many what?" The man attempted to answer, his cheek smashed into the dirt.

Kirin paused before answering, as if he was figuring out his own question. "How many more of you?!"

"A lot. More'n you can take on. Hundreds! Let me go, and you might live if you start running now."

"No good at farming, no good at fighting, and no good at lying. That's all I needed to know." Kirin removed his boot from the man's face, immediately dropping to replace it with a knee on his shoulder, and drew his dagger.

"Okay, okay, wait! Look, mister." The man attempted to reason with Kirin. "Them creatures, the fallow… they'd attack our town, eatin' our people. Every time, they'd stop after they got one of the little ones." Valia hugged the child closer, pressing one of her ears against her shoulder and covering the other with her palm. "Once we saw the effect they had on our crops, we gave 'em what they wanted, and they'd become docile for a season. Might as well use 'em to our advantage, eh? It's survival. A fair exchange really. We did what we had to do. It was them or us."

"*Them*? This innocent child you abducted?"

"We didn't 'ave any more of our own! We gave 'em our animals, but that only satisfied them a few days. What do you expect, us to just lay down and die?"

"Look at you now." Kirin put his dagger to the man's throat and stared at the man as a vein on his forehead looked like it may burst.

Valia watched in silence as she picked up her rings and quickly placed them back on her fingers. She felt comforted to have some power back at her command, almost fearing Kirin's wrath would somehow turn on her.

"You don't deserve my dagger." Kirin sheathed it, then released the man. He walked over to the third man, now lying quiet and still on the ground, and picked up the rope he'd been carrying.

"Thank ya, mister," the man said as Kirin returned. "Glad you can see reason. I was just doing—"

Kirin yanked him up by the collar and slammed him against a tree. He took the man's sword, threw it on the ground, then quickly tied the man to the tree before he could recover from the blow.

"'Ey, hang on," the man protested, fear finally beginning to show in his eyes. "'Ey, no, come on." The man wriggled but was already tightly secured to the tree. Kirin finished some final knots, secured his whip to his back, and turned to Valia.

"Time to go," Kirin said, looking again up at the sky. He turned toward the horses and offered Valia a hand.

Valia stood up, carrying Alie, still in shock and speechless. She dared not protest Kirin's methods after all that had happened. They walked toward their horses which stood patiently amidst the chaos.

"You can't leave me here! There's still fallow around!" Kirin and Valia kept walking, paying the man no more attention as they mounted. Valia situated Alie in front of her, and the child grabbed a fistful of Bird's mane. To Bird's credit, she allowed this with minimal fuss.

"This ain't no death for a man. Come back'n fight me!" The man began hurling curses and insults as they secured their gear, mounted, and started off down the road. "Coward! I hope you fall forever down Turiyel's Pit! May your family have their breath stolen by a weirwight! May your damned bleeder woman drown in the Vast Blue! Curses on you!" They couldn't hear him anymore, but that last one made Valia's skin crawl.

They picked up their pace as umbra darkened the sky. With Valia's hearing still heightened, she could hear the nightmarish screeching of fallows behind them—this time somehow sounding quicker and fiercer.

It was a cruel end for a cruel man. Was *Kirin* also cruel for setting the man up to die in that way? Had she made a mistake in not heeding her father's advice to stay away from him?

Valia felt saddened by what Kirin did, though she wasn't sure it was wrong, either. She couldn't exactly have arrested the men and brought them back to Wyra to stand trial for their crimes. The man from the inn, too. She'd always been raised to value a proper process for the kingdom's criminals, even the worst kind. But... she couldn't deny it felt good to know these treacherous men were no longer out there. No longer able to cause harm to Avania's people—*her* people.

As the sky lightened again, they slowed their pace. Valia looked at Kirin, who rode slightly ahead of her and Alie. His head turned slightly, as if he knew she was looking.

"Sorry, Valia. I'm sorry you had to witness all that. Justice often isn't kind or pretty outside cities like Wyra."

Valia didn't respond. This time, she was the untalkative one.

"But it makes no sense," Kirin continued. "Fallows are nocturnal. I've never seen one in the light of day before recently." He sounded frustrated. "You've seen the crops elsewhere. You've heard of the droughts. There's no way this place would flourish as much as it is without the fallow receiving regular feeding. Look." He pointed to the nearest cherry tree as they rode by. The cherries, which had been deep red and perfectly round not long ago, had already begun to rot on the branches.

Valia looked at Kirin again and their eyes met. His face was softer now as he looked at Valia. Caring. Emotional, even. He quickly turned his head forward.

"What shall we do about Alie?" Valia finally spoke.

"Alie?"

"The child. Alie, where do you live?"

"With mama and papa." Alie fixed her green eyes on Valia. "Where's mama?"

"We'll bring you to her, sweetheart."

With one hand wrapped around Alie and the other on the reins, Valia followed Kirin along the road. They passed another field, where golden wheat started to slump and turn a dingy tan. In saving Alie, they seemed to have doomed the village—if anyone even remained.

nce they were back in the forest, Kirin slowed and dismounted. Valia handed Alie to Kirin before dismounting herself. Kirin took the child and held her securely with one arm. He seemed like a natural holding her, causing Valia to wonder if he had experience with children. The thought never crossed her mind until now, but it was entirely possible this man she knew next to nothing about had children of his own. Once Valia was on the ground, he handed Alie back to her.

"This might hurt for just a moment." Valia used the pointed ring on her index finger to quickly prick the child's palm. A bead of blood rose and Alie howled with indignation. Valia pressed the blood to her sight ring and whispered a spell. Alie fell silent as a constellation of stars rose in the air in front of them, one for Alie and two for her parents.

Next, Valia used the family-finding spell and a tracking spell to place Alie's family on a map. It seemed they lived on a farm near the village that fed the fallows.

"See," Valia said as she straightened and handed the map to Kirin, marked with a drop of blood where the farm was. "Magic is wonderful. It's incredibly useful."

"I never said it couldn't be," Kirin said.

"We go home now?" Alie asked hopefully.

"Yes, sweetheart. Home." Valia and Kirin exchanged glances.

They mounted the horses again. Alie seemed to be in better spirits now that she was free and going home. She accepted a drink of water and the final slice of slightly stale bread Valia had brought, which she gnawed on as they rode. When she finished, she began to sing to herself.

"Flora is here, and Flora is there. Flora comes from everywhere. Look in the sky, and look in the sea. The Flora is anywhere you can be."

It was a catchy tune Valia remembered from her own childhood, and she soon found herself humming along. The child was warm in her arms and smelled like both dirt and soap. She reminded Valia of when Litia had been small.

They arrived at Alie's family farm. Kirin insisted on going in first and Valia accepted without argument. She stayed outside, holding Alie back to stop her from running in after Kirin. Shortly after him entering, a slender woman with red hair came flying out of the house. As soon as Alie saw her, her eyes lit up and she lifted her arms to her mother. The woman scooped Alie into her arms, pressed her close, and spun her around. Then she turned to Valia.

"Thank you," she said, her eyes full of tears. "We didn't know where they took her. My husband has been looking everywhere. I've been here, praying to Flora that she might be returned to us."

"As soon as your husband gets back, you need to leave." Kirin emerged from the house. "It isn't safe here anymore."

"I understand." The woman sniffled. "I won't let anything else happen to Alie."

Valia pressed a few florans into the woman's hand. "For the journey." The woman accepted the florans with a grateful smile, but her eyes lingered on Valia's rings a moment too long. She lifted her gaze to Valia's and, for a moment, they stared at each other. Valia got the feeling there was a question in the woman's gaze, of who Valia was and why she had such rings.

"Time to go." Kirin broke in. "I recommend you seek refuge in the capital."

"Thank you," the woman said again. "Flora watch over you."

"You as well." Valia nodded, though Kirin turned away as if the horses required his immediate attention.

"Bye bye," Alie called from her mother's arms. She waved a chubby hand and Valia waved back, then followed Kirin to the horses.

"Fallows in broad daylight," Kirin muttered as they rode on. "Fallows being fed by villagers. Not long ago, fallows were scary bedtime stories. Now, I've personally slain four, and I hope to never encounter one in the dark."

"How could they do that?" Valia asked. "Sacrifice children like that?"

Kirin's expression was grim. "We need to be careful. This isn't the Avania you know anymore."

"I believe it." Despite how annoying he could be—and more recently, terrifying—Valia was glad again to have such a capable man by her side. She was still wrapping her head around the fact he had defeated several men, not to mention a nightmarish creature, by himself, all in the same battle. She would never have been able to save Alie on her own. She probably would have died trying, if the man in the inn hadn't gotten her first. It was a sobering thought, and the thought crossed her mind Kirin was being underpaid.

But seeing him put himself in harm's way to save the child told her something, too. He wasn't just obsessed with hunting creatures for bags of coin, even if that was the show he put on. He'd claimed not to be a good man, and while he'd certainly scared her at times, that's not what she saw. Slowly, she began to see another side to him—something deeper and more complex than good or bad. He was flawed, he'd been hurt in the past, and his scars were more than physical. Something about him was *real*.

They rode on, both lost in their own thoughts. Rescuing Alie had delayed them, but by Valia's calculations, they were still nearly halfway to the coast. They stopped in another town to buy more provisions. Valia waited with the horses while Kirin went into the market since he was less recognizable. As dusk closed in, Kirin found a clearing off the road, and they made camp for the night.

Valia was more than a little on edge after beginning her day by being attacked in her sleep, followed by an encounter with a monster that shouldn't exist, then almost being captured by strange men who sacrificed children. Every small sound in the forest, from an owl hooting to the rustling of branches, made her jump.

She felt a little better when Kirin made a fire, and they roasted the sausages they'd bought earlier that day. Once she'd had a little time to rest, she realized there was one thing she could do to help the situation. Valia got to her feet and used her surge ring to grow the bushes and vines surrounding the clearing into a tightly woven thicket higher than Kirin's head. Kirin jumped when she began to cast, then looked uneasy until Valia finished and sat back down, with a hand on his dagger.

"It'll be safer this way," she told him. "Now, no one and nothing will be able to approach us without hacking through the vines."

"And just how are we going to leave?" Kirin asked. Valia grinned.

"I'll part the vines in the morning. Simple."

She felt better again now that they were safely cocooned in vegetation, but the dark was still oppressive and Valia couldn't help worrying about bears and manticores and all the other creatures that could easily be lurking in the bushes, sizing them up. A manticore could break through the walls easily...

"Let's talk," Valia blurted. Kirin looked at her as though she'd sprouted a second head.

"About?"

"I don't know." Valia didn't want to admit she was scared, but she also didn't want to sit in silence and worry about what might be out there. "Here's an idea. We can do a challenge. The loser has to tell a story."

Kirin sighed. "What's the challenge?"

"Who can break a bigger branch." Valia gestured to the clearing around them, which was illuminated by the flickering firelight.

Kirin stood, lifted a branch that was as thick as Valia's arm, and broke it over his knee with a firm crack. Then he sat down again, picked up the stick that his sausage was on, and went back to his cooking. It was hard to tell, but Valia was almost certain he looked a little smug from the way he leaned back against the log behind him and the way the corners of his mouth had ticked ever so slightly upward.

"Hah." Valia looked around the clearing and selected a fallen oak log as thick as her torso. She used her gale ring to split the log neatly in half with a soft crack. One half rolled slightly forward, revealing the tree's growth rings inside in a smooth cross-section.

"Using floramancy is cheating. What did you have to sacrifice for that little show?"

"Just my firstborn child." Valia smirked. "It was just a seed spell. And floramancy isn't cheating. You never said it was off limits, and neither did I. Now, tell me a story."

Kirin looked like a man who'd just been asked to sing an impromptu opera. He sighed. "I don't have any good ones."

"Come *on*." Valia held herself back from rolling her eyes so as not to discourage him. "You travel the world slaying evil monsters and wicked men. You must have at least one good story."

"Plenty of bad ones." Kirin paused and looked over to the horses. Perhaps he realized Valia was looking for comfort and distraction—not a reminder of the day they'd had. "Alright. I'll tell you about my first time hunting a creature." Valia perked up and playfully rested her chin on her hands.

"In a village near where I was born, people claimed to have seen a great beast in the forest just past the last row of homes. It had been stealing their vegetables for seasons until, one day, it had almost trampled a young boy who was out tending sheep and scattered the flock. That boy was the headman's son. He'd claimed it was a wild, rabid unicorn—thrice the size of a horse. As he was known for his skill in taming wild animals, we took him at his word.

"The headman posted a bounty on the beast for three hundred eyes." Valia gave him a confused look. "Trominite coin... Surely the princess of Avania would know the name of Trominite currency?" Valia shot him a glare but didn't respond. "Anyway, seeing as how my previous work had me earning half that in a season, I took the job. I was young and foolish, thinking I had nothing to lose.

"I set off into the forest. Right away, I came across a set of hoofprints. They were broad and deep and meandered up slopes and through streams. I followed.

"The further I went, the more I believed the boy's description of the creature. Apart from the hoof prints, I noticed snapped branches I imagined were struck with a long horn. And what else would roam the woods like this, attacking shepherd boys and stealing vegetables? A regular horse would simply be grazing on grass in the nearby plains." Kirin paused to take a sip of water and Valia leaned forward.

"I knew you had a good story. I didn't even know unicorns existed anymore."

"Indeed. I remembered from somewhere that the best way to catch a unicorn was to drop onto it from above. I got it into my mind that I would drop onto the unicorn, capture it, and ride it through town as proof I'd been successful.

"Finally, I found a grove where the unicorn seemed to be living. The tracks led into the grove, and I spotted a few long mane hairs at the entrance of a small clearing surrounded by a thicket of dense vegetation—not so different from what you've created here. I climbed up a tree and lay in wait. Just as it was getting dark, I heard the clip clop of its hooves. I took my chance and dropped down, but missed its back and landed in a bush. I quickly got to my feet and leaped onto its back before it could get away. It was startled and broke into a run, dodging narrowly in and out of trees and descending hills at breakneck speed, and every now and then attempted to buck me off. Up close, I saw it was brown, not white as I had expected, but I was still convinced. I managed to gain control of the unicorn and brought it to a stop just outside the village. In the lamplight, I saw it. I had captured a horse."

Valia burst into laughter. "A horse?"

"A horse." Kirin nodded long-sufferingly. "That horse." He nodded toward his nameless mount.

"But you were so sure it was a unicorn."

"I was. I didn't question the report given to me."

"Did you get your pay?"

"Sort of. The headman's son had clearly exaggerated the size of the beast and hadn't wanted to admit to a horse he couldn't tame. The village was hesitant to pay the full amount when I'd merely captured a horse, but they gave me fifty eyes and agreed to let me keep the horse."

"This is the best story ever. And now we have a name for your horse!"

"What?"

"Unicorn!" Valia began to laugh again. "We'll call him Unicorn!"

"No, no." Kirin shook his head firmly. "He doesn't need a name. He's not a pet."

"Come on. Hey, Unicorn!" Kirin's horse turned his head slightly toward Valia. "See? He likes it."

Kirin chuckled. "Fine. Call him Unicorn, if it pleases Your Highness."

"I will." Valia lay back against the soft moss beneath her. She felt more relaxed now. Her dinner and the story had done the trick.

"You're impossible."

"You're funny." Valia yawned. "Thanks for the story."

"Thanks for building our cage of vegetation."

"You are most welcome." Valia yawned again. "Okay, I think I'll sleep now. Good night, Kirin."

"Good night." There was a long pause, in which Valia heard only the crackling of the fire and the hooting of a faraway owl. Then Kirin added, quietly, "Valia."

CHAPTER SIXTEEN
LUCK

alia awoke the next day to warm sunlight streaming over her face. She sat up, rubbing crust from her eyes, and a cloak fell off her. Valia frowned at it. It was black and made of thick wool—it must be Kirin's. He must have put it on her while she'd slept.

Valia brushed leaves and moss from her hair with her hands and scanned the clearing. Kirin was already awake and saddling Bird. Unicorn stood patiently beside him, his saddle already on. The fire was now a neat pile of coal, and their bags had been packed.

"Good morning." Kirin tightened the last buckle on Bird's saddle and turned to Valia. He looked as refreshed as if he'd spent the night on a soft bed, while Valia felt stiff and tired. It made her wonder even more what his life was like. How much time did he spend sleeping on hard ground instead of in that small hut she'd seen? "I was about to wake you."

"How did you sleep?" Valia stood and brushed more leaves and moss off her trousers. She was grateful the chill of fall hadn't fully set in yet.

"Let's get moving. We're on pace to reach the coast by tomorrow."

"I also slept fine, thanks for asking." Valia smiled sweetly and went in search of her waterskin.

"Can you take down the..." Kirin gestured broadly at the wall of foliage surrounding them.

"Mhm." Valia took a long drink of water, then used a seed spell to disentangle the vines. The vegetation receded until it lay flat on the ground.

Kirin and Valia finished preparing their horses. Valia used a stump to climb onto Bird's back, while Kirin performed his usual expert vault onto Unicorn. Valia remembered his story from the night before and grinned to herself. It was nice to know Kirin had a side to him that could make fun of himself and agree to call his horse Unicorn.

They rode for a while before rejoining the main road. As before, this route was far more crowded, but Valia and Kirin made good time on the well-maintained road. They passed a few small villages without stopping, but in the third, Kirin took a side street into a market district.

"Stay here," he told Valia. She slid off Bird and nodded.

"Alright."

He soon returned with a wrapped bundle in his arms. Valia wanted a longer break but didn't complain when Kirin mounted right away, and they set off again. Once they were out of town, Kirin opened the bundle, brought Unicorn alongside Bird, and handed Valia a pair of thin black gloves.

"What are these?" Valia asked, turning the gloves over in her free hand.

"Gloves."

"Right, I got that, but why? It isn't that cold yet."

"To hide your rings."

Valia slid the gloves onto her hands. She could still remove them quickly to cast, and Kirin was right. Her rings were too noticeable to be constantly on display. Still, it felt foreign and unnatural to be unable to touch her rings at a moment's notice. Her hands felt itchy and uncomfortable with the gloves on.

"It's not forever."

Valia looked up to see Kirin watching her with his usual enigmatic expression.

"I know." She tugged at the finger of one of the gloves. "How about another competition?"

"No floramancy this time."

"Floramancy isn't my only skill." Valia considered. "Okay. Let's guess how many cows we'll see in the next stretch of road. I see a travel marker up there, so we can count from this to the next one."

"Ten," Kirin said.

"Then I'll go with eleven."

Kirin looked mildly offended. "Why?"

"It's a classic strategy. I used to play games like this with my sisters all the time, and you always want to hedge someone in. This way, if there are more than ten cows, I'm guaranteed to win." For the first time, talking about her sisters didn't make Valia's chest ache. She felt a little guilty about it, but it was nice to be able to bring them up without wanting to cry.

"Okay, we'll begin now." Kirin gestured to the travel marker, which was a small wooden pole that had been painted red at the bottom, to indicate they were in the southern Avanian region of Sarona, and orange at the top, to indicate they were traveling east. The marker on the other side was painted blue, to indicate that travelers going the other direction would head north. At the top was a number that counted the spans from Wyra.

Almost immediately, they passed a herd of cows on the left. Valia quickly counted seven and shot Kirin a confident grin.

"We're not even a quarter of the way in, and I'm already winning."

"I'd say I'm winning. I doubt we'll see many cows in the forest ahead."

Kirin was right. They rode into a small stretch of forest and were surrounded by trees for a short time. Valia began to worry that she might lose the bet. When they emerged though, she spotted another herd just ahead.

"Ha!"

"Nope." Kirin pointed to the sign that stood between them and the field of cows. "It's your turn to tell a story."

"Fine. Lucky you." Valia took a moment to think. "When I was very young, perhaps five or six, my parents took my sisters and me to a river just outside the palace. We went to that river often back then, before things started getting more difficult in Avania. Anyway, we were all playing by the river, making flower crowns out of daisies. Even though I was young, my flower crowns always came out the most beautiful."

"So modest."

"No, it's true. But it's hard to take all the credit. The flowers wound together of their own accord and sprouted new petals even after I'd plucked them. That's when my mother noticed that I had a particular affinity with plants and suggested that I should have an attunement ceremony right away, instead of waiting until the age of ten, as is more common. It was a magical day for me. The sun was bright, the water was cold, and I felt such freedom away from the palace. But more than that, I felt *loved*. Not only by my family, but by the Flora too. It's one of my most treasured memories."

"Sounds nice." But there was an edge in Kirin's voice.

"Are you uncomfortable because I'm talking about floramancy again?"

Kirin glanced at her with those unreadable eyes. "I wonder what the Flora wanted with you so young."

"What the Flora *wanted* with me?" Valia frowned.

"Princess. Haven't you ever wondered what the Flora wants? Why it chooses some people but not others? Why it allows some spells but denies others?"

"The Flora wants... balance," Valia said, but even she heard the hesitation in her own voice.

"Perhaps a better question, then: What is the Flora?"

"It's..." Valia gestured at the trees around them, the horses, the sky. "It's what holds us all together. It's the life force of the universe."

"If that's so, why don't all people use floramancy instead of just Avanians?"

"I..." Valia shook her head. "Not everyone chooses the Flora, and not everyone is chosen."

"Chosen." Kirin shifted on the ground. "That happens in your attunement ceremony, isn't that right?"

"Yes." Valia glanced at him, then away.

"And what happens in this ceremony?"

"Don't you know?"

Kirin shook his head. "The details of attunement ceremonies are not shared with people like me."

Valia hesitated. Her attunement ceremony was a treasured memory, just like the story of the day making flower crowns, and she wasn't sure she wanted to share it with someone trying to make it out to be something sinister.

"Well, a powerful floramancer leads the ceremony," she said. "It begins with a sacrifice of blood from the lips from the initiate. The floramancer offers the initiate a drink of sap water brought from a sacred tree deep in a forest somewhere. Then, the initiate makes a vow. A vow to serve the Flora and be part of the sacred network of life that the Flora flows through. Finally, the initiate places their lips upon the wood of a living tree and allows their blood to sink into it. We call this the *vow of blood and sap*, because we exchange our blood for a drink of the Flora's sap. We connect ourselves directly to the flow of the Flora."

"Right. And this all seems perfectly normal to you?" Kirin's steely eyes were intense now. "It doesn't seem at all strange that the Flora requests your servitude? And your blood?"

"I..." Valia felt uncomfortable. Perhaps she had made a mistake in sharing this memory with a Trominite man. "Maybe we should talk about something else."

"Hm." Kirin glanced at her, his gray eyes resting on hers for a long moment, before he spoke again. "Another competition?"

Valia felt more than a little shaken by Kirin's line of questioning, but if he was ready to move on, she was, too. "Alright. I believe it's your turn to come up with something."

"And, if I'm learning from your lead, I should choose something I can easily win. Perhaps a knife throwing competition."

"I might do better than you think."

"No floramancy."

For the rest of the day, as they rode through the scrubbier forests further from Wyra, they engaged in more small competitions. They threw knives (Kirin won), played a memory game (Valia won), and finally, as dusk set in, they made camp on a side path and competed to see who could collect more food for dinner. Valia brought back an armful of edible leafy greens and several handfuls of sweet late-season blackberries, while Kirin returned with two large fish.

"Who won?" Valia asked as they settled into a clearing. Kirin cleaned and prepared the fish while Valia raised her wall of greenery and started the fire.

"We both do. We get to eat a full meal." Kirin draped a cut of fish over two sticks he'd laid across the fire.

"Agreed. We'll call this one a draw, then." Valia began to wash the greens with water from her skin. "We'll reach the coast tomorrow, right?"

"I believe we should be there by mid-morning."

The fish suddenly smelled less appetizing as Valia's stomach knotted in nerves. She'd traveled a long, dangerous way already just to visit the Savani. What if they couldn't find her? What if the Savani answered her questions, but Valia didn't like what she heard? What if they got lost and drowned in the Vast Blue?

"Are you alright? Valia?" Valia looked up to see Kirin holding out a slightly charred slice of fish wrapped in a leaf. She took it from him.

"Thank you. Yes, I'm alright. I'm just a little anxious about meeting the Savani."

"It'll be fine. What could go wrong when it comes to a reclusive blood prophet who may or may not exist?" Kirin looked up from his own piece of fish and noticed Valia's worried expression. He added, "Really, I'm sure it'll be alright. You'll get the answers you're looking for. One way or another."

"I hope so."

"I'll... press a circle for you." Kirin held up his right hand with the thumb and forefinger touching. "That's what you Avanians say, right?"

"Right." Valia copied the gesture. "What do you say in Tromin?"

"In Tromin, we salute the moon." Kirin made a fist, which he pressed to his chest, then lifted to the sky.

"Alright." Valia did the same. "We need all the luck we can get, don't we?"

"We'll make our own luck." Kirin lifted the fish off the makeshift roasting platform he'd constructed over the fire.

They ate their fish and greens, finishing with the berries for dessert, then lay on opposite sides of the fire. Valia was grateful for her new gloves with the chill in the air. As she was on the edge of sleep, she heard a familiar hissing from the forest. It was the same sound she'd heard as they'd ridden into the village on the first night, and in the fields of Meadowstead. She sat up and, in the light of the dying fire, she saw Kirin looking back at her. He held a finger to his lips.

For a long moment, they sat in silence, staring at each other. The hissing died away, replaced by the normal noises of nighttime in the forest. Still unsettled, Valia lay back down, but sleep didn't come for a long time.

CHAPTER SEVENTEEN
EYE

The next day, Valia awoke before Kirin. This hadn't happened since that first night in the inn before their return to Wyra. Valia yawned and sat upright, then looked across the fire at Kirin. His eyelashes were splayed on his cheeks, and he looked peaceful—not at all like the hardened man he usually was in wakefulness. Valia noticed dried blood on his lower lip, likely from their encounter two days ago. Valia resisted the urge to watch him longer, but the memory of their kiss in the draevori cave resurfaced in the soft predawn light. They'd overcome quite a lot together since then.

Quietly, Valia stood, wrangled her hair into a braid, and fetched the waterskins from their bag. There was a river nearby where she could fill the skins so that they'd be ready to leave once Kirin awoke. Valia quietly parted the thicket of vegetation, then closed it behind her to protect Kirin in his sleep.

The river wasn't far. Valia walked down the hill, following the sound of running water, and soon came to the bank of the river. The water was cold and clear. It pooled in places, reflecting the pines and oaks towering above them. Valia caught sight of her own reflection and paused, staring down at the woman in the river. She was no longer the helpless, drained woman Kirin had rescued from the draevori cave. Nor was she the soft, pink-cheeked princess she'd been before that. Valia saw someone else now. Someone powerful. Someone with purpose.

Turning away from her reflection, Valia quickly filled both waterskins, then began to pick her way back up the sloped hill toward their camp. She must have overshot, though, because she soon came upon the narrow road they'd taken the evening before.

Valia turned in the direction of their camp and began to follow the road. It was still early, so she was alone, and the dirt crunched softly beneath her boots. As Valia was about to reach the place where she and Kirin had turned into the woods, she spotted a poster nailed to a tree.

Turn away from blood magic and embrace the eternal eye.

Below the text was a simple, broad circle, with a smaller one in the center.

Valia stared at the poster for several long moments. Had this been here yesterday when they'd made their camp? The parchment was still crisp, not yet weathered by extended time in the elements, and Valia had the sinking suspicion it had been put here during the night.

Turn away from blood magic. That part was clear. Whoever had made the poster clearly didn't approve of floramancy. Valia pressed her thumb against her rings in comfort, glad she hadn't yet put her gloves on.

The second part was more obscure. *Embrace the eternal eye.* What did that mean?

Valia bit her lip, then turned away from the poster. It sounded like something Kirin may have more insight into what it meant once she woke him.

The sight Valia found when she returned to camp, though, was of a shiny blade slashing through the wall of vines from inside.

"Kirin?"

"Valia!" His voice was louder and wilder than usual. Valia used her power to part the wall of vegetation and came face-to-face with Kirin, his dagger held up in mid-slash, his feet bare, his eyes wild. When he saw her, he grabbed her hand and pulled her into the protection of their camp, then scanned the forest outside. Seeming satisfied that she wasn't in imminent danger, he turned to her with a scolding, expectant stare. Clearly, he wanted an explanation.

"I went to get water." Valia held up the full waterskins.

"Why is it that whenever you wake before me, your first instinct is to run off into the forest?" Kirin ran a hand through his hair. "How am I supposed to keep you safe when you keep disappearing?"

"Kirin." Valia grabbed his free hand and tugged so that he fell a step closer to her. "I'm safe. I'm sorry I left without you, but I'm safe."

"You're safe." He seemed to deflate slightly from the wild energy of a few moments ago. Then his eyes turned steely. "Next time, wake me when you do."

"I will. Sorry." Valia looked down, feeling chastened, as Kirin released her hand and went to put his boots on. Soon they were on the road again, and the mysterious poster fell to the back of Valia's mind.

Before long, Valia noticed distinct changes in the vegetation. The trees grew shorter and more gnarled as the undergrowth thinned out. She spotted a few seagulls flying overhead and calling out to each other in indignant squawks. There was the scent of salt in the air and the dirt on the road slowly gave way to sand. Valia even spotted a few palm trees, and it took all her resolve not to pull Bird to a stop so that she could press her hand to one and see what kind of power it could offer her.

After a pleasant and peaceful ride along the coast, they reached the town of Belisport. Kirin checked to make sure Valia wore her gloves before they reached the first few houses. She held up both hands to confirm they were firmly in place. The town was moderately sized, with worn stone houses painted in bright colors. They rode through a small market, where Valia caught sight of her favorite orelai fruit stacked in colorful towers and fresh fish on blocks of ice that must have been magically made.

"Do you know exactly where the Savani is?" Kirin asked as they passed the market. "I doubt there will be signs for her."

"The lore states that her island lies somewhere in the Vast Blue between the towns of Belisport and Canin, and that if you search for her and are worthy, you'll find her."

"She has to deem you worthy?" Kirin raised his eyebrows.

"We're worthy… I think. But we definitely still need a boat."

"Right." They rode through town toward the docks, where they dismounted. There was a row of hooks to tie up horses, along with a bored looking girl who took a few florans from Valia to watch the horses. They'd barely finished tying up Bird and Unicorn when three different merchants strode toward them.

"I can offer you the best deal on a boat," the first said.

"You're seeking the Savani, aren't you? His boat may be cheap, but it'll fall apart before it ever reaches her."

"Such nonsense from these two," the third chimed in. "What you want is a pleasant, guided trip with me at your side to help you ride the waves. I assume neither of you is an experienced seafarer?"

Kirin and Valia exchanged glances. It seemed everyone knew they were looking for the Savani. Was it really so common for people to come looking for her?

"You." Kirin nodded to the second merchant, a tall, slim woman with a cunning glint in her eye. "How often do people come here looking for the Savani?"

"Oh, all the time."

"And how often do they find her?"

The merchant hesitated. "Less often, but surely *you* won't have any issues. So long as your hearts are pure and your intentions are good, you'll row straight to her."

"Right. And how much do you charge?"

"My rental fees are nominal, really," the merchant told him. "Especially for a young couple like yourselves. I'd be happy to give you a discount. I do require a safety deposit, though."

"Not me," the third merchant, an athletic-looking young man around Valia's age, chimed in. "Since my tours are guided, there's no need for a deposit."

"And how often do *your* customers find the Savani?" Valia asked. The three merchants turned to her as if seeing her for the first time.

"All the time," the third merchant told her.

"Lies," the first merchant put in. "His clients rarely find anything but fish. Miss, do I know you from somewhere? You look familiar..."

"No, I don't believe so," Valia told him, her heart rate increasing. "I haven't been to Belisport before."

Kirin glanced at Valia, then jutted his chin to the second merchant. She shrugged her assent, and Kirin turned to the merchant. "We'll take your boat."

The other two merchants fell away, grumbling, while the second merchant showered them with compliments as she exacted a rental fee and safety deposit enough to purchase the boat anywhere else.

Valia handed over the payments without haggling, even though it left her with little coin with which to pay Kirin. They were so close now, and she didn't want to turn down the boat they needed.

"Beautiful day today. You'll have a wonderful time out there," the merchant told them as she ushered them down the dock. Her boat was small but looked well-cared-for and seaworthy. The merchant helped Valia and Kirin into the boat, then handed them a pair of oars. "Flora guide you!"

With that, she gave their boat a strong shove away from the dock, and they were on their way.

Kirin arranged the oars, then dipped them into the water. The boat skimmed across the surface, bobbing slightly on the waves, and Valia took a deep breath of the fresh, salty air. She'd been so caught up in finding a boat, she'd barely noticed the view.

The ocean stretched as far as she could see, all sparkling cerulean blues and rolling whitecapped waves. The sky above was equally blue, with the cloud cover of early morning having burned off into a beautiful day. If Valia didn't look back at the town of Belisport, with its mix of brightly painted cottages and large stone buildings, it would be easy to believe they were in the middle of the ocean. She understood now why the waters surrounding Avania were called the Vast Blue.

"It seems like a lot of people come here to look for the Savani," Valia said.

"I've seen this kind of thing before," Kirin told her. "When there's a place or a being of great power or interest, people build a whole tourist infrastructure around it. In Tromin, there's a deep cave said to be able to heal any ailment or bring someone back from the dead. Even though most people who enter never even return to the surface, people keep attempting to explore it out of hope or desperation. Merchants claim to be able to increase a person's chances of success, but they're just as desperate, just for coin. And not brave enough to explore the pit themselves."

Valia's heart sank. "So, do you think the Savani doesn't really exist either?"

"I don't know," Kirin admitted. "But I've actually heard of her before, I think. Just not by that name. If she's really a powerful floramancer, you might be able to sense her."

Valia closed her eyes and broadened her senses. She heard the slap of the waves against the boat and the soft creaking of the oars in their sockets. She heard the screech of seagulls and the faraway sound of bells back in Belisport. On instinct, Valia tugged off her gloves, reached out with a finding spell, and felt a tug. She couldn't explain exactly what it was, but she felt drawn to it in the way birds are compelled to migrate in advance of the changing seasons.

"That way." She pointed northeast. "I felt something. I'm not sure what."

"Alright." Kirin adjusted his course and continued to row in slow, powerful strokes. The use of her powers brought back the memory of the poster from that morning, and Valia leaned forward.

"I saw something strange today. There was a poster with a slogan, something about letting go of blood magic and embracing the eternal eye. And there was a full circle below with a smaller one in the center. It looked like the moon. Do you know what that means?"

There was a long pause as Kirin continued to row and, for a moment, Valia thought that he might not answer her at all. Then he sighed. "I'm... familiar with the concept. The circle represents the Ev... the moon, as you say."

"Okay..." Valia stared at him for a long moment, but he didn't say anything else. "Continue, please."

"Well, as I'm sure you know, there are people out there who don't... approve of floramancy."

"Like you?"

"No. Well, kind of, but it's different. There are people who believe that floramancy and floramancers are wrong. That exchanging blood for power is twisted, and calling on an unknown being like the Flora is bound to create more problems than good."

"Right. I know that. That still sounds like you." Valia crossed her arms. "But what was the part about the eternal eye? And who put it there?"

"The eternal eye is the moon," Kirin told her. "Metemancers gain power from stones fallen from it. Those stones don't require the power of a being like the Flora, and it uses power that would be released anyway. In Tromin, metemancy is used instead of floramancy. My dagger is partly made of this metemantic material." He looked at her from the corner of his eye as if worried Valia might panic.

"So is your token," Valia said slowly. "That's why I couldn't use my power on it." She bit her lip. "Are you a metem, then?" She didn't want to believe that the man she'd grown close to over the last few days was a metemancer, but even if he was one, he was still Kirin—*wasn't he?*

"No. I prefer to draw on my own strength. But the material on my dagger does give it a boost. It can drain or release energy on impact and regenerates it when it gets nicked or broken. Others have weapons completely shaped from metemantic stone. When the weapon strikes something, it reacts with the power inside."

Valia felt relieved. It was one thing to use a metemantic material as a tool and another completely to be a metem. If most people where Kirin was from were metems—or perhaps she should say metemancers—it also made sense his dagger would be made with a metemantic material.

"That's why anyone who sees your dagger wants you to leave. My father. Poriev." The pieces were starting to fall into place, but she had another question—one she wasn't sure she wanted to know the answer to. "Do you agree with the people who hung the poster?"

"Not with them," Kirin said, quickly. "They've gone too far."

"What do you mean?"

Kirin's eyes met hers steadily. "There are some people who would do anything to stop a powerful floramancer. Or even a minor one. Then some would murder anyone associated with floramancy at all."

"Like whoever put the bounty on floramantic rings."

"Yes. Not just that, though. There was a metemancer who brought deceased animals back to life to hunt down a village floramancer. A healer."

"That's why things have been so strange in Avania," Valia filled in. "These... people are doing all these things."

"Not exactly. Or, I don't think so, anyway. Not all those who oppose floramancers are metemancers. And metemancers weren't always as powerful as they seem to be now. No one was able to reanimate the deceased before. And creatures like the fallows aren't supposed to exist at all. There's a shift of power in Avania. Can't you feel it?"

"I—" In that moment, there was a hollow *clunk* against the bottom of the boat. Valia and Kirin both sat up straighter and looked around. "What was that?"

"I'm not sure." They both sat very still for a long moment, then it came again. *Clunk.* A short moment later, a small hole the size of Valia's palm and perfectly round, fell away from the bottom of the boat. Instead of the rush of seawater Valia expected, though, a round, dark shape appeared in the hole.

Kirin immediately went for his metemantic knife, but Valia reached out, grabbed his arm, and shook her head.

"Wait," she whispered.

Kirin muttered something that sounded like "I don't see any bear cubs in the sky," and, although he kept his dagger ready in his hand, he didn't strike.

The dark shape flicked around and fluttered closed to reveal dark blue skin. It opened again and, in that moment, Valia realized she was looking at an eye. Kirin must have realized the same thing, because his eyes widened. He made a stabbing motion with the dagger, then raised his eyebrows at Valia. She shook her head again and raised one finger to her lips.

Then, Valia stilled her mind. She thought only of the question she had come to ask. She drew on the Flora and held her power ready in the palms of her hands. Not threatening, but *showing*. A long moment passed. The eye blinked once more, then suddenly they were moving.

The motion came so suddenly that both Valia and Kirin fell back, Kirin landing on top of Valia. He managed to brace against the sides of the boat in time so that his full weight wasn't on her, but Valia was still acutely aware of his closeness and the heat from his body. He quickly scrambled to a seated position and helped Valia up. They clung to the sides of the boat as they flew through the water, moving fast enough that whitecaps appeared on either side of the boat.

"What is happening?" Kirin hissed.

"I think this creature is her guardian," Valia replied. "I think it's bringing us to her." It no longer seemed important to be quiet, seeing as their progress through the water made a lot of noise as well.

"And if it's decided we're not worthy and is taking us to its lair to eat us instead?"

"Then you can stab it."

Kirin readied his dagger with a wide stance. He always looked more comfortable with a weapon in his hand, as though they were an extension of himself—like Valia and her rings. Valia got the feeling he would rather fight the sea creature than allow himself a single moment of vulnerability or doubt.

Valia peered over the front of the boat and spotted a small island with a tall, jagged mountain in the center quickly growing closer. She pointed to the island and Kirin nodded.

As they neared the beach, the creature gave them a final shove, and they careened across the water and smashed into the land. The force of impact sent Valia and Kirin tumbling out of the boat and onto the sand, knocking the breath out of Valia. She brushed sand out of her mouth and gasped for air as she rolled onto her back. Back in the ocean, the creature disappeared into the depths, but not before throwing one long tentacle into the air in a gesture that looked suspiciously like a wave.

"Are you alright?" Kirin asked. He sounded like he'd had the wind knocked out of him as well.

"Yes, you?"

"I don't think we'll get our deposit back." He nodded to the boat, which had split into two upon impact with the island's shore. Something about the comment struck Valia as impossibly funny and she began to giggle. The giggling turned into full-out laughing, and soon Valia was lying back on the sand, clutching her stomach as waves of mirth rolled over her. Kirin, propped up on an elbow beside her, looked down at Valia as though she'd had her wits addled by a well-placed curse.

"*The deposit,*" Valia managed to gasp between fits of laughter. "We're stranded on an island." More laughter. "It belongs to a potentially dangerous prophet." Another round of giggles. "There's no way off! And you're worried about *the deposit.*"

"Obviously, I'm worried about other things, too." But Kirin was grinning.

"Okay." Valia pushed herself back up to a seated position, took a deep breath, and got her giggles under control. "Shall we?"

Kirin nodded and got to his feet. He was covered in sand, which he began to brush off, and Valia did the same. Her lighthearted laughter quickly turned back into nerves. The creature had judged them worthy of seeing the Savani. What it would have done if they weren't worthy, she didn't want to consider. But there was still no reason to believe the Savani would have the answer she sought, and Valia would only be able to ask a single question.

"I'm guessing she'll be up there." Valia pointed up the steep slope of the craggy peak, at the top of which perched a white marble structure that stood out against the dark rocks and vegetation.

"Good guess."

Together, they set off up the slope, Valia with her gloves off and Kirin ever ready for trouble.

CHAPTER EIGHTEEN
SECRETS

he closer Valia came to the marble structure, the more worried she became. First, there was the question of how this structure had come to be on the island in the first place. From this distance, it appeared as a temple. Wide columns of pure white marble, seemingly untouched by weather or time, stood in the front. Behind the columns, an open door led somewhere Valia couldn't see.

"Do you know the question you'll ask?" Kirin wondered.

"Yes. I'm ready."

He nodded. "If something goes wrong, I'll be ready too."

Valia's stomach twisted at the thought of something going wrong. Whoever lived here was powerful enough to have built this temple, which meant they were undoubtedly more powerful than Valia. Still, she felt better with Kirin by her side.

Together, they climbed a small set of stairs and passed under the columns and through the door on the other side. To Valia's surprise, the interior of the temple didn't match the exterior at all. In fact, the interior looked like any other cottage. There was a kitchen along one wall filled with fish, a loaf of fresh bread, and strands of herbs drying on the ceiling. Along another wall was a bed with a neat patchwork quilt. And in the middle, cross-legged and with a peaceful smile on her lovely face, sat... a girl.

She was perhaps sixteen or seventeen, with long blonde hair in a braid over one shoulder. Her eyes were so blue they made the water and sky seem dull and pale. Valia got the sense that staring into those eyes for too long would be a mistake and quickly looked away. The girl wore a simple white gown, which was as spotless as the outside of the temple.

"Hello, Valia," she said in a high, sweet voice. "I'm so glad you're here." She said Valia's name with a strange inflection, as though there was some kind of power in the word.

"Are you... the Savani?" Valia asked.

"Please, come. Sit." The girl—the Savani—gestured to the floor in front of her. Valia exchanged a glance with Kirin, who looked overly tense. Putting her misgivings to the side, Valia took a deep breath and sat in front of the girl.

"May I have your hand?" the Savani asked. Valia held out one hand palm up, and in a flash, the Savani pricked her palm with a long needle. She pressed the blood to a pendant she wore around her wrist. She hummed, low and thoughtful, and tilted her head to the side. Her big, too-blue eyes were unblinking.

"Okay, Valia," the Savani continued in that high, sweet voice. "Let's get the unpleasant part out of the way. Every question comes with a price, and I must collect payment."

Valia's blood ran cold, but she nodded. "What's the payment?"

"A core memory. One from your youth. You will lose this part of yourself forever, Valia. Do you accept?"

Valia didn't look back at Kirin, though she sensed his presence standing watchfully behind her. She knew what she would see in his eyes: warning. She also knew she couldn't listen to his concerns. This was bigger than either of them.

"I accept." Then Valia hesitated. "Kirin, do you remember the story I told you when I lost the cow competition?"

"I remember," Kirin said from behind her. "But—" Valia shook her head, and he fell silent.

Once again, the Savani pricked Valia's palm. She pressed a drop of blood to the bracelet on her other wrist, then took Valia's hand. Valia closed her eyes and offered up her memory, the memory of the day she'd discovered her power. She remembered the chain of daisies in her hands and the way her sisters had smiled at her. She remembered the cool of the water and the warmth of her parents' arms. She remembered...

The summer day melted into a swirl of gray nothingness.

Valia was no longer sure which memory she'd given up, only that there was a hollow place in her chest where it had been. She flicked her eyes open and resisted the urge to scramble backward. The Savani was no longer a teenager. Instead, a young girl of perhaps twelve sat in front of Valia. She wore the same unsettling smile and had the same unblinking blue eyes, staring straight at her.

"How did you do that?" Valia asked.

The Savani raised her eyebrow. "Is that your question for me, Valia?"

Valia shook her head quickly. "No."

"Then what is?"

"I have a living sibling," Valia said. "I'm not sure who it is. Maybe one of my sisters, or—"

The Savani shook her head. "Flora returns only silence from your sisters. They are gone."

"Then someone else, maybe," Valia told her, trying to ignore the crushing blow of hearing once again that her sisters were gone. "It must be. I cast a spell and saw that I have a living sibling, somewhere. I just can't figure out who it is. Something seems to be blocking my magic."

The Savani went pale. "You're sure of this, child?"

It was strange to be called *child* by someone who looked like a child herself. Valia nodded.

The Savani took Valia's hands again, but this time, she used a drop of her own blood against one of her pendants. Her eyes glazed over, and a long moment passed. Then she jolted as if returning to her body, her mouth falling open.

"What?" Valia asked.

"Three peaks. Stone and ruin. Free from sin. Birthplace of the burning light!" The Savani blinked with a look of calm distress on her face. She took a moment to recompose herself before continuing. "King Aran and Queen Ellara came to me, just once, at the dawn of their reign. As all Avanian rulers do. When I took their hands, I had a terrifying vision. I saw that if they had a son together, he would bring ruin to Avania. I saw crops burning, people all over the country fleeing toward Wyra, creatures of old coming back to life—the balance of Flora destroyed alongside the royal family."

"That's happening," Valia said softly. "All those things. They're happening." She hesitated. "Are you saying I have a brother?"

The Savani nodded. "Flora touched him, just now, for a moment, somewhere in the north. But the same thing blocking your magic now blocks mine. His exact location is unclear."

Valia felt tears prick at the backs of her eyes. "If my parents had a son together, why didn't I know about him?"

"An infant's exile would be a shameful secret."

A tear spilled down Valia's cheek and she took her hand back from the Savani's to wipe it away.

"I'm sorry, child," the Savani said, and for a moment, Valia saw her as an old woman, tired of the weight of the world. Then the moment passed, and she was a stolid child again.

Valia pushed to her feet and stumbled back. Kirin's arm went around her shoulders protectively.

"And *you*. Kirin now, is it?" The Savani bored her eyes into him. "Has this journey been as you've expected?"

"This isn't about me. I'm only here to protect her." Kirin's eyes narrowed and his arm around Valia's shoulders tightened slightly.

"If only that were so." The Savani tilted her head to the side, those deep blue eyes locked onto Kirin's. "Do you want to know what you'll choose?"

Valia looked into Kirin's eyes and got the feeling a secret conversation was taking place in front of her. She now had more questions for Kirin, but right now, thoughts of her brother were overwhelming enough.

"We've heard enough." Kirin took a step back and Valia followed.

"Very well. You'll find a boat on the western beach." The Savani pointed, staring blankly forward. "Flora be with you. *Both of you.*"

Kirin took another step back, looking unsettled. Valia went through the door and Kirin followed. Then, they were walking back down the path. Their steps grew longer and more hurried until they were practically running.

"I have a brother," Valia said, her voice sounding choked even to her own ears.

"Could she be wrong?"

"No. I have a brother. It all makes sense now." Valia came to a stop and faced Kirin. "My father refused to speak to me or to let anyone else speak to me when I asked about a living sibling. My mother was terrified before having Litia and I once overheard her sobbing to my father with fear that 'it would happen again.' The Savani is telling the truth."

"And even if you do, what then?" Kirin spread his hands. "She said a prince would lead to Avania's ruin, and clearly that's happening. Whoever he is now, he's dangerous, whether that's ultimately his fault or not."

"I still have to find him. I need to apologize for what my parents did and, if he's really causing all these problems in Avania, I need to stop him."

"You don't even know where to look. 'North' isn't enough."

"Maybe my father does." Valia began to jog down the hill again and Kirin fell into step beside her. "We need to go back to Wyra. We need to find him!"

"Valia." Suddenly, Kirin's arms were around her. The unexpected contact brought tears to Valia's eyes, and she found herself melting into the warmth of Kirin's arms. He smelled like sea salt and campfire smoke and pine. His shirt was rough against Valia's cheek, and she could feel the firm contour of muscles beneath, but his arms were gentle around her.

"I just don't know what I'm supposed to do," she whispered.

"We'll figure it out." Kirin rubbed his hand across her upper back. His voice was soft, close to her ear. "You're not alone."

"Right... I'm not alone because I have a mercenary who's only here because he's paid to be." Valia stepped out of his embrace and crossed her arms over her stomach. "How lucky I am."

"Really?" Kirin raised his eyebrows. "You think I'm still here because you're paying me? You do realize I haven't actually been paid?"

"So, you want payment right now?"

"No. You're not listening. Valia, I'm here with you because..." he hesitated. "I'm not here for the coin."

Valia looked up at him. "You aren't?"

"No." Kirin's eyes skated away from hers.

"Well, then what *are* you here for? Tell me, Kirin, because I don't understand."

Kirin paused, thinking carefully about his next words. "I... I don't know exactly, Valia. The world is changing, and I'm figuring out where that leaves me. I've already told you, I'm not a good man. But I'm trying to make up for the things I've done."

"And protecting *me* accomplishes this how, exactly?"

"I'm figuring that out."

"Hm," Valia grumbled, unsatisfied with his answer. "Well, how can I trust you, when I don't even know what it is you want?"

"I can see how important this is. Not just to you or your family, but to Avania. Maybe to the world. You can trust me, Valia. You have your mission, and I have mine. I'm going to get you to your brother. You won't make it without me." Valia stared into his eyes for a long moment, trying to read his face for clues into his motivations. She was still confused by the Savani's comments toward him. She also wasn't sure how to respond to his assertion that she wouldn't make it without him—even though he *was* probably right.

"We should get moving," she said, deciding to let his words sit without a response.

Valia started walking down the path toward the western beach, and Kirin closely followed. Despite the overwhelming realization that she had a brother—one who her parents must have cast out like three-day-old bread—she felt better than before. She knew what she needed to do now, and who she needed to find.

She still had questions about Kirin, but she *did* feel, deep down, she could trust him. She felt he would stay by her side, not because she was paying him, but because he wanted to.

For now, that was enough.

"Valia."

She glanced at Kirin, then turned her gaze back to the rocky path below. "Yes?"

"You gave up a memory to the Savani. Do you know which one?"

"No. I just know it was something important. I can feel it missing."

"You told it to me. Would you like to hear it?"

"Oh…" Valia hesitated. "Yes. Please."

"When you were a young child, you went down to the river with your family. It was a beautiful day, with blue skies and cold water." Kirin's gaze was focused on the path as well, not looking at Valia. "You made a flower crown out of daisies, the most beautiful of all your sisters'. The flowers practically wove themselves at your touch."

"The most beautiful? How modest." Valia's heart pattered in her chest at the story. It felt like déjà vu, as though she'd heard it before but couldn't quite place it. That made sense, of course, since it was her story, even if she couldn't remember it.

"That's what I said when you told me. When your parents saw what you did, they knew the Flora had… chosen you, and that it was time for what you called an 'attunement ceremony.' You felt loved that day, not just by your family, but by the Flora, too. It was very special for you."

"That sounds nice." Valia searched for the memory in her own mind, but it wasn't there. "Thank you for telling me."

"Does it make it better, to know it happened even though you don't remember?"

"I suppose." Valia bit her lip and picked over a particularly rocky section of the path. Ahead of them, the ocean grew closer and Valia spotted a neat row of wooden boats on the beach below. The Savani had prepared well for her guests. "Was it hard to tell me a story about how I discovered my floramantic powers?"

"No. I know it means a lot to you."

Valia ran her fingers over her rings and tried to remember the little girl she'd been, weaving flower crowns with her sisters. But the thought felt sour. Even if that had been a special day for her, her brother—whoever he was—had been excluded.

She had to find him. And with Kirin by her side, she was certain she could.

CHAPTER NINETEEN
PRACTICE

he journey back to Belisport in the Savani's boat was uneventful. Valia and Kirin were both slightly tense, half expecting the sea creature to thud against their boat again, but they returned to shore without incident. When they pulled up to the dock, the same three merchants were sitting on the edge playing a complicated game of dice. They all looked up in surprise when Kirin leaped out of the boat and tied it neatly to a bollard.

"You actually saw her, didn't you?" the merchant who'd rented them the boat asked. She looked from Kirin and Valia, who were still wet and sandy, to the shiny boat and back, her expression appraising.

"We did," Kirin confirmed. "But... we also lost your boat."

"I'll take that one in exchange," the merchant offered.

"Fine by me," Kirin said. He looked at Valia, and she nodded her consent.

The merchant returned Valia's deposit and went to admire her new boat. Valia was fairly certain the Savani's boat was better than the one the sea creature had destroyed. The merchant had gotten a splendid deal out of this. It didn't matter; Valia had no further use for a boat.

Kirin retrieved Unicorn and Bird, tipping the bored girl who'd watched them for her trouble, and they rode out of town without speaking. Valia's throat ached as though she'd swallowed broken glass—half from holding back tears, and half from the burn of using a lot of magic in the last few days.

They rode quickly for a while, speaking little and not pausing for breaks. Valia felt a strong need to get away from the coast and the realizations she'd come to there, and Kirin seemed to feel the same.

The horses began to tire, though, and they slowed their pace.

"Something is bothering me," Kirin said in a low voice.

"What is it?"

"The Savani mentioned your parents giving your brother away, but wouldn't the kingdom have noticed your pregnant mother, then no child arriving?"

"Presumably. That's something else my father will need to explain." Although, with his previous hesitancy to answer even her most basic questions, Valia wasn't convinced he'd be helpful. "Something's been bothering me, too."

"Yes?"

"The Savani mentioned that you would be making a choice. What was she talking about?"

"I couldn't say. She could have meant anything." But Kirin's eyes skated away from hers as he answered. The broken glass feeling grew stronger. Just when Valia thought she and Kirin were understanding each other better, there were more secrets.

They rode on without speaking further, each lost in their own thoughts. The only sounds were the clip-clop of the horses' hooves and the rustle of the wind in the trees. Occasionally, they passed travelers heading the opposite direction, most of them looking worn and tired. There weren't as many refugees on this part of the road, and Valia wondered if the south had been less affected by the destruction sweeping the rest of Avania.

Then, in the distance, Valia heard a fainting hissing sound. She turned to Kirin, who looked back at her with serious eyes and held a finger to his lips. Valia's heart began to race. It was their fourth time hearing this strange sound.

They'd been riding along the main road, which had been filled with other travelers since they'd set out. Now, though, it was suddenly empty, as though every other traveler had been warned not to be here right now.

Kirin pulled Unicorn to a stop, so Valia followed suit. When he slid off the horse's back and onto the ground, she followed him, pulling her gloves off as she did so. There was no point in hiding now, and every reason to be ready for what may come. Kirin's whip was in his hands, and he looked ready for a fight.

The hissing sound grew louder, then abruptly cut off. Valia's gaze swept the tree line, but she couldn't see anything out of the ordinary. For a few long moments, Valia and Kirin stood side by side, waiting for an attack that didn't appear. Finally, Kirin glanced at Valia.

"Hmm."

"What *is* that?" Valia tried to keep her voice calm, but the hissing alarmed her more than most of the other creatures they'd come across. Something about not being able to see whatever it was made her uneasy.

"I don't know." Kirin's eyes were back on the trees. "It doesn't seem to mean us any harm. At least not directly. It's had plenty of opportunities to attack."

"Then what does it want? It can't be a coincidence that we've heard it four times now."

"My best guess? It's watching us." Kirin glanced at Valia again. "Reporting our movements to someone else."

"Like my father?"

"I doubt it. His spies tend to be more obvious."

Valia's chest tightened. "So, someone is spying on us?"

"It could be something else. Either way, we can't let it stop us with a sound." Kirin turned back toward Unicorn.

As soon as he turned, the trees parted and a bear emerged from the woods, its lips pulled back to reveal long, sharp fangs. Unnatural fangs. Without hesitating, the bear pounced at Kirin in a long, jerky movement, its claws extended toward his back.

Acting on instinct, Valia shoved at the bear with her power, drawing on her gale ring and a basic incantation. The animal was so large that her efforts glanced off its huge bulk, but it did slow the bear enough for Kirin to turn and strike with his whip. The sharp tip struck true on the bear's shoulder. Dark blood spurted out, but it otherwise had little effect. The bear let out a low growl and swiped at Kirin, who rolled out of the way. Its leap carried it too far and its claws missed Unicorn by inches. The horse whinnied in fright, his eyes turning white.

"Go!" Valia called, compelling the horses with her link ring. Both horses took off down the path, and the bear faltered for a heartbeat as though it might heed her command, too. In that moment, Kirin lunged with his dagger, slashing across the bear's neck. Again, blood spurted, but the animal still seemed unfazed. It prowled a few paces back, then swung its large head slowly toward Valia. Its eyes were deep blue, and, despite her panic, Valia felt a momentary burst of déjà vu. Then, the bear swiped at her, and she lost all rational thought. Valia dove out of the way. As she regained her feet, she ran her thumb across her rings, desperately searching her mind for a spell that could affect a beast this large.

Kirin was already on the move again. He leaped onto the bear's back and stabbed downward with his dagger, then swiped across the bear's neck. The bear staggered a few more steps, then fell to the ground, dark blood blossoming over its matted fur. Kirin rolled away to avoid being crushed under the creature's weight as it flopped down, unmoving. As soon as he was on his feet again, his gaze sought Valia, and he leaped over the bear's immobile form to her. His hands were on her shoulders in a heartbeat as he scanned her.

"Are you alright?"

"Yes." But Valia was looking past him at the bear. She couldn't quite believe what had just happened. Kirin gently tilted her chin toward him. His gray eyes were full of concern, and he was close enough for Valia to catch his smoky, salty scent again.

"Are you sure? Did it get you anywhere?"

"I'm sure." Valia looked up at Kirin. "Did you see it, too?"

"See what?"

"Its eyes. That was no ordinary bear. From the state of its fur and its movements, I think it may have been reanimated. Do you think whatever creature was hissing brought the bear to us?"

"Maybe."

Valia stepped around Kirin and knelt beside the bear. Beneath its thick fur, its skin was cold—too cold for an animal they'd slain only moments ago. A chunk of fur came off in Valia's hands and, disgusted, she brushed it away. She looked back at Kirin, whose face was expressionless.

"What do we have here?"

Valia looked up to see a farmer sitting atop a wagon of hay. With a blink of surprise, she realized the road was relatively full of travelers again.

"A bear," Kirin told him grimly. "I wouldn't linger long here."

"You kill it yourself?" the farmer asked.

Kirin came to Valia's side and held out his hand to help her up. "Come. We should be going."

"Impressive. You must be strong. Do you two need a ride?" the farmer pressed.

"No," Kirin said bluntly.

"I'd be happy to give you two a ride," the farmer repeated. Valia looked at the farmer again and saw that his eyes were trained on her—more specifically, on her hands. With a worrying jolt, Valia realized her gloves were still off and that her rings were, once again, in full display. *Well.* There was no point in being subtle now. Valia pressed blood to her link ring, looked up at the man, and repeated the same word she'd spoken to the horses: "Go."

"I'd best be going." The farmer lifted his reins, nodded to Valia and Kirin, and rode off. Valia quickly searched for her gloves, found them on the ground, and slipped them back on. Once she'd straightened herself with her rings hidden again, she noticed Kirin looking at her appraisingly.

"Yes?"

"I didn't know you could control people."

"I can't. Not really. It's the same thing I did with the first bear we met, and with the horses just now. The farmer wasn't sure if he should leave, so I pushed him to go. If no part of him wanted to leave, it wouldn't have worked."

"That's... good to know." But Kirin still wore a strange expression. Valia looked away. Up ahead, she spotted their horses, standing near a field of corn. She started off toward them at an adrenaline-fueled pace. If Kirin wanted to take offense at the magic she'd used to keep them both safe without hurting the farmer, that was his problem.

Kirin fell into step beside her. "Exactly how powerful are you?"

Valia glanced at him. "Clearly, not very. That bear would have killed me had you not been here." She hesitated. "A lot of things would have by now. I want to learn to fight like you."

"What?"

"I need to be able to defend myself. Clearly, as long as we're roaming the kingdom looking for my brother, we're going to face creatures like this. I can't rely on you to kill them all for me."

"I don't think you realize how dangerous you already are." Kirin seemed half impressed, and half concerned.

"Again, clearly not. What happens if you're faced with more than you can handle yourself? Two is better than one."

"You're right. You do need to be able to defend yourself." They reached the horses and, without missing a beat, Kirin held out his hands to help Valia onto Bird's back. She let him. "Wait. How do I know you didn't just mind control me into agreeing?"

"I didn't! You'd know."

"Does the passerby know?"

"Well, maybe later he will, if he thinks deeply about it. But we'll be long gone by then. I've been with you for days... *You'd know*."

"I suppose I'll have to start 'thinking deeply' about all our interactions."

"Kirin, stop it. I wouldn't with you. You asked me to trust you, so trust *me*. I'm really not as powerful as you imagine." She downplayed herself slightly, knowing she probably *could* nudge his thoughts if she wanted. For some reason, though, the thought of breaking Kirin's trust in such a way twisted her chest with a pang of guilt.

"Alright, fine. Then we'll have to raise you to my imagination, in case your imagination about me being faced with more than I can handle finds us." Valia wondered if he'd suddenly changed his mind, or if he'd merely been teasing her all along. "We'll start tonight."

Valia tried to ignore her nerves at the thought of that. She'd never been the warrior Daria was, but times were changing, and her heart was still racing from the bear attack. This bear had been different from the first one they'd encountered. The first one had been willing to kill them, but only in defense of its cubs. This one seemed to have no thought beyond obliterating her and Kirin—mostly her. It had been another creature reanimated by a metem, Valia suspected.

They made camp early while the sky was still light. Kirin collected water and caught a rabbit while Valia found a tree with slightly wizened pears and foraged for edible greens. They met back at their campsite, where Valia wove a protective network of dense greenery. Kirin started a fire near one edge of their camp, leaving a large, open, relatively flat space in the center. They finished at nearly the same time and turned to each other.

"So, how do we do this?" Valia asked. "Do we practice on a tree or something?"

"I'm being underpaid if a tree can kill you," Kirin said lightly. "You'll practice on me." He was already shedding his dark cloak to reveal an equally dark-colored shirt underneath. Valia could see the ripple of his muscles under the thin fabric. He set his whip and dagger on the ground.

"I don't think so." Valia crossed her arms. "What if I hurt you?"

"You won't," Kirin said confidently.

"Keep in mind, I have powers, and you're unarmed," Valia pointed out.

"Remind me what you need me for, then?" he pointed out.

"Okay, so perhaps I should be worrying that I'll get hurt. Either way, you're not selling this." Valia shook her head disparagingly.

"You're safe, Valia. You won't hurt me, and I won't hurt you." Kirin's gray eyes were fixed on Valia's. "The only way you can learn to fight is to go up against a real opponent. What you said before was right. There may come a time when I alone am not enough. Especially since we're looking for your brother who, according to a backward-aging child, is responsible for the destruction throughout Avania. I can't take you to your certain death."

"Okay." Valia bit her lip. "So, we just... fight?" She lifted her hands into her idea of a fighting stance and Kirin's mouth quirked into a smile.

"Yes. Unless that's beneath you, Princess." Kirin began to circle her. Valia felt a rush of nerves that came out as an anxious giggle. Kirin raised his eyebrows and Valia fell silent. She pulled off her gloves, letting them fall on the ground beside her, and flexed her fingers.

"Do I try to attack you?" she asked.

"Yes, try."

Valia pressed her gale ring and sent a shove of power at Kirin—not enough to hurt him, but enough to knock him off his feet. He pivoted as if he were a door being opened, easily avoiding the wave of power, then lunged at Valia. As she scrambled for another spell, he grabbed her wrist and pulled her toward him, spinning her so her back was against his chest. With his other hand, he grabbed her free arm and pressed her palms together. Their first bout was over before it began.

Valia should have been thinking about how easily he'd defeated her, but her mind was focused on his closeness and the feeling of his broad, rough palms on the backs of her hands.

"How did you dodge my spell?"

"You telegraph your casting. It's understandable. You've never needed to disguise your spells before. I saw your finger reach for your gale ring and knew to move out of the way. Whenever you fight, you default to that spell, which might not always be your best strategy. And now that I've pinned your hands, what will you do?"

"What if I used instinctive magic?"

"Then you'd better defeat me the first time. It would hurt you as much as it would hurt me, or more." Kirin released her and strode to the far side of the open space as Valia turned toward him again.

"How did you know to hold my hands like that?"

"Common sense, really." Kirin's eyes skated away from hers. "If your power comes from the rings on your fingers, all I have to do is disable them. They're a weak point, and this isn't my first time fighting a magic user."

"Right." Valia bit her lip. "You've fought floramancers before." It wasn't a question.

"Metemancers, too. Capturing the hands is the best way to restrain anyone, floramancer or not. But keep in mind it's harder to capture than to kill. There are quicker and easier ways to kill."

Valia thought of the man who'd attacked her with a knife in the inn. Even if Kirin had no intention of hurting her, he was still a dangerous man capable of unhesitating violence. He was quicker to act than even her impulsive father. She shouldn't forget that.

"Should we try again?" Valia asked. She was tired, cold, and hungry, but she couldn't give up after such a bad first showing.

"Yes. Whenever you're ready."

"Ready."

This time, when Kirin began to circle, Valia put her hands behind her back. She wasn't some novice who needed to look at her rings to cast. As Kirin came closer, then fell back, she pressed her lumen ring. The ground beneath Kirin's feet appeared to turn into a bed of snakes and, when he looked down, she struck out with another wave of force. This time, it hit Kirin and tossed him back several feet, but he leaned into the force and rolled before returning gracefully to his feet.

Valia pressed her advantage and dove toward Kirin, hoping to catch him off guard. He was ready for her, though, and within an instant he'd swept her feet and knocked her onto her back. He landed on top of her, slowing her fall with one arm while posting off the other, then quickly pinned her hands above her head. Their faces were inches away, and his body radiated a heat which cut through the chill evening. It was infinitely more satisfying than sitting by the fire, though Kirin would need a link ring to get her to confess it.

"Better. Good trick with your hands behind your back."

"I shouldn't have come toward you."

"No, you shouldn't have. But keep in mind that I'm not using any weapons right now. If I were, keeping your distance wouldn't be enough, depending on my weapons."

"Right." Valia sighed. "I can't even fight you while you're un-armed. How am I going to fight something that actually wants to kill me?"

"Practice." Kirin pushed to his feet and held out a hand to help Valia up. "Do you expect to master combat after two bouts?"

Valia rubbed her throat, where the broken-glass feeling had returned. Her head was throbbing, too. "I might need a break. I've used a lot of magic today."

"Then we'll eat." Kirin led the way to the fire. Valia picked up her gloves and cloak and put them both back on. She didn't like covering her rings when she didn't need to, but it was cold tonight, and she was glad for the added warmth.

"How did you learn to fight?" Valia asked as Kirin skewered a chunk of rabbit on a sharpened stick and handed it to her.

"I had teachers," Kirin said.

"So did I, back at the palace. My sisters and I all learned sword fighting and archery, though only a little compared to Daria."

"Sword fighting and archery?" Kirin raised his eyebrows. "Why not floramancy for combat?"

"I probably could have learned if I'd wanted to, but I didn't. Times were easier then; my sisters and I didn't have to know how to fight. Daria took an interest in it, but I liked making plants grow or healing wounds, not magic that hurts people."

"Maybe you're looking at it wrong," Kirin suggested. "Sometimes you have to hurt people to prevent them from hurting others. Maybe you can use plants to help you do that."

"Maybe." Valia considered. "I'll try tomorrow... How long will it take us to return to Wyra?"

"Depends on how much trouble we find along the way."

"I don't know what I'll say to my father," Valia admitted. "I need him to tell me the truth, but there's no reason for him to tell me now if he wouldn't before. I just need to know where he left my brother."

"Confront him with what you know." Kirin pondered for a moment. "I'm sure you could use your powers to make him tell you. I'm sure some part of him wants to."

Valia frowned. "That's out of the question. It might not work on him even if I wanted to. He's been trained against manipulation. And even the attempt would be high treason. I already told you, Kirin, I don't go around manipulating people to my will." Valia sighed. "I know my floramancy makes you uncomfortable."

"'Uncomfortable' is a word for it. Like you've said, your Flora seems to have a special interest in you. You might not be so powerful now, but..." Kirin looked at her over the fire. "What happens when you are? Too much power can corrupt even the most noble."

"Do you have some personal experience with that?" Valia tilted her head, her annoyance giving way to curiosity.

"I've... seen a few different sides of power." Kirin hesitated. "Your rabbit is done."

"Oh." Valia took the stick off the fire and slid her dinner onto a broad leaf. "Thank you." When she looked up at Kirin again, he looked deeply involved in cutting a shriveled pear into slices, and Valia decided to let the conversation fade away with Kirin's reticence. She didn't push. Kirin's past belonged to him, and if he wanted to share, he would.

She wished he would.

CHAPTER TWENTY
WAYWARD

The next three days were filled with little more than riding, sleeping, and practice fights. Valia fell asleep each night in their makeshift camps with her muscles sore and her head aching. She awoke each day feeling barely better. Still, she pushed on. She needed to get back to Wyra and speak with her father, and she needed to learn to fight.

For his part, Kirin didn't mention floramancy again. He was more talkative than he'd been on the ride to the coast, but he still didn't speak unless Valia asked him questions. Mostly, she kept their conversations to light topics about what they planned to eat that night, how she could improve her fighting technique, and the history of the towns and forests they passed. Slowly, they worked their way back through the farmlands and forests. The closer they got to Wyra, the more buildings there were, and the more travelers and refugees.

On the final night before they reached Wyra, Valia almost defeated Kirin in a skirmish. She managed to use a vine to entangle his feet and almost captured his hands, too. At the last moment, Kirin burst out of the vines with a jumping roll that ended with him pinning Valia once again. She still felt a strong sense of accomplishment. She'd come close to winning. Even Kirin had said so.

At mid-morning the next day, they arrived at the outskirts of Wyra. By silent agreement, they stopped outside the gates of the city to regroup.

"I can't go in with you," Kirin said. "My presence would only make things more difficult."

"I know. That's fine." Valia dug into her satchel and handed Kirin the purse of coin she'd taken from the palace at the onset of her journey. "Here's your payment, for taking me to the Savani and back. I know you don't owe me anything, but if you'd wait here..."

"I can't take this." Kirin handed the purse back to Valia. "I told you on the Savani's island I'm not here for coin. I'm still not. Go. I'll be here."

"I hear you." Valia pressed the purse into Kirin's hands again. "But I insist that you take it. Whether you're here for coin or not, we made an agreement that I intend to honor."

"How honorable of you. Fine." Kirin put the purse into his satchel. Then, he sat on a stump and took a small blue book Valia had never seen before out of one of his bags. She couldn't tell if his comment was serious or if he was teasing her. He didn't look up as Valia mounted Bird again with the help of a second stump and rode through the gates into Wyra.

It was strange to see the city again. Valia hadn't left that long ago, but she felt like a different person. Now she *knew*, rather than suspected, that her parents had kept something important from her.

It was even stranger to leave Kirin behind. For many days, they'd been side by side almost constantly, riding, eating, sleeping, and fighting. Valia had grown used to his warm, safe, and often silent presence.

More than used to it. A memory flashed through Valia's mind, of Kirin pinning her to the moss the day before, his face only inches from hers, as he'd remarked on how quickly she was learning. His hands had been on hers and his warmth had spread through the thin layers of clothing that separated them. If he'd leaned a few inches closer—or if Valia had—their lips would've touched.

Their kiss in the draevori cave had been to break the illusion, not because of any feelings between them. Purely a calculated, problem-solving maneuver. Now, Valia wondered if she *did* feel something. Maybe he did too. If not for the payment, what was he really staying for? Why did he find it so important to escort her on her mission?

She shook her head slightly to clear it. Her romantic curiosities were of little concern, all things considered. There were much more important, realm-altering matters at stake than what amounted to a crush. She'd gotten used to traveling with Kirin and, if she needed to, she could get used to traveling without him again.

As Valia rode through the streets of Wyra, she half expected someone to shout that the princess was back and for guards to descend upon her. Yet, with her hair bound back in a braid and the plain trousers of an everyday traveler, no one seemed to recognize her. It was liberating, and it gave Valia an idea.

When she reached the edge of the palace, she didn't go to the main gate. Instead, she brought Bird around to an unguarded section of the wall. There was no need for anyone to watch here, since the wall was smooth and five times as tall as Valia, making it near impossible for a thief or invader to climb over. Valia was no thief or invader, though.

She tied Bird to the trunk of a nearby tree then stood, hands on hips, gazing up at the wall. There was no reason, really, why she couldn't just stride in through the main gate and demand to be taken to her father. Yet some deep part of Valia wanted to show her father—and herself—that something had changed. She was no longer the innocent, rule-following princess she had been, and she deserved answers.

Valia glanced around the alley to make sure it was deserted, then climbed the tree she'd tied Bird to. The horse eyed her suspiciously but didn't move beyond lifting her forelegs a few times. At the top, Valia shimmied out on the branch that came closest to the palace wall and paused to survey her next move. She was still too far to jump onto the wall, and several guards would be patrolling the top. She waited until she understood their movements, her legs growing stiff from holding the branch, then slipped off her gloves and used a seed spell to encourage the branch to grow over the wall. She swung down and dropped gracefully onto the top of the wall, then used another spell to curve the branch away to make her entry less obvious.

Quietly, she crept along the wall into the nearest guard tower. One of the guards, a young man with bright red hair and a slightly too-large uniform, approached the tower. Valia muttered a veil spell. It wouldn't be enough to prevent her being found for a long time, but it was enough to make the young guard's eyes skim over her as though she were as much a part of the tower as the racks of arrows or canteens of water. Once the guard passed, Valia hurried down the stairs into the gardens, where she breathed a sigh of relief. Many people lived and worked in the palace, so one more wouldn't be noticeable as long as no one had spotted her wall-and-tree-based acrobatics. As Valia walked, she slipped her gloves back on.

She made a beeline through the gardens toward the palace. There was a higher chance she'd be recognized once she was inside, but she thought she could make it as long as she kept moving and didn't make eye contact. Instead of going inside right away, she circled the palace wall until she found the entrance to the kitchens and descended into the warm, fragrant rooms. It was almost lunch time, and it was easy to spot the food that would be going to her father: half a roast duck decorated with fruit, accompanied by rolls shaped like swans. It was too fancy to be anyone else's meal. The smell of food was enough to make Valia's stomach grumble. She'd eaten enough to survive in the woods, but stringy wild rabbit and bitter greens weren't anywhere near as enticing as the food here.

A young serving boy lifted the platter and, struggling slightly under the weight, carried it toward the stairs. Valia followed him and, once they were alone in the hallway leading out of the kitchen, tapped his shoulder.

"I can take that," she said in her kindest voice. The boy looked relieved.

"Thanks, miss."

"Where is the king today?"

"His private dining room."

Valia bobbed a curtsey and headed for her father's chambers with the platter balanced in her arms. There was a close call when she passed one of her father's advisors in the stairwell, but he didn't seem very interested in the trousers-wearing serving girl—despite her lack of a proper uniform—and walked by without a second glance.

Valia knocked on the door before pushing it open. Her father was sitting at his table with a pile of papers spread in front of him, his brow creased in worry. He didn't look up when Valia entered.

"Just set it down," he said gruffly. "Thank you."

Valia walked over and dropped the platter onto his desk with enough noise to get his attention. King Aran looked up at her.

"Hello, father."

"Valia." He stood, almost knocking over a stack of papers. "Where have you been? Do you have any idea how worried I've been?"

Valia felt a momentary stab of guilt for the stress she'd put her father through by disappearing, then shoved the guilt away. Her father was the one who had lied to her and tried to make her doubt her own magic.

"I'm well enough, father. But we need to talk."

"Does anyone know you're back? We need to get you to a healer." King Aran reached for the bell beside his table, but Valia stopped him with her hand on his.

"No healers. We need to talk. I left to find out who my missing sibling is, and that's what you're going to tell me."

King Aran let out a frustrated sigh. "I've told you a hundred times, there is no other sibling. I thought you would give up after bothering everyone in the palace, but apparently you had to risk your life and worry me sick first. If your mother were here—"

"Stop lying, father." Valia felt anger bubble inside her, but she kept her voice calm. "I know I have a brother."

King Aran's mouth opened, then closed, looking rather like one of the fish Kirin had pulled out of a river.

"What makes you think you have a brother?" he asked, finally.

"I found the Savani," Valia told him. "She told me everything: that I have a sibling she can't locate, that she gave you and Mother a prophecy about sons, everything. You can't lie anymore."

King Aran inhaled, then let his breath out slowly. His expression was calculating. Valia waited, half expecting him to try to lie again.

"Your mother never wanted you girls to know," he said. "She made me swear not to tell you."

"As you've reminded me, my mother isn't here." Valia sank into the chair across from her father and rested her elbows on her knees. "Please. I must know. Now more than ever, because I've seen what's happening in Avania. And if the Savani's prophecy is correct, my brother has something to do with it."

Her father ran a hand across his brow and sat back down. "I guess there's no keeping it from you now. My daughter, bold enough to seek out the Savani. Fine. If you want to know..." He took another deep breath before continuing. "You said the Savani told you about the prophecy. That if your mother and I ever had a son, that boy would bring destruction to our family and all of Avania. The same destruction you say you've seen now. Well, your mother and I were terrified, but we still needed an heir. If we didn't provide one, it would bring a different kind of destruction to the land we loved. So, we tried, and your sister Samalia was born. We were overjoyed.

"Then, without planning for it to happen, your mother fell pregnant again, and Daria was born. We began to hope. Perhaps the prophecy wouldn't matter if we only had girls. We grew too confident, and your mother fell pregnant with you. Your mother went into labor, and you were born. Oh, how we celebrated our third little girl. And then... the boy came."

"I have a twin brother," Valia said softly.

"Yes. The only people in the room were me, your mother, and the healer. We asked the healer to leave and sat together, holding our children. There were two options before us: keep the boy and raise him as our own, hoping the Savani was wrong, or kill him and protect the country."

"You didn't..." Valia whispered, her voice giving away her horror.

"We did neither. Instead, we agreed to send the boy away. I had heard of a monastery far in the northern Nelirrhi mountains where magic of all kinds is forbidden. The Sacred Triant Monastery. We hoped that, if the boy grew up there with no knowledge of who he really was, that catastrophe could be prevented, and he could live a good life. We brought in Poriev, and he agreed to take the boy there alone. He left under the cover of darkness. We swore the healer to secrecy with a blood vow, and we told everyone else only one child had been born. You."

Valia was reeling. There was so much she needed to ask, no matter how much she feared the answers. Still, one question rose to the top. "So, my brother's still there? In the monastery?"

"We don't know anymore. But you must understand, Valia, your mother and I made a mistake when we sent the boy away. We should have killed him."

"What?! How can you say that?" Valia stood. Her hands were shaking with a mix of anger and horror.

"Don't you see? The balance of power in Avania has shifted. Metems are growing more powerful, and our family and county have been shattered, just as the Savani predicted. That boy is doing this, Valia. He killed your mother and your sisters. He's responsible for the rise of dangerous creatures, the bandits, and everything else."

"How? How can you be sure a boy my age is responsible for all this?" Valia asked.

"It's all exactly as the Savani prophesized," King Aran told her. His eyes looked hollow. "Valia, I lost your mother and your sisters. I can't lose you, too. We did the best we could."

Despite herself, Valia believed him. They'd faced an impossible choice when her brother had been born, and they'd tried to do the right thing. Yet she also knew she could never forgive her father. It was one thing to eliminate a threat to the country. It was something completely different to exile an innocent baby out of fear for the future it may bring. How different everything might have been if she'd grown up with her twin brother by her side. If he was the one causing all this, perhaps growing up in a loving family would have been enough to prevent it. Perhaps the prophecy was self-fulfilling.

Still, her brother, a stranger, had also killed her mother and sisters, if her father was to be believed. No matter what else had happened, that was beyond forgiveness, too. Valia now stood in the center of this terrible mess, her hands full of the broken threads of her family.

"What are you going to do about it?" Valia asked softly.

"What I've been doing, Valia! Do you think I've merely been managing refugees and distributing grain?" Aran took a deep breath. "I'm sorry. I suppose there's no use treating you like a princess any longer. Here is the state of things. The monastery is in Kanalear. Any direct use of force would be an act of war against Kanalear. A war we cannot presently afford. I've sent men... scouts at first, then more formidable mercenaries. Men who cannot be linked to us. It's not the same place it was when we sent him there, Valia, whether he's still there or not. I know, because none of those men have returned, and the state of our country has only worsened. I've spent the better part of the season courting this idiot ambassador for full military access. They are stalling, Valia. Delay after delay. Claiming to be investigating on their own. But what have they done?

"What would *you* do, Valia?" King Aran asked. For the first time, it wasn't the question of a father doubting the opinions of a child, but of a man seeking counsel wherever he could find it. "This boy killed my wife and daughters. He's destroying the entire country, as I was warned he would. What other option do I have than to send an army and deal with the Kanaleans after? The madness in Avania must end."

"Let *me* go." Valia folded her arms. Her heart pounded, but she was determined. "Let me find him. Let me deal with him."

"I won't allow it. He'll kill you."

"He'll kill any troops you send too," Valia countered. "He already has, by the sound of it. I'm his twin. If anyone can convince him to stop, it's me."

"No." King Aran shook his head. "After all that's happened, what makes you think he can be convinced? And what happens when he isn't? You have an immense gift from Flora, Valia, but you have never learned to wield it."

"I will. I'll figure it out." Valia stood. "I need to find him. I need to apologize. And if he's really doing all this and won't stop, I need to stop him. I'll do it, father."

"Valia, no." King Aran reached for her, but Valia tore off her glove and held up her hand, threatening to prick her thumb. Her father froze.

"I'm going. You can't stop me." Valia said.

"You wouldn't dare." There was a slight hesitation in her father's voice. "Where did this spirit of yours come from?"

"I love you," Valia said. "You'll always be my father. But I must fix this. It's the only way."

Her father slumped back in his chair as Valia got to her feet.

"Don't send your forces yet," she said. "Give me a head start."

"I can't do that," King Aran replied. He looked older and more weathered than ever now. "If they can stop him, it will save you. I *will not* lose you too, Valia."

"Please." Valia took several steps back until her back was to the door. "Just give me a head start."

"I pray Flora guide you to your senses, dear daughter. I don't know when you became so obstinate."

"One more thing." She hesitated, her hand on the door handle. "What's his name?"

King Aran shook his head. "I don't know. We didn't name him. If we had, we never would have been able to let him go."

With that, Valia stepped into the hallway, shutting the door carefully behind her. Then, she broke into a sprint. She needed to get back out of the palace and find Kirin. She needed to ask him to travel north with her, to the monastery. She needed to deal with her brother. Despite her courage in front of her father, Valia knew she couldn't do it alone.

She needed him.

CHAPTER TWENTY-ONE
NOTICE

alia didn't have much time before her father locked down the palace. Most likely, he'd already summoned his personal guards while she ran down the hallway. If she didn't leave the palace before the rest were alerted, she might not manage to leave at all. He would confine her to her rooms and place her under perpetual surveillance, believing he was doing the right thing. Clearly, he was willing to do almost anything for what he thought was right—even if that meant sending away his own newborn son.

Valia forced herself to slow her frantic pace to a walk. Running would only draw more attention. After a few paces, Valia spotted a narrow supply closet and ducked inside. She took a deep breath and looked around. There were no uniforms in the closet, but there were linens. Valia unfolded a pillowcase and knotted it over her hair, hoping it would look like a scarf many female laborers wore to protect their hair from dirt and sun. There wasn't much to be done about her clothes. She'd look more conspicuous running around with a bedsheet tied around her waist than she did now.

Valia reached for the Flora and drew on a trunk spell to alter her appearance as she looked at herself in her looking glass. Wrinkles and age spots formed on her skin. Valia added another veil spell to discourage wandering eyes from lingering upon her. Finally, instead of wearing her gloves, Valia hid her hands in her sleeves so she'd still be able to cast quickly if needed.

Valia slumped forward and bent her knees slightly, abandoning the regal posture Avanian princesses were ingrained with. Finally, she threaded a basket of linens onto her elbow and opened the door. No one was in the hallway—yet. She set off toward the kitchens at a brisk pace, hoping she wouldn't pass anyone on the way.

A horn sounded out. Within moments, three palace guards came jogging toward her, their boots clopping against the stone floor. The palace tower's bell began to ring, alerting the rest of the palace and the city below. Valia looked down at her basket of linens, and the guards flew past her with hardly a glance. She slumped in relief but kept moving.

At the far end of the hallway, Valia descended to the kitchens and slipped out the same way she'd come in. A few of the cooks and scullery maids gave her confused looks, but no one stopped her. Once she was outside, Valia set down the basket of linens and made for the wall. Several more soldiers passed her, their eyes alert, but Valia wasn't sure whether they were looking for her or just making their rounds. Just after she'd passed them, one guard called out.

"Madam?"

Valia froze. She turned back, her heart thumping in her chest. The soldier, the same young red-haired man she'd hidden from in the tower on her way in, scanned her.

"Madam, are you alright? Your face…"

Valia lifted a hand to brush her cheek. The skin felt wrinkled and loose. "Yes, thank you, young man." She tried to affect the friendly, slightly maternal voice she'd heard older women use. Valia pressed her link ring. "There's no cause to concern yourself about me."

The guard straightened and saluted her, then fell back into step with his companions. Valia didn't have time to dwell on the fact she'd used controlling magic for the second time in a few days. Just like with the farmer, she believed this was justified. She only used it when she had to, and she wasn't hurting anyone. If anything, it prevented her from having to.

Quickly, Valia climbed the stairs to the wall. "Hey!" a voice called from a guard stationed along it. He ran toward her. "You can't be up here."

"Just getting some fresh air." Valia kept walking toward the edge of the wall.

"Madam, this area is off-limits." The guard strode toward her, his steps quickening. "Stop!"

Valia reached the edge of the wall and leaped over without hesitation. She was near the same tree she'd used to get over the wall on the way in, so as she began to fall, she reached out with her powers and coaxed the branch toward her. It swung in her direction and Valia managed to catch it, her hands slipping painfully on the rough bark. Her head began to throb, and her throat gave a warning burn. The branch lowered Valia until she was able to drop onto the cobblestones a few paces from Bird.

The guard's head appeared over the wall above, alarmed and confused. As Valia got to her feet, her right ankle throbbing from a slightly skewed landing, he disappeared as he called out to the other guards.

Valia grabbed for Bird, untying her reins with shaking hands, and lifted herself onto the horse's back. With her heart still pounding and her headache intensifying, she encouraged the horse into a full gallop toward the city gate where she hoped to find Kirin.

He'd claimed he wasn't helping her for the coin, and that would be put to the test now. Valia had imagined gathering a few supplies, more florans, and some proper food at least, but there had been no time. If he stayed with her for the next part of the journey, they'd have to make do with what they had, and she wouldn't be able to offer any sort of payment until they returned. *If* they returned.

Valia and Bird burst out the city gates. Valia looked toward the stump where she last saw Kirin. He wasn't there. Valia's heart dropped. After everything he'd said, had he just left her? She was a wealthy Avanian princess after all—*the* Avanian princess, now—and he was a mercenary. Perhaps he was just playing her for the coin, and now that she'd paid him, he'd reconsidered the risks of her journey. She'd considered this as a possibility, but it still stung far more than she'd imagined.

It didn't matter. She would figure it out on her own. Tears began to well up in her eyes, but she continued on at full pace. She felt alone and betrayed. By Kirin, by her father, by her potentially murderous brother. It seemed as if no one was on her side.

Just then, she heard a galloping horse behind her. Had her father's guards caught up already? She urged Bird faster with a sharp nudge of her heels.

"Valia, stop!"

She knew that voice. She looked behind her. It was Kirin. She wiped the tears from her eyes and pulled Bird to a stop as Kirin reined in beside her.

"Kirin."

He frowned at her. "Valia?"

"Yes, obviously."

"What happened to your face?"

Valia touched her cheek again. "Oh. It's a disguise. Why? Does it look wrong?"

"Yes, and no... It's a good disguise."

"Well, it shouldn't last long." Valia felt tears burning at the backs of her eyes, this time from the relief of knowing Kirin hadn't abandoned her.

"How did it go?"

"My brother's at a monastery in the Nelirrhi mountains," she replied. "Or, at least he was. Will you come with me? I can't pay you yet, but—"

Kirin got to his feet. "Enough of that, Valia."

"If you're coming, we need to leave now. My father locked down the palace. He might lock down all of Wyra to stop me. He thinks that if I go looking for my brother, I'll die."

Kirin shot her a concerned look. His expressions were still hard to read, but Valia had gotten better at deciphering them.

"Did you consider that he might be right?"

"He may be," Valia admitted. "I don't want to die. But I also need to find my brother and stop him. And I need to apologize. He was cast out as a baby. That never should have happened. And if he's really the one who killed my family... his family... well, I need to know."

"I won't let you go to your death, Valia."

"Then stay!" Valia tugged the reins a little too hard and Bird whinnied unhappily. "Sorry, girl. I just... Kirin, make your decision. My father would rather I be locked up than let me make mine. Stay if you want, but don't you dare try to hold me back like him."

"Valia." Kirin glanced at her with caring eyes. "I meant I'll protect you. I'll prepare you on the way."

"Oh... then why didn't you just say that?" Her tone softened, but she was too annoyed with his misleading choice of words to thank him. Instead, she started Bird along the road again at a canter, and Kirin followed.

They turned onto a main road, then took a small track that went north. "Kirin, there's more. I believe my father is sending an army to the monastery across the Kanalean border. We must get there before they do. If he's truly powerful enough to cause so much destruction throughout Avania, he'll kill those soldiers without hesitation. And if he isn't, the soldiers will kill him before I have a chance to talk to him, and Kanalear will finally have their cause for war against us."

"So, you're telling me I've now picked a fight with the Avanian army? Great. Just after I was finally approved to stay here."

Valia glanced at Kirin, ready to retort that he still had a chance to back out, but saw that he was grinning. She found her lips quirking into a matching smile.

"Don't forget, the king isn't pleased with our little mission."

"Good bonus. I was getting bored of being here legally already. So much less fun."

"I figured. I wanted to help. I made sure to mention it was specifically you who convinced me to be disobedient," Valia teased. Kirin chuckled. They slowed their pace, the road empty behind them. With no present need to hurry, they didn't want to exhaust the horses before their journey even began.

They rode for a while without talking. Valia absently stroked Bird's mane and Kirin seemed focused on the horizon, where the dark shadows of mountains were barely visible.

"Do you think you'll go back to Tromin once all this is over?" Valia asked after a while.

"No. I'm not welcome there anymore, either," Kirin said simply. Valia glanced at him again. He was still smiling, but his eyes were shuttered.

"Why? Did you anger their king, too? Run away with the princess?"

"It's a council, not a king. I'm still surprised you don't know these things. But... no, not exactly."

"Well, *exactly* how do you make so many enemies while ridding the world of dangerous creatures?"

Kirin's smile took on a wry edge. "I wasn't always hunting creatures."

"Right." Valia stroked Bird's mane again. She was getting used to Kirin and his secrets, but she was no more at peace with how much he was hiding than she'd been when they'd first met and he'd refused to tell her his name. It was frustrating that Kirin knew everything about her, while she still knew so little about him.

"I would tell you," Kirin said suddenly, as if he'd read her thoughts, "but how—"

"But what? But I'm some little girl to be protected from the truth? Like my father keeping my brother from me?"

"No. *But how* do I explain? You need to know something else first."

"Well go ahead, then."

"I'm not a mercenary. Not really. Never have been."

"So you lied? What are you?" Valia bit her lip.

"I'm just a man. And I never claimed to be. I just never corrected you."

"Okay. So how exactly did you come to look for me in the draevori cave? Was that not a mercenary contract?"

"Hardly. It was a deal I'd made with your father for my freedom."

"Your freedom? What do you mean?"

"Here, look. My payment for returning you safely." Kirin removed the round wooden chit from his saddlebag. He tossed it to Valia, and she caught it.

Valia inspected it. It was light and soft to the touch and had the king's seal engraved into it. She recognized this material. It was brinwood, the same as the one grown in the gardens of Palace Annulus. Valia had attempted to cast with the brinwood tree before, curious what powers it might offer her. Her powers never seemed to flow through it, but holding it now in this form gave her the feeling that it was somehow solid and *true*. Perhaps that's why it was used together with the king's seal.

Valia flipped it over. On the other side, it read: *By royal decree and favor of King Aran Martev, let it be known that Kirin Adante, having been granted remission of past transgressions, shall dwell within the realm under the watchful grace of the crown. By this writ, all subjects are commanded to uphold said clemency and hinder not his passage nor settlement.*

Valia ran her thumb over it again, feeling its subtle power. "So, what are these transgressions?"

"I hunted floramancers," Kirin confessed.

Valia froze. The color drained from her face. She stared at him with both disbelief and suspicion as she ran her thumbs over her rings.

"What? You said—"

"Not like them. They were the reason I left Tromin and sought refuge in Avania. The floramancers I hunted deserved it." He appraised her reaction. "Do you still trust me?"

Valia paused for a while, looking him up and down in an attempt to gauge her own feelings. "I don't know. Should I?"

"I... I can't answer that for you," Kirin said, looking straight back at her.

Valia turned away as her eyes welled up with silent tears. She quickly wiped them away. She felt overwhelmed and exhausted and didn't know what to think. Who exactly was this man she'd aligned herself with? Perhaps she *had* made a mistake in not listening to her father about him. Still, it was too late to turn back now. She needed Kirin to reach her brother. And regardless of what he had just told her, she strangely felt no doubt in her heart that she could trust him. She looked back at him and found his eyes still fixed on her.

Kirin broke the silence as if reading her mind. "Valia, it's not too late. You could go back to the safety of your palace. I'm sure your father would welcome you with open arms, and you could work with him to find your brother."

Valia looked away. "That's not going to happen. He'll kill him. I'm still going, with or without you. I'm not going back."

"Don't you miss the palace?" Kirin's question sounded genuine. Valia considered.

"Of course there are things I miss. It's comfortable. I had a cup of chocolate every morning in bed, and there's a rooftop spot with an amazing view of the stars. But it was a different place when I was young, and before... before everything. Before I learned what I know now. When... *if* I return, it won't ever feel the same." They both stared forward for a long moment.

"Yes. I understand." There was a depth of emotion in Kirin's words, and Valia thought of the painting of the man, woman, and boy she'd seen in Kirin's house. With what he'd told her about leaving Tromin, perhaps he really did understand. "I'm still with you, if you'll have me. I'm sorry I didn't tell you sooner."

Valia looked at him with softer eyes but didn't answer. They rode on, letting the conversation fall away with the setting sun. By silent agreement, they followed smaller roads through fields and forests to reduce their chance of running into bounty hunters or Avanian patrols in the wide-open Kaelvi Plains. Valia stopped once to drink a little sap water, which took the edge off her headache.

Eventually, they found a grove of elms and made their camp. As had become their rhythm, they both gathered food before Kirin started the fire and Valia prepared their protective wall of greenery. It was harder tonight because of all the magic she'd used that day.

"Your face looks normal again," Kirin said as they sat by the fire.

"Just what every girl wants to hear," Valia joked, attempting to bring some lightness into the heavy day.

"I am a master of flattery," Kirin replied, deadpan, and Valia laughed. "We'll skip tonight's training."

"Why? Are you scared I'll win?"

"Your adventures in Wyra were enough learning for the day. It's no easy feat to escape the palace of a capital city without being caught. You've proven yourself capable today." Valia blushed at his compliment.

He was right; it was no small feat. Despite the lackluster palace guard in the draevori illusion, Palace Annulus was secure, now more than ever. Maybe she *was* more capable than she gave herself credit for.

"Besides," Kirin continued, "tonight may be the last night you'll get any real rest before we cross into Kanalear. It's only going to get more dangerous the further we travel north."

"Fine." Valia said lightly, absorbing his compliment but still anxious about the danger ahead. "Then... find another way to distract me from my worries. Teach me something."

Kirin stood up, then sat back down next to Valia. After a moment to think, he asked, "Do you know where metemancers draw their power from?"

"Dead things," Valia replied quickly.

"No. Not really. That's something Avanians say to make it sound bad. They extract power from rocks that have been falling from the sky for hundreds of cycles. Rocks that used to be part of the Everwatcher, as it's called in Tromin. You know it as the moon. It used to be bigger, but it's breaking apart slowly over time."

"Rocks," Valia repeated. "From the sky. But your dagger is made of... ash?"

"That's what it looks like, sure. The rocks eventually lose their binding with the repeated use of their power. They turn to darkened dust, so that's what it looks like on the outside as parts begin to fall off." Kirin frowned at her. "You really didn't know any of this as the heir to Avania?"

"It's not like we attend a class on metemancy as children, other than that it's..." Valia paused, searching for the right word to replace *bad*, *evil*, and *perverse*. "Dangerous." She paused again. "Isn't it hard to find these rocks?"

"If you don't know how to look. There's a record of every reported shooting stare."

"Stare? Don't you mean a shooting *star*?" Valia asked.

"No, a stare. That's what we call it when they fall. Common mistake. Anyway, then... someone... seeks it out. Their energy is unstable following an impact, and they've been known to affect the wildlife. Someone must be called to secure the area before it can be extracted. And of course, not all who call themselves metemancers are equally capable of extracting the rocks' power."

"Sky rocks from the moon. The Everwatcher. Shooting *stares*." Valia shook her head. "Now I've heard everything."

"Just imagine how floramancy sounds to Olanthians. Drawing your own blood and offering it to a fickle entity which may or may not give you what you want at its whim."

Valia slipped her gloves back on, then put on her cloak and draped a blanket over her knees. Darkness had fallen and autumn was in full swing now, leaving the nights colder than before. In the mountains, it would be even colder. Valia shivered at the thought.

"Are you cold?" Kirin slid closer to Valia and put his arm around her. She rested her head on his shoulder.

"A little. I'm alright."

"I'll gather more wood for the fire."

"No, it's okay. Let's eat. I'm starving." Valia pressed her finger to her flux ring to warm her hands and feet against the evening chill. She pushed a little extra warmth through the air toward Kirin, hoping he would assume the warm air came from the fire instead of from floramancy.

He didn't seem to notice. Or if he did, he didn't seem to mind.

CHAPTER TWENTY-TWO
LINGER

he next day, they rode north through fields and forests, over streams and up hills, the mountains looming ever closer. Valia had read about the Nelirrhi mountains in textbooks and seen paintings, but seeing them rise up from the earth in jagged, snow-covered crags with her own eyes was a completely different experience. Just as when they'd ridden south, the further they got from Wyra, the more the enormous farms turned into self-sufficient farmsteads and the wilder the vegetation became. Despite her general apprehension at their mission, Valia felt more at home, and more able to breathe, when she was further from civilization. Perhaps some things were better than chocolate in bed each morning.

That night, they made camp in a grove of pines and oaks interspersed with viny lianas and wildflowers. Valia was grateful when her wall of greenery went up, both because it meant she didn't have to ride anymore that day, and because the branches obscured the mountains on the horizon. Blocking them from her sight helped her forget that their end goal would likely be less enjoyable than their journey.

After a few practice bouts of fighting under an orange-and-gold sunset, Valia began to feel something different. All the tactics she'd tried against Kirin, though unsuccessful, were ready at the back of her mind. She felt her powers stretch, as though she were running after sitting still for a long time. When they fought for a third time, she created a bird illusion that swooped at Kirin's head. He dodged, right into a thick, viny liana that snagged his legs and pulled him to the ground. He rolled, but the vine dragged him toward a vine-wrapped tree. The spell became harder to maintain as Kirin struggled, but with the press of her surge ring, Valia was able to hold it. The liana pulled him flat against a sturdy oak and wound around him until he could no longer move.

Valia strode across the clearing and stopped in front of him.

"How's it going?" she asked sweetly.

Kirin looked down at the vines that were now completely wrapped around him. "I think you won."

"Did I?" Valia tapped her lip with one finger. "It looks like I did. Wow. You were bested by a princess. The minstrels will sing of my accomplishments." She gave a little twirl.

"I never expected anything less." Kirin pulled at one of the liana's tendrils. "...Care to let me go now?"

"I suppose so." Valia tapped blood to her surge ring and the vines retracted enough for Kirin to slip between them. "I think it's time for a real challenge."

"Should I use a weapon?" Kirin suggested.

"Maybe not that much of a challenge. But how about a competition? Instead of betting a story this time, we can raise the stakes."

"Okay. If I win, you have to go a day without floramancy." Kirin brushed the last vine away from his feet, which it seemed hesitant to let go of.

Valia rolled her eyes. "You just want to fight me without my powers tomorrow because you're worried that I'll defeat you all the time now."

"Maybe." Kirin grinned and stepped away from the vine, which followed him snakelike along the ground. "Are you doing this?"

"No. I think it got inspired." Valia gave the liana a firm look. "Enough." The vine flopped into stillness, and she looked back up at Kirin. "And if I win?"

"You won't." Kirin circled her. "But just for the sake of the agreement, anything you want."

"Anything?" Valia raised an eyebrow. She tucked her hands behind her back and paced opposite Kirin, keeping the clearing between them. Kirin jumped a little at a rustle in the bushes, perhaps looking for another illusion, but Valia wasn't about to try the same trick twice.

Kirin's gaze returned to Valia, and he paced, his hands at the ready. Finally, Valia muttered something under her breath and glanced at a tree behind Kirin's back. Just as she'd hoped, he assumed she was casting a spell and took advantage of her distraction to pounce across the clearing toward her. Valia pivoted out of his way and grabbed a low-hanging tree branch. Using a slight magical boost, she swung up until she was sitting on the branch, then used a push of power to raise the branch until it was out of Kirin's reach.

"Is this a new tactic?" Kirin asked, circling below her now. "Or are you stuck?"

"I'm stuck," Valia said. "Come help me. I'm just a poor, helpless princess in a tree." She batted her eyelashes.

"Convincing." Kirin leaped into the air to grab for Valia's leg but missed as the tree branch carried her slightly higher. "Are you going to come back down?"

"Maybe," Valia called cheerfully. She reached her powers toward another branch, which swooped Kirin's feet out from under him. He fell to the ground, and she swung down from the tree branch and landed with her feet on either side of him and a stick in her hand.

"It's a dagger," she told him as she pressed the stick to his throat. Not one to give up easily, Kirin rolled, pulling her with him, so that he was on top of her. He pinned the hand with the stick to the ground, so Valia released the stick and reached for the liana again, hoping to use it to pull him off her. Kirin rolled them both out of the way but misjudged the distance the liana could strike. It grabbed him by the foot and pulled as Valia rolled backward onto her feet.

This time, though, Kirin was ready for the vine. Before a second tendril could grab ahold of him, he batted the first vine away and reached for Valia's hands. Valia struck with the liana again, but this time she was the one who misjudged. The vine swept them both off their feet and flat onto the ground. Valia glanced at Kirin and they both began to laugh.

"Who won that time?" Valia asked.

"The vine." Kirin was grinning. "Did you do that on purpose?"

"Yep. I wanted to knock us both flat on our backs." The liana was twirling around their ankles, so Valia gave it another stern look, and it relaxed onto the ground.

"Is there a reason why it's so eager?" Kirin asked.

"Probably. Lianas are sometimes used in surge rings, so I suspect it was particularly excitable for that reason." Valia lifted a hand to her hair, which had collected leaves and sticks while they'd rolled across the ground. "If the vine won, who gets the reward?"

In an instant, Kirin rolled onto Valia and pinned her hands. "Maybe I won."

"Or maybe we can both have something we want," Valia suggested. She aimed to sound playful, but her words came out a little breathier than intended. Perhaps she was still winded from the vine knocking her down.

"What might that be?" Kirin's warmth and weight pressed against Valia, his eyes bored into her, and his mouth lingered inches away. Not for the first time, Valia remembered their kiss in the draevori cave.

"Kiss me." Valia said. Again, the words came out too breathy, but it didn't seem to matter. Kirin's eyes darkened from raincloud gray to the color of a winter storm.

His lips parted slightly; Valia's gaze followed the motion. She'd felt passing attraction before—interesting young noblemen visiting the palace for one reason or another—but nothing as strong as she felt in this moment. From the way Kirin gazed at her, she suspected he felt the same way. What would it be like to kiss him now, without the excuse of dispelling a hostile illusion?

The moment stretched. Valia was aware of everything: the press of a small stone against her right calf, the sound of a bird calling in the distance, the crackle of the fire not far away. Yet, she was aware of nothing more acutely than Kirin. She could practically feel his heart beating. His hands were gentle on hers, no longer pinning her to the ground, but holding her hands lightly as he rested on his elbows. If Valia lifted her head, just slightly, her lips would touch his.

Kirin abruptly rolled off her and got to his feet. She felt the absence of his warmth and as though she were missing one of her rings.

"Kirin?" Valia scrambled to her feet and followed him toward the fire. "What happened?"

Kirin turned back to her, his face neutral again. None of the emotion she'd seen just moments ago remained. "Our food is going to burn," he said calmly.

Valia bit her lip and crossed her arms protectively over her stomach. "I'm sorry. I thought…"

"It's fine." Kirin sat and removed the roasted rabbit from the makeshift rack above the fire. "Let's just eat."

Valia looked away from his cold expression. It seemed her attraction had been one-sided after all. Perhaps it was merely the result of so many days spent in harsh conditions, relying on him. A false attraction borne from the risks they faced, and her desperation for some sort of relief. Perhaps there was nothing there at all.

Still, the way Valia's chest felt a little too tight and the way Kirin studiously avoided her gaze made her think that there was more to it. Perhaps Kirin still thought of her as little more than a coddled princess, unable to make her own way in the world.

They ate in silence. Kirin passed Valia a skewer of rabbit meat and she handed him a handful of bright blackberries that stained her palm with purple juice. Valia ached for something to break the uncomfortable silence, but she didn't know what to say.

Once they'd eaten, Kirin lay down on the far side of the fire, one hand resting on his whip, and closed his eyes. It was too early to sleep. They usually would have spent a little while talking or sitting in companionable silence, but tonight was different. Her heart heavy, Valia lay down on her side of the fire, drew her blanket over herself, and tried to sleep.

Instead, she studied the stars in the night sky. She found herself wondering, not for the first time, if there were others out there truly like her. Usually, the thought was comforting, but tonight, she just felt lonely.

How silly, Valia thought. They were on a dangerous journey that could easily lead to death, so Valia had bigger things to worry about than Kirin not wanting to kiss her. It was better this way. She could focus on finding her brother and dealing with him without any distractions.

Valia eventually felt sleep overtake her and slipped seamlessly into a dream.

Valia sat by the riverbank. Her sisters laughed and played around her, all of them children, including Valia. In her hands, she held a flower crown that bloomed of its own accord. The whole thing felt familiar somehow, as if this wasn't the first time she'd been here, as so many dreams did.

"Vali! Look here!"

Valia looked up to see a young boy with raven-dark hair and bright blue eyes sitting across from her. In his hands, he held a roughly shaped and faintly glowing rock. As he watched, the rock cracked neatly along the center and bright blue light spilled out. He looked up at Valia and they grinned at each other.

Then the boy's eyes glowed the same electric blue as the light in the rock as his wide-eyed smile narrowed into a glare.

"You shouldn't be here. Go away, Vali."

With a gasp, Valia sat upright. Her heart raced, and she instinctively tore off her gloves. Slowly, the clearing came back into focus. The fire was barely alive. The moon illuminated Kirin's dark form across the fire. He was looking at her.

"Valia?"

She cleared her throat. "Yes. I'm fine."

"You cried out in your sleep," Kirin said. "What were you dreaming about?"

Valia shook her head. "Nothing. It doesn't matter. Kirin, I'm so sorry about earlier today."

"Valia, don't give it another thought." Kirin laid back down. "Sleep. We'll need our rest for tomorrow."

Valia lay back down and did her best to banish all thoughts of Kirin and the strange dream from her mind.

CHAPTER TWENTY-THREE
CLOSER

irin awoke first. By the time Valia opened her eyes, he'd already put out the last remnants of the fire and packed their things. Valia sat up, her blanket falling from her shoulders, and squinted at him.

"Oh. Did I sleep too long?"

"No." Kirin tightened the saddlebag on Unicorn's flank. "But now's a good time to get moving."

"Alright." Valia got to her feet and folded her blanket, her heart still heavy. Clearly, they wouldn't be able to fall back into their old, playful patterns after last night's fiasco. It was back to the reticent mercenary—or whatever he was—that Valia had known before. *Great.*

Valia took down the wall of greenery, then they both mounted and set off. They followed a country lane that seemed to curve back and forth unnecessarily, which slowed them down significantly, but was still preferable to the main roads. After a while of awkward silence, Valia decided that it was time to return to her old tricks.

"Lovely day isn't it?" she called out to Kirin.

He glanced at her. "Yes. Nice weather."

"We haven't been attacked since the bear before Wyra," she continued. "And I haven't heard the hissing thingy, either. Do you think it'll be easier going from here on?"

"Probably not."

"Have you been in this area before?"

"A few times."

"What were you doing here?"

Kirin glanced at Valia again. "It'll be faster if we don't talk."

"How, exactly? Do the horses struggle to wade through the vibrations coming from our mouths?" She took a breath. "Kirin, I'm really sorry about yesterday." Valia pulled Bird closer. "I've apologized more than once. But please, this journey is hard enough without you giving me this weird silent treatment."

"I'm not being silent. We're still talking." Kirin flicked Unicorn's reins, and the horse picked up his pace.

"Flora strangle me. This is fun."

They rode in silence a while longer. As the day wore on, Valia began to wonder if she'd imagined the Kirin from the last few days, the one who'd joked with her, grinned at her, and looked at her as though she was somehow special. The Kirin who felt like a childhood friend grown into a man. Comfortable, safe, and *warm*—but dangerous, too. He was still courteous enough. He answered direct questions, although mostly with one or two words. He suggested breaks at regular intervals and shared his waterskin with Valia when hers ran out before they could find a stream. Yet, he was no longer particularly friendly, either.

The further they rode, the less frequently they passed any form of civilization. Northern Avania wasn't heavily populated, and the few people who chose to live here tended to be isolated for a reason.

Valia knew stories of metemancers who hid in the north, as well as floramancers driven mad by their power, and the nix who preferred not to have any part in the Avanian kingdom. The stories said that strange creatures rarely seen in the rest of the kingdom tended to live here, too—though they seemed to be everywhere now.

When night came, they picked a spot away from the road and set up camp. Valia was a little surprised when, after they'd gathered food, walled off the clearing, and started a fire, Kirin got to his feet and asked if she was ready.

"Really?" Valia asked.

"You still have lots to learn, and little time for it," Kirin replied.

"Fine." Valia removed her gloves, and they began to circle. Valia's heart wasn't in it, though, and Kirin was able to quickly pin her hands. He let go immediately and took a long step away from her.

"Seriously?" Valia crossed her arms. "I get it. You aren't attracted to me, and you don't want to kiss me. That's fine. But now you won't even touch me while we're practice fighting? Really?"

"What?" Kirin looked genuinely startled.

"*What*, what?" Valia replied sharply.

"It's not like that," Kirin said.

"You ran like I was possessed by the Flora when I asked you to kiss me," Valia pointed out. She felt more hurt than angry now. "Today you barely spoke to me. And now you won't touch me. What other conclusion am I supposed to draw?"

"Valia." Kirin took a step closer. "I shouldn't have been distant with you today. That wasn't fair."

"...It's fine." Valia hugged her arms around her stomach now. "Can we just go back to normal now?"

Kirin sighed. "I want to be clear. The reason I didn't kiss you isn't because I'm not attracted to you."

Valia's eyes narrowed. "Well, that clears things up."

"What I mean is…" Kirin ran a hand through his hair, making it stick up almost straight. "I don't want you to get hurt."

"Oh, *please*," Valia scoffed.

"No, listen to me. You're something different, Valia. *Someone* different. If I told you I'm attracted to you, those words would be… inaccurate. Not that I'm not. You're gorgeous and you act like you don't know it. You're smart. Witty. You handle uncomfortable situations with grace. You restrain your power. Mine, too. You stopped me from making a mistake with that ridiculous eye under our boat. The bear, too."

Valia's face lightened, a little blood rushing to her cheeks. "Well, then. I'm listening…"

"Come here. Sit down."

Sheepishly, Valia followed Kirin back to the fire and sat cross-legged across from him.

"You're the princess of a kingdom in an invisible war. Heir to it. You're a floramancer. I'm a…"

"A what?" Valia asked, eager to finally hear what he called himself.

Kirin was a man who could masterfully dispatch half a dozen men and an otherworldly creature at the same time, but it seemed as if words and feelings would finally do him in.

"Bad things tend to happen to people I care about." Kirin sighed. "When we were in my cottage, you saw a painting, right? Of me as a child?"

Valia nodded.

"In the painting with me were my parents. When I was six, a phoenix attacked our village. Phoenixes are normally peaceful and passive, as I've since learned, but there was something about this one that wasn't right. It burned crops and picked off small livestock, mostly chickens, and came back every so often.

"Just as the village was growing truly concerned, a man arrived. Tall, with the deepest blue eyes and hands full of rings. Not just rings, either. He wore several amulets on a chain around his neck and had more in his pockets. He asked around about the phoenix, and it became clear he'd been trying to tame the creature to his will.

"At the time, I only knew what my parents told me, which was that he'd come to relocate the phoenix so we'd all be safe. The man sat in the center of our town. Many of us gathered to watch. Floramancy is uncommon in Tromin, so it was unusual to see one in action, but at the time it was more exciting than alarming. The fear of floramancy in Tromin... well, it came later."

Valia sat, listening to Kirin, as a bad feeling grew in her chest. Kirin gazed into the fire, as though he were still that little boy in the village square watching the first floramancer he'd ever seen.

"After a while, the man managed to summon the phoenix. It flew to him, squawking and breathing little bursts of fire, its eyes darting around at all the people gathered. I held my mother's hand so tightly that I must have hurt her. The man managed to control the phoenix for a while. He made it fly loops over the crowd. People cheered. Not my parents, though. My father decided we'd seen enough and that it was time to leave. We started back toward our home, and that's when we heard it. A loud, tortured cry. The phoenix had broken free of the man's control, and it began to attack again. This time, instead of attacking chickens, it attacked people.

"There was no rhyme or reason to what it did. It just clawed at everyone in sight, breathing bursts of fire and crying out. I'm not sure if it had been driven mad or if it was just lashing out after whatever the man had done to it. Everyone screamed and ran and finally the phoenix flew off into the sky, away from the village.

"I'd been pushed to the ground as people ran. When I got to my feet, I saw bleeding, injured, and dying people all around me.

Including my parents. I ran to find the man, who had protected himself with floramancy from the phoenix, and begged him to save my family, but he just shook his head and smiled. 'Floramancy doesn't work like that,' he said. 'And anyway, I'm not done with that phoenix.' I asked if he was going to kill it, and he laughed. 'And waste all that power?' he asked as he walked off."

Kirin finally raised his eyes to meet Valia's. "After that, I... well. I was on my own for a long time, Valia. I was lost in hurt and anger. I've done things I'm not proud of. There was someone else who came along, someone who showed me the value of restraint, like you. She's... gone now. I fear involving myself with you will bring you the same fate."

Valia came around the fire to Kirin. There, she sat beside him and took his hand in hers.

"I'm so sorry, Kirin. I can understand why you hate floramancy so much."

Kirin gave a short, humorless laugh.

"What happened to the floramancer and the phoenix?" Valia asked. "Did you ever find out?"

Kirin's eyes met hers in the firelight. "When I was older, I looked for them." Kirin held her gaze. "I killed him."

"If that's what you did that you aren't proud of... well, I think it's understandable. That floramancer was responsible for your parents' deaths, and probably the deaths of many others. If you hadn't killed him, more people would have been hurt." Valia still held Kirin's hand in her own.

"Thank you, but that's the least of it."

"You could tell me. Maybe I would understand." Valia knew the floramancer who'd killed his parents wasn't the only floramancer Kirin had killed, but she'd come to know him well over their adventures together. If he'd killed anyone, she was sure he had a good reason.

Kirin glanced at her. "Maybe you're right. But not tonight."

"Okay. Thank you for telling me about your parents."

"It's been a long time since I've spoken of them."

Valia shifted a little closer. "What were their names?"

"My mother was called Annelin, and my father Petr."

"What were they like?"

"My mother was the village midwife." Kirin smiled slightly. "She was always drying herbs and making concoctions, so our cottage always smelled like sage, sarcochilus, and lavender all the time. And she had a bag of knives and clothes and medicines she took to every birth, which I found terrifying because I wasn't sure how the knives were involved."

Valia laughed lightly and Kirin's smile widened. "And your father?" she prompted.

"He was a farmer. In rural Tromin, my mother would have been expected to help him, but he always supported her working as a midwife. He hired boys from the village to help instead. He was in the fields most of the time and always came back with sunburns and dirt under his nails. I often joined him in the mornings before the sun got too hot to help him tend the fields."

"Sounds like he was a good man."

"He was." Kirin ran his thumb over the back of Valia's hand. "Tell me of your mother and sisters."

"Oh… Okay." She composed herself, not expecting to speak about them, but happy for the opportunity to do so. "My mother was the smartest woman I'd ever known. Her name was Ellara. Despite being very busy with the affairs of the country, she always had time for me and my sisters." Valia bit her lip. "It's harder to think of her now, knowing what she did to my brother, but I do have many good memories of her. As a child, I thought she was the most wonderful person in the world. She always cared for the Avanians who needed it most, even when they couldn't do anything for the country. Refugees and orphans. 'They're all Avania's children,' she'd say. My mother even liked the generally unliked animals, like rats and snakes, because she felt that they had an undeservedly bad reputation. She said that they didn't choose to be born as they are and are only trying to survive like the rest of us." Valia smiled.

"Did she have powers, like you?"

"No. Neither of my parents did, beyond the basics. None of my sisters were particularly powerful, either. They all waited until the usual age to get their attunement ceremonies, although I got mine earlier…. I can't remember why."

"I know why. That's the memory you gave up to the Savani." Kirin ran his thumb along Valia's palm again. "The one I told you about, when you were at the river with your sisters, and you made your flower crown bloom."

Valia's dream, of being by the river with her brother, flashed through her mind, but she set it to the side. "Oh. I see… Um, then Samalia, my oldest sister… well, she'd prepared to be queen all her life. She would have been wonderful at it. You might think I have the posture of a princess, but she had the *presence* of a queen. When she entered a room, everyone stopped what they were doing because it always seemed like she had something important to say."

Kirin smiled. "I imagine she often did. Did she look like you?"

"She had blonde hair and was very fair," Valia said. "We didn't look similar at all. Actually, I don't really look like any of my sisters. They all took after my mother."

"Whereas you look more like your father."

"Exactly. Do you look more like your mother or your father?"

"I'm not sure. I only have the one painting, and I don't really remember. But people used to tell me that I looked like my father when I was young." Kirin met her eyes in the firelight. "Is there anything else you want to ask me? Something not about my family?"

"It's okay, Kirin." Valia shook her head. "I can wait. Tonight, we can just talk about the people we miss."

And so, they did. Long after the fire had turned to embers, after the stars had come out in the sky, after the owls had ceased their dusk hooting and the forest around them stilled, Valia and Kirin talked. They shared stories from their childhoods, of the games Valia had played with her sisters, of the knowledge of plants Kirin had learned from his parents. It felt like a kind of magic, talking about the people who were gone. Valia could almost believe their families were here with them, sitting in the clearing around the fire, listening to the stories, too.

There *was* a lot Valia wanted to ask. Kirin said he'd done things he wasn't proud of. He'd hunted floramancers, whether they were like her or not. This, along with the Savani's comment about him needing to choose, made Valia certain they would eventually have to have an uncomfortable conversation. But not tonight. Tonight, they reminisced, hands and hearts warm in each other's.

"It's cold tonight," Valia said when their stories finally wound down into companionable silence.

"Perhaps we should preserve our heat by sleeping closer?"

"To preserve heat. It only makes sense." So, they laid down, side-by-side on the hard ground with their blankets draped over them.

When Valia awoke in the morning, her head was resting on Kirin's shoulder and his arm was wrapped protectively around her. Sometime in the night, they'd been drawn together like sun and moon at umbra.

CHAPTER TWENTY-FOUR
BLUE

he next day was long and hard, leaving little opportunity for more heart-to-hearts. In a way, Valia was glad. It had felt special, almost magical, talking to Kirin about their families, but it left her with more questions than answers. Questions Valia wasn't sure how to ask, and Kirin didn't seem ready to answer. It was easier that their time was filled with foraging and navigating rough terrain.

The morning after their conversation by the fire, the hissing sound returned. It followed them on and off for a while, then disappeared just before umbra.

"Be ready," Kirin warned grimly. He pulled his whip from his back and checked his dagger at his ankle while Valia pulled off her gloves, her heart thudding in her chest. When the hissing had begun, they'd talked about trying to find a town or clearing in which to fortify, but no towns were nearby, and there wasn't enough vegetation to gain a substantial advantage. Instead, they'd ridden on, unable to afford a lengthy distraction. Above, the sun began to darken. Shadows grew long as the moon covered a tenth of the sun, a fifth, a quarter.

As soon as the sun disappeared behind the moon, the manticore attacked. It came flying out of the forest, claws outstretched, aiming straight for Valia. Valia's heart skipped a beat, and, despite all her training with Kirin, her first instinct was to send a shove of power at the creature. It was enough to knock the manticore off course, where it plowed into the ground, its sinewy body flipping over its scaly head before it landed on its feet. She followed up her push of power with a damper spell that made the creature slow as though it were moving through mud.

Kirin's whip cracked, first flicking against the manticore's shoulder to draw its attention, then wrapping around the creature's long neck. Kirin pulled the whip taut as he leaped off Unicorn's back and stabbed at the creature's eye with his dagger. The manticore rolled, already shaking off Valia's damper spell. Its tail struck at Kirin.

Kirin dove out of the way as Valia slid from Bird's back and reached for the vegetation around them. There were no vines nearby, so Valia reached for a yew with low, gnarled branches that stood just off the path. She hadn't wanted to attack Kirin with a branch, but there was no need to hesitate when it came to the manticore. After making sure Kirin had rolled out of the way, Valia brought the widest branch smashing to the ground with all the force she could muster. It caught the manticore in the middle of its back, pinning it to the ground.

The creature shrieked, writhing snakelike in an attempt to free itself, but the branch was heavy. Valia reached for another surge spell to send tendrils of the branch down into the earth, further securing the creature. With the manticore pinned, Kirin wasted no time driving his dagger through one of the creature's eyes. It thrashed for a moment longer, then lay still.

Kirin pulled his knife from the creature's eye, wiped it on his shirt, then looked up and met Valia's eyes. Unlike after their other encounters, he didn't immediately run to her to ensure she was unhurt. Instead, he gave her a slow nod, his eyes never leaving hers—acknowledgement that they'd fought together and won.

"Is it dead?" Valia asked. Her heart was still racing, but she felt calmer than she'd expected. This had been completely different from her disastrous encounter with the manticore outside of Wyra.

"Seems to be." Kirin walked along the length of the manticore's sinewy body, hopped over the log, and went to its tail. "Well done with the branch."

"I hesitated." Valia shook her head. "I still pushed power at it, even though I've learned that isn't the best tactic."

"It worked." Kirin used the blade of his dagger to cut neatly through the creature's tail. He took the sharp tip, which he wrapped in waxed paper and put in his saddlebag.

"What are you doing with that?" Valia asked. She was still filled with nervous energy and wasn't sure where to look.

"I had an idea. I've been wanting to add one of these to the end of my whip, ever since I fought the manticore near Abynth. That one's tail shattered in the fight, so it was unusable." Kirin crossed to Valia. "How do you feel?"

"Good." Valia bounced a little on her toes. Her hands were shaky. "I feel like I have too much energy."

"That's the adrenaline. You aren't hurt?" He reached for her, straightening the hem of her shirt and brushing her arms as though dislodging invisible dirt. Valia wanted to point out that he was the one who'd been rolling around the forest floor, but bit back her comment. Feeling Kirin's warm hands on her arms, so gentle after the way he'd fought the manticore, felt too good for her to say something that might stop him.

"No, I'm alright." She lifted her gaze to meet Kirin's gray eyes. She noticed once more how much taller he was than her and how solid his presence was. His nearness made her shakiness subside, especially as his hands trailed down her arms to her hands.

"Good." The corners of Kirin's mouth lifted into a grin. "We don't make a bad team." He flipped her hands over and examined her thumbs.

Valia smiled back, and the simple gesture relaxed her further.

"Does this hurt?" Kirin wiped his thumb across a trail of blood from one of the pricks on her thumb.

"No, it's alright. I was trying to cast quickly, so I wasn't as careful as usual. If this is the only injury I have from our first successful fight together, I'll call it a win."

Kirin grinned, his seriousness melting into something softer. "I imagine you would have had a trail of healers running after you if this had happened in Wyra."

"You have no idea." Valia grinned back. "But floramancers heal quickly. And for a small prick like this, even a princess is expected to care for herself."

"You poor thing." Kirin brought her hands together, sandwiched between his palms, and squeezed for a moment before letting go. "Shall we continue? We can discuss how to improve our technique in the next fight."

Valia chuckled. "Excellent. Can the next fight be hunting down the hissing thing? Eventually, it's going to bring a creature we can't defeat."

"Don't underestimate yourself. Or me." Kirin turned back toward Unicorn, revealing his shirt had been torn over his right shoulder blade. A trickle of blood seeped into the fabric below the tear.

"Kirin?" Valia grabbed his other arm to stop him. "You're hurt."

"It's just a scratch," Kirin said, as calmly as if he were talking about the weather. "It's not deep." He gently removed her hand from his arm.

"Let me look at it," Valia insisted. "Come on. Take off your shirt."

"First you want to kiss me, now you want me to take off my shirt." Kirin turned back to her with a teasing grin. "A bit forward, Princess."

Valia rolled her eyes, though inwardly she felt relieved things weren't awkward after their heart-to-heart. "Come on. Let me see."

Kirin pulled his shirt over his head. Sure enough, the scratch wasn't deep, but blood was seeping through the cracked skin and trickling down his back. Valia went to Bird to fetch her waterskin, then used it to wash the excess blood away.

"May I use floramancy to fix this?" she asked. She was aching to press her surge ring to speed the healing process; her thumb was already dancing over her ring.

"Absolutely not."

"Come on." Valia moved in front of Kirin so she could see his face. "You refuse my help, even if it means you'll suffer more, when I could fix you immediately?"

Kirin shook his head. "Valia, this is not suffering. Pain can be a useful teacher, and this will heal on its own in a few days. If you want to get a clean bandage from my bag, that would be helpful."

"Fine." Valia went to fetch a bandage, which she carefully laid over the scratch and wrapped around Kirin's shoulder. With the immediate wound tended to, she noticed a network of scars across Kirin's back. Some looked minor, while others were broad and seemed dangerous. Beneath the scars, she couldn't help but admire his body. It was no wonder he always moved so effortlessly in his fights.

"What's this from?" She traced a finger over a particularly long slash on Kirin's lower back.

"A former friend. Leander." Kirin's smile was slightly strained. "We had a... disagreement."

"What kind of disagreement leads to a scar like this?" Her finger was still on the scar. With a little floramancy, she could heal this too, but she got the feeling Kirin wouldn't want that—even if he'd approved of floramancy. He seemed like the kind of man who considered his scars as much of himself as she did her rings or her nose. "Who is Leander?"

"Not who I thought he was. Like I said, *former* friend." Kirin turned away from her touch and shrugged his shirt back on. "Come on. Let's keep moving. We have a long way to go."

Valia groaned. Kirin was right. They had a long way to travel, but she was exhausted from days spent on the move and from the fight with the manticore. She was tired of him hiding so much about his past, too, but she was willing to be patient. Kirin looked at her in surprise.

"Are you alright?"

"Yes. I'm just tired. Who knew that trying to save the kingdom would involve so much riding?"

Kirin chuckled. "Especially when trying to outpace a potential army behind us. Need a break?"

"No, no. It's fine." They remounted the horses and set off. Valia listened closely for another bout of hissing, but whatever creature had made the sound seemed to be gone now.

That night, in their camp, Valia struggled to create the usual protective wall of greenery. The further north they went, the scrubbier the plants were. The area was mostly spruces and firs, neither of which were particularly conducive to being knitted together into protective walls. By the time Valia finally managed to create a more-or-less impenetrable boundary, she was tired and had sacrificed a lot of blood.

"We'll skip our spar tonight." Kirin said as Valia slumped by the fire.

"No, it's fine. I can do it."

"The manticore was enough," Kirin pointed out. "Rest will be more beneficial when we don't know tomorrow's challenges."

"Fine, if you insist. You *are* injured. And rest does sound nice."

After dinner, Valia helped Kirin affix the manticore's tail spike to the end of his whip. Kirin spent a short time attacking nearby trees and invisible enemies to get a feel for the new weapon.

Valia liked watching him go through his paces with complete focus. Usually, when he fought, she was distracted—either by him attacking her in a play-fight or by whatever monstrosity he was fighting. It was rare to see him like this.

"Kirin?" Valia said, once he'd finished his drills.

"Mhm?" Kirin coiled his whip.

"A competition?"

Kirin's eyes narrowed and his mouth crooked into a grin. "What happened to rest?"

"That tired, are you? Don't worry, nothing too taxing. Just a little game to keep my mind busy, please?" Valia got to her feet and arranged three sticks into a triangle on the ground as Kirin watched curiously. "Let's throw pinecones into the triangle. Whoever gets closer wins."

They both sat by the fire and selected pinecones from the ground. Valia tossed her pinecone underhand. It made a perfect arc though the air before plopping into the middle of the triangle. Kirin narrowed his eyes, judging the angles, then tossed his pinecone, which rolled across the triangle and knocked Valia's pinecone into the dirt outside the playing field.

"That's cheating," Valia complained.

Kirin grinned, flashing his teeth in the gathering dark. "Tell me a story."

Valia considered. "You told me how you got your horse. I'll tell you how I got mine. In my family, you could get a horse when you turned twelve, if you agreed to care for it yourself. I swore up and down that I would be the most conscientious horse owner the kingdom had ever seen, so my mother took me to a farm outside of town to choose my horse. Just the two of us. It was a rainy spring day, but I refused to be disheartened by anything.

"When we got there, my mother took me to a field full of horses. There was every kind of horse: dappled brown and white, black as night, foals and older horses. No unicorns, though." Valia winked and Kirin snorted.

"There never are," he said.

"I was drawn right away to one horse. She was gorgeous, gray with a white mark on her forehead, and she was also wild. The farmer told us that she had resisted every effort at training and that she'd kicked him, once. He also pointed out that she was too tall for me and that I'd never be able to ride her without help.

"But my mother took my hands and said, 'Valia, if you know something is right, you'll find a way.' So, I went into the field, held out my hand to the horse, and pressed my link ring. I sent her every thought of safety and love that I had, and I called her to me. She walked over and nuzzled my hand. It still took seasons to make her a proper royal horse, but she was *my* horse from that moment on."

"How enlightening." Kirin smirked. "You picked the stubborn, difficult horse too large for you."

Valia laughed. "Yes, you and Star are basically the same." Across the clearing, Bird whinnied. "You're great, too, Bird."

The night was cold with a piercing wind. Once again, Valia and Kirin slept near each other to conserve heat. Once again, they awoke the next morning in each other's arms. And, once again, they didn't discuss it in the light of day. Instead, they packed up and kept moving. The mountains grew closer, and the terrain grew rougher, but they still had a way to go.

In the morning, shortly after they'd started traveling again, the hissing noise returned. Kirin and Valia exchanged a look and wordlessly prepared themselves for battle. They scanned their surroundings.

"Valia." Kirin subtly nodded his head in the direction of the road ahead and held up three fingers. Valia looked and spotted three men. They were armed with bows and knives and blended into the tree cover. If Valia hadn't been on alert from the hissing sound, she might not have noticed them until the first arrow struck.

Kirin swung his whip into his hand, but Valia signaled for him to wait with one hand. Kirin nodded and rested the whip on his legs.

Taking a deep breath, Valia reached out with her powers. The trees the men were hiding in twisted to life. Evergreen branches wrapped around them, pulling their hands flat to their sides. The men began to shout and hack at the branches to no avail. Valia had them all neatly pinned.

Kirin gave Valia an approving look, and they rode past the three would-be bandits, who stared at them in confusion.

"Filthy blood mage!" one shouted at Valia. "You'll pay!"

"They'll be able to free themselves eventually," Valia said to Kirin in a low voice once they were out of earshot.

"Too bad."

They rode on for a while, following a narrow stream filled with clear water up a rocky slope.

"Something doesn't add up." Kirin ran a hand through his hair. "With that hissing sound."

"I was thinking the same thing. At first, I thought it was someone tracking us so that they'd know when to attack. That made sense with the creatures, but it doesn't make sense with the bandits. Unless you think whoever controls the hiss hired them?"

"I doubt it. They weren't ready for us at all. I'm starting to think the hiss might be warning us of trouble, rather than bring it."

Valia nodded slowly. "I may want to retract what I said about hunting it down. But what about the first time we heard the hiss, when we were going into the town? I thought it stopped because the danger had passed."

"Maybe it did. Or maybe..." Kirin's brows drew together in consideration. "Maybe it warned us about the man who attacked you in the night."

"And the third time, when we were camping in the forest? Nothing attacked then either."

"I'm not sure."

They rode quietly for a while, then Valia inhaled quickly.

"Wait, maybe I know. The next morning, after we heard the hiss in the night, I saw the poster with the circles on it that I told you about. It looked fresh, and I suspected that it might have been put up while we were sleeping. What if the hiss was warning us about that?"

"Maybe." Kirin didn't look entirely convinced. "Why would it be warning us, though? I don't know of any creature that does that."

"Neither do I. This could be one of them. Maybe it's a spell cast by someone who wants to help us?"

"Like who? I wouldn't be so sure. I'm suspicious of anything that won't show its face."

Valia scanned the forest. "Well, next time we hear it, we'll see what we can do."

The next night, in their enclosed clearing, Valia pulled off her gloves in preparation for a fight, and Kirin picked up his whip.

"What's the plan?" Valia asked, gesturing at the whip.

"You're winning about half the time when we fight hand-to-hand," Kirin pointed out. "I think it's time for you to face off against an opponent with a weapon. Plenty of creatures have tails like this." He unfurled the whip and snapped it in the air above his head. Valia's eyes widened.

"You're definitely going to take my ear off with that thing."

"Consider it a donation to the Flora?" Kirin flicked the whip back and forth as though it had a mind of its own. "Don't be afraid."

The first fight ended as soon as it began. Kirin snapped the whip out, caught Valia around the wrist from across the clearing, and pulled her to him. Valia tripped over her feet as he pulled her against his chest, spun her around, and clasped her hands.

"Will the minstrels sing about *my* accomplishments now?" Kirin asked, referencing Valia's comment after her first win. His voice was soft in Valia's ear and sent shivers down her spine. She found herself leaning back against him instinctively.

"That *was* impressive," Valia admitted. "It didn't even hurt." She stepped out of Kirin's arms and assumed the singing position she'd been taught as a child in the palace before anyone realized she hadn't inherited Queen Ellara's musical prowess. "Oh Kirin, mighty and strong," she sang. "He fights monsters and creatures all day long."

Her song was cut off, though, by Kirin bursting into laughter. He was so overcome with mirth that he bent over, slapping his thighs with his hands, looking like a boy who'd just heard the world's funniest joke.

"Hey!" Valia put her hands on her hips. Kirin caught sight of her expression and managed to pull himself together.

"Sorry. But I have to say, Valia, though you may be talented in many areas, your singing skills need work."

"Can *you* do better?" she challenged. "I bet my last apple you can't."

Kirin straightened up and took a deep breath in, then out. Valia hesitated. He looked, for all the world, like a man who was about to sing beautifully. Then, he opened his mouth. "Princess Valia, she wields magic so well. Is there a limit to her powers? None can tell!"

Now it was Valia's turn to collapse into giggles. "It's a good thing confronting my brother won't involve any singing, because we'd absolutely fail."

"Hey." Kirin put a hand on his chest. "I'm a talented singer."

"Who told you that? A deaf squirrel?"

"Well, it wasn't deaf when I'd started..."

Valia giggled again. She liked this side of him, the side willing to show off his horrible singing skills and laugh at himself.

"Let's go again."

This time, Valia was ready. As Kirin circled, the whip flicking in his hand, she reached out. Childhood lessons taught her that the Flora was in almost everything alive, from people to trees to animals. Even in the metal bars of the draevori cave or maybe the air around it, Valia had been able to find a little bit of the Flora. Valia imagined that she was standing in the midst of a vast network of Flora, alive in the trees and the animals around her. Alive within *her*. She sensed Kirin, though only vaguely, and reached further. There it was. His whip was made of leather, with a wooden handle and the tip of the manticore's tail. All those materials had once been alive. They had once pulsed with the energy of the Flora.

Valia pressed her surge ring, and the whip began to writhe in Kirin's hand like an oversized snake. His eyes widened as he struggled to regain control, while Valia seized the moment to dive across the clearing and press a hand to Kirin's throat.

"You can do that?" Kirin asked as his whip relaxed in his hands, returning to its previous inanimate form.

"I reached for the materials in your whip," Valia said. "The ones that used to be alive. The Flora is still within them."

"I don't think most floramancers can do that," Kirin replied in a low voice. "These materials aren't alive, you know. I thought 'dead things' was how you were taught metemancy was used. Then again, your rings..." He tilted her chin back with one hand, his fingers gentle against her skin, and gazed into her eyes. Valia found herself looking up into his eyes. From this close, she noticed that they weren't *all* gray—there were small green and black flecks in the irises.

"Um, Kirin?"

"You have blue eyes," he said.

"I do." The moment, and the phrase, could have been romantic, but Valia got the feeling something else was going on.

"But they're dark." Kirin released her and let out a soft puff of breath. "Dark blue."

In an instant, Valia realized his concern. People and creatures who had used too much magic, or who had had too much magic used on them, ended up with the dark blue eyes Valia had seen on the Savani and on the creatures that had attacked.

"I... don't use that much floramancy," Valia said.

"But you do. That's the thing." Kirin lifted his hands as he began to pace. "Your minor spells are powerful enough to require a much bigger sacrifice from someone else, but not from you. I've seen what these kinds of powers can do to people. Floramancy especially, but metemancy too. And it can't do all this." He made for the fire, where he sat. Valia followed, feeling uncertain.

"Listen, I'm always careful. I only use minor spells, and I don't sacrifice too much."

"I know. But the biggest sacrifice I've seen you make was your vision when we first met. I'm sure some of the spells you've done since then have been just as major, but your sacrifices have been smaller. Have you given much more than blood since then?"

"Not really..." Valia sat beside Kirin. "Most of these spells are on plant material, which is easier for me to manipulate. It's different."

"Valia, please. Think about it." Kirin turned and took her hands, looking down at her rings. "The Flora decides who is powerful and who isn't. It's decided *you* can be powerful without much cost. Haven't you stopped to think about why that is?"

"Not really." Valia took her hands back and put them in her lap. "I haven't. But even if you're right, and the Flora does favor me in some way, why is that a problem? Maybe, since I need to confront my brother who may be powerful in his own right, the Flora wants to ensure that I'll be strong enough."

"Maybe..." Kirin looked away from her, into the fire. "But what happens after?"

Valia followed his gaze. Perhaps Kirin was right. Recently, she'd been able to conjure illusions and move materials faster and more easily than ever before. Still... Valia had always been strong, though mostly unapplied. Maybe this was nothing more than her strength blossoming under adverse conditions, like moss across a rocky surface.

"I don't know," Valia admitted. She glanced at Kirin. "But I'm far more worried about my brother than about the Flora, which has always helped me." She spread her arms to encompass the forest around them. "The Flora is a force for good. For balance. For life."

Kirin leaned closer, his eyes flashing in the firelight. In a low voice, he asked, "How can you be so sure?"

Valia didn't answer for a long time. Eventually, Kirin began roasting the fish for their dinner, and conversation moved on to the path they'd need to journey across tomorrow (across a rocky field into the foothills of the mountains, if Kirin's maps were to be trusted) and how far they were from the monastery (perhaps two or three days, if they kept pace). Still, Kirin's doubts played in Valia's mind as they lay in the dying light of the fire and under the moonlight.

Valia had never questioned the Flora before. It had always been there for her—a warm, bright power that helped her do more than light candles, sprout flowers, and heal scrapes. When Valia was young and would sit at the top of the tower at night, she'd imagine that the Flora was there with her, all around her—as she'd been taught since she was a child—and felt comforted. Now, Valia wondered. If the Flora was really so benevolent, why had it let people like the floramancer who'd killed Kirin's parents grow so powerful? Why had it given Valia such power, but not her sisters who'd surely deserved it just as much? Why had it led the Savani to tell Valia's parents that a son would bring ruin?

In that moment, the thought of the Flora humming in every tree and owl and blade of grass around her wasn't as comforting as it used to be.

CHAPTER TWENTY-FIVE
INTENTION

ou're quiet today." The statement was so unexpected that Valia almost tipped into the river. She and Kirin were crouched by an icy cold river, refilling their water skins after a long morning of riding.

"If *you're* saying that, it really must be something." Valia adjusted her footing on the smooth rocks beneath her, took a drink from her waterskin, and put the cap on. She straightened, overbalanced a little, and felt Kirin catch her elbow to steady her.

"You're just usually much... chattier."

"Do you miss me?" Valia smiled and nudged Kirin with her shoulder. "I thought my chatter annoyed you."

"Never." Kirin smiled a slow smile, then ran a hand through his hair. "Mostly never."

Valia chuckled. "Well, it's nothing. I've just been thinking. About the Flora... about everything." Kirin bit his lip, and Valia's eyes followed the gesture. They hadn't spoken about anything romantic in the least since that night by the clearing. Still, Valia couldn't help but feel drawn to Kirin. It was a beacon in the darkness to felt cared for in his softer moments. "I've been thinking about our upcoming confrontation with my brother."

"As have I."

"Good." Valia hesitated, shifting her weight from foot to foot. "You said I was powerful, and that my power might exist for a reason. Perhaps it does. Perhaps my power is the only thing that can defeat my brother... if it comes to that."

"Maybe. Unless the Flora has chosen other champions."

"Champions?" Valia wrinkled her nose. "I'll agree that the Flora may have its own motivations in choosing who becomes powerful, but 'champion' seems like a stretch."

"What did you want to say?"

"Well, what if I can't fight?" Valia looked up at Kirin. "What if I'm incapacitated or injured or otherwise unable to use my powers?"

"Then that would mean I'm dead," Kirin said in a low voice. "I'll keep you safe. No matter what."

Valia's knees went a little weak at his words, though she preferred he just listen to her full thought. "Just listen. When you win our fights, it normally ends with you restraining my hands. I'm useless without my hands, and I'm not confident enough that I can prevent their capture. It's an obvious weakness, and I wonder if that's why the floramancer from your childhood had more than just rings. So, Kirin... if I'm incapacitated and can't use my powers... maybe you can." She braced herself for his response, which she knew wouldn't be positive. Sure enough, Kirin's eyebrows shot up.

"Explain?"

"It's possible for one person to draw on another's power. It's difficult, and it can go wrong, but as long as both people are in sync, it can work."

"So, you want me to use floramancy? Through you?" Kirin summarized, still confused.

"I know you don't want to. I know you've experienced the worst sides of Flora." Valia reached for his hand. "We'd only do it as a last resort. Isn't it better to have the option to cast together and not need it, than need it and not be able to? Shouldn't we at least try it?"

"You make a fair case." Kirin gave a gruff sigh and turned away. "Give me time to think about it."

"Of course..." she said, gently. Though, with only a couple days left of riding, Valia was eager to have an answer.

For the rest of the day, it was Kirin who was mostly quiet as they rode. Just as they'd seen the night before, today's road mostly wove over a large, rocky field. Valia couldn't help but think there was something unnatural about such a large open area where nothing grew. In the distance, the mountains loomed, wreathed in a cloak of fog obscuring any detail. In her current mood, they felt more threatening than beautiful.

As they rode, Valia took a drink from her waterskin. The water inside was so cold it made her throat burn, and she instinctively pressed her ring to warm it up. As she took another sip of the now palatable water, a morbid idea struck. She could so easily change the temperature of water. Perhaps she could do the same with blood?

Valia stowed the waterskin again, her heart constricting. She didn't like the idea of freezing someone's blood, even if that someone was a creature about to attack her. She certainly couldn't test the idea on Kirin, but it was a good strategy to keep in her palm.

By nightfall, they were back in a forested area. This far north, there were few farms or other travelers, so it wasn't hard to find a place to set up camp. Today, while Valia created a weak wall of vegetation from the scrubby trees that surrounded them, Kirin sharpened his weapons. When Valia finished, he put away his dagger and came to sit with her.

"I have an idea," Valia said.

"What is it?"

"New competition. If I win, you'll try floramancy with me. If you do, you don't have to."

"You'd leave such a big decision to chance?" Kirin asked.

"Not chance. Skill. Come on." She nudged his shoulder with her own. "At least it'll help move the decision forward. You don't have much longer to make it."

"What's the competition?"

"Hmm... I used to play a game with my sisters where we'd take turns stacking rocks as high as we could without the pile toppling. Can we try that? Do you accept?"

"Fine." Kirin reached for a large, smooth stone, which he placed on a flat patch of ground. "I'm winning."

Valia stood and circled the clearing until she found a good stone, which she added carefully to Kirin's. "Your turn."

Kirin scanned for his own rock, which he placed carefully on top. The pile wobbled slightly. "I should get something if I win, too. Seems a bit one-sided."

"Beyond not having to do floramancy?" Valia added the next stone. "You ask for so much. Who's the spoiled princess now?"

"I never said you were spoiled." Kirin carefully balanced the next rock.

"You thought it." Valia added another. "What happens if we run out of rocks in the clearing before the pile falls over?"

"Good question."

They both held their breaths for a long moment as Kirin placed his next rock. The stack didn't fall, though, and Valia went looking for another rock to add. When she added it to the top, the pile began to lean, then tipped over, rocks rolling across the ground.

"Hm." Disappointment rushed through Valia. She had hoped that Flora indeed flowed through all things, including these rocks, and would somehow help her win. It had been such a simple game with such an important outcome, but she had lost. If Flora was in them, it didn't want Kirin to use it.

"I'll try it," Kirin said.

"What?" Valia lifted her gaze to Kirin's eyes.

"I'll try floramancy with you."

"Thank you." Valia's heart stirred at his words. It meant a lot for a man like Kirin, with all he was and all he'd been through, to say that.

"Let me be clear," Kirin continued, holding up a hand. "I'm only doing this because I agree that we should have all possible options available when we face your brother. The priority is to fight as we've been doing."

"Our priority is peaceful negotiation," Valia reminded him.

"Right. Of course. Our *second* priority is to fight as we've fought. Only if there's no other option, only if it would save your life, will I do floramancy."

"My life, or yours," Valia corrected. Kirin made a noncommittal noise and Valia stepped closer, taking his hand with her gloved one. "My life, *or yours*," she repeated. "We both need to survive this, Kirin."

"Sure. That would be my preference too." Kirin's eyes skated away from Valia's, but she kept her hands in his until he looked back at her and nodded. "How do we start?"

"Let's start by kneeling." Valia sank to her knees. "Casting from a kneeling position is easiest."

"Why is that?"

"I don't know. It just is. Maybe because we're closer to the ground, where the Flora is."

"Isn't it in the air too? All around us? Maybe it's because the Flora likes a show of submission and supplication," Kirin suggested under his breath. Valia gave him a sharp look.

"Maybe you'll feel differently once you feel it." Valia removed her gloves and pressed her palms together. "Alright. We need to be touching, skin to skin. Anywhere can work. Give me your hands."

Kirin took her hands between his own, as he'd done dozens of times during their sparring sessions. This time, he cupped them gently, palms up, so that Valia could still access her rings. For a moment, the way his hands enveloped hers was all she could think about.

"Now what?" he asked in a low voice.

"Do you know the three basic parts of floramancy?"

"I suppose you're going to tell me."

Valia gave him another stern look. "I am. Listen closely."

Kirin raised his eyebrows. "I was never a particularly attentive student."

"Perhaps you just didn't have the right teacher."

"Are you the right teacher, Princess?"

"I don't know. My favorite teacher when I was young always gave me and my sisters sweets when we did well."

"Got any sweets?"

"Does leftover rabbit from yesterday count?"

Kirin made a face. "Shall we get started?"

"If my student is ready to take this seriously, yes." Valia sat up a little straighter. "The first thing you need for floramancy is a conductive material. Depending on what you're trying to do, you'll need different materials. Do you know what my rings do?"

"Some of them."

"Well, don't worry. There's a song for children to help learn. Are you ready?"

"For you to sing?" Kirin grinned. "Can't wait."

Valia took a deep breath. "Prism strengthens all we do," Valia sang in a soft, low voice. "Null disables me and you. Flux exchanges hot and cold. Gale force winds move fast and bold. Link persuades and shows the way. Lumen makes light, night and day. Sight makes information flow. Surge makes all things move and grow."

"Beautiful," Kirin said. Valia rolled her eyes. "So, which will we use?"

"It depends on what we need to do. But in a fight, I'm guessing we'll want surge or gale."

"Alright. You said there were three parts. What's next?"

"Sacrifice. Since the power comes from me, I'll be the one to make the sacrifice. Which, in the spells we'll practice today, means a drop of blood. In joint spell casting, it's theoretically possible for you to make the sacrifice as well, but it tends to have stranger results."

"And what if I try to cast a spell that would need more than blood? Say, bending metal bars like you did."

"It would most likely fail. Between the two of us, I'm more powerful, so if I opposed the spell you were trying to do, it just wouldn't work. Or something strange would happen."

"I don't love the idea of 'something strange' happening. In fact, this all seems rather undependable." Kirin looked around the clearing as though the shadows might come to life. Valia was almost amused by his concerned expression, though she tried not to show it. The mere whisper of something completely natural to her made him worry. Though, given his past, she could understand his apprehension.

"It probably won't. And we're starting small and safe. Don't worry. Alright, the final element of the spell is the intention. An incantation or prayer. That, you'll have to do."

Kirin looked alarmed. "What do I say?"

"You just reach out to the Flora." Valia shrugged. "It's hard to describe. Some small spells, like lighting a candle, have specific incantations that everyone knows. To light a candle, for instance, you'd say, something like 'to you I pray, a tiny flame to light my way.'"

"Does it have to rhyme?"

"No. But for bigger spells, you mostly need to make something up. It's more of an intention than anything. A feeling. Powerful floramancers often think of what they want and don't need a specific prayer, but beginners often need to articulate an incantation to prevent any misunderstandings."

"Let me guess, *you* mostly just think of what you want."

"Mostly. But you'll need an incantation. Try not to think about it so much. Are you ready?"

"I suppose." Kirin still didn't look pleased.

"Try to make light," Valia suggested. "That shouldn't be too difficult."

"Okay. Teach me the incantation."

"Hm." Valia considered. "Try picturing a ball of light in your mind. Like the ones I've made, but smaller. Then say something like 'bright in the night, we bring the light.'"

"Really?" Kirin wrinkled his nose. "It sounds like a nursery rhyme."

"It *is*. This is what we teach young children who are just learning about floramancy. Once you're older and more experienced, you can simply hold your intention in your mind. You'll feel it."

"At least it'll be easy to remember." Kirin frowned at Valia's hands, which were still cupped between his own. "So, I need to take your blood now?"

"Yes. Just prick my finger with the ring. Don't worry, I do this a hundred times a day. I'll live."

Kirin gently pricked Valia's finger with her needle ring and used his finger to transfer a drop of her blood onto the lumen ring. In a low voice, he muttered, "Bright in the night, we bring the light."

Nothing happened. Kirin sighed and released Valia's hands to run his fingers through his hair.

"It's fine," Valia said. "You'll get it."

"With time, maybe. Time we don't have the luxury to spend on this." Kirin sighed. "We'll reach the monastery soon, if your father's troops don't catch up to us first."

"Try again." Valia held out her hands. "You can do this."

"Maybe a different spell?"

"Let's stick with the light. It'll be easier to contain and dispel if there are any issues, and it'll help you learn the principles that will apply to any spell. Just remember, focus on your intention and reach out with your mind. Imagine the light rushing in from somewhere else: from the stars, from starflowers, from the fire, anything."

They tried again and again with no results. On the fourth try, a tiny flicker sparkled in the air between them, making Valia gasp. On the eighth try, Kirin was able to conjure and maintain a small ball of light that floated between them.

"See?" Valia grinned in the light of the orb. "We did it."

"I'm not sure how we'll use this," Kirin pointed out.

"You have the basics now. The more powerful your intention, and the higher the sacrifice, the easier the spell will be. And the more connected to the Flora you are, the easier it will be."

"I'll leave the Flora connecting to you." Kirin rolled his neck. "Is floramancy always this tiring?"

"Yes. I used to nap after every floramancy lesson when I was a child."

"I may do the same." Kirin yawned. "But first, we spar."

"Are you sure?" Valia was skeptical; Kirin looked half asleep already.

"I'm sure." Kirin stood, fetched his whip, and squared off against Valia. Valia swung a small branch at his feet to serve as a distraction, but in his exhausted state, Kirin didn't see the branch coming and fell flat on the ground. Valia hurried to him, half concerned, half amused, as Kirin chuckled.

"Okay," he said, looking up at her from the ground. "Maybe floramancy takes more effort than I thought."

"No." Valia widened her eyes and dropped her jaw as though this were shocking news. "I never would have guessed. If only someone would have told you!"

Kirin grunted and held up a hand. "Help me up, at least?"

Valia took his hand. Instead of letting her help him, Kirin tugged so that she tumbled to the ground and landed on top of him. He rolled over to pin her to the ground covered in pine needles as Valia giggled.

"I can still win, even if I'm tired," he said.

"Only with trickery." Valia grinned up at him, then rolled so that she was pinning him. "This was my victory."

Kirin protested halfheartedly as Valia helped him to his feet. They spent the rest of the evening around the fire, eating leftover rabbit from the day before. There wasn't much to eat in the area this far north, especially with the barren ground they'd been riding over most of the day. The rabbit was enough to warm Valia's stomach and lift her spirits, though. Kirin gave her an extra portion, even though she tried to refuse, reminding her of her need to replenish her lost blood.

When the time came for sleep, Valia rolled to face Kirin, trying to ignore the pull she felt to kiss his stubbly cheek or rest her head on his shoulder. Somehow, despite riding and fighting all day, he still smelled pleasant.

"Thank you for trusting me enough to try floramancy today."

"It was never *you* I doubted. I still don't trust floramancy," Kirin admitted. "I felt nothing, good nor bad. And how you prick your finger with that ring all the time…"

"It's not so bad." Valia brought her hand out from under the blanket and held it up in the dying firelight. The side of her thumb was covered in tiny pinpricks, but they were shallow and already mostly healed.

Kirin took her hand and examined it. "All these pricks look quite unpleasant for a princess."

"Not really. And you're one to talk. How is your back after the manticore?"

"I've barely thought about it. It was just a scratch."

"What's on my thumb is far less." Still, Valia didn't take her hand from Kirin's as he examined the pinpricks from every angle. It was nice to be cared for, even though she really was fine. "Doesn't metemancy require sacrifice?"

"No. Since the energy is stored in the rocks I told you about, it doesn't take much to let it out. Once they're used, the rock crumbles into dust."

Valia yawned. "That's nice."

"All power has its sacrifices, I suppose," Kirin continued. "Even if those sacrifices aren't immediately visible. With floramancy and metemancy, but with any other kind of power, too. A king's power brings its own sacrifices."

"And the power of Kirin Adante?" Valia asked. "What do you sacrifice to be able to defeat any creature that comes your way?"

"Friends. Family. My way of thinking. My way of life." Kirin ran his thumb along Valia's rings. "Fighting for *any* cause means giving something else up. When I was young, after the man killed my family, everything seemed simple. Blood magic was bad. Anything that could defeat it was good. The older I got, the more I recognized that *nothing* is that simple. Nothing is black and white, all good or all bad."

Valia held her breath. It seemed Kirin was skirting the edge of revealing more about himself.

"What do you mean, it wasn't that simple?" she asked, when Kirin didn't immediately continue. He released her hand and rolled toward her to face her. Valia's head rested on her pack and Kirin's on his arm. In the dying firelight, she could just make out the glint of his eyes and the edge of his face.

"Back in Tromin," he said carefully. "I started an organization that aimed to reduce the influence of floramancers. The Watchers, we called ourselves. When I was in charge, we hunted creatures driven mad by floramancy. We captured and killed floramancers, too."

"Oh," Valia said softly. "You told me that. About you hunting floramancers."

"We only ever hunted floramancers who were wreaking havoc. And we only killed them as a last resort."

"I believe you." Valia's heart beat hard in her chest.

"That's not all." Kirin sighed and ran his free hand through his hair. "After a while, more radical elements joined the organization. They believed *all* floramancers needed to be disposed of, whether they'd done anything wrong or not, because it was only a matter of time before power like that corrupted. They began placing bounties on floramantic charms and rings, much like the one carried by the man in the inn. The bounty doesn't say it, but it's understood as a bounty on floramancers themselves. Destructive or not. Man or child alike.

"I tried to stop it. As angry as I was with floramancers, I knew not all of them deserved to die. But by that point, my followers had grown strong, and the radicals outnumbered me. I lost a lot of people that day, either killed or consumed by a corrupted ideology. In the end, I came to Avania."

"You fought with your own people?"

"They fought with me. One man led the charge to reform the organization. Leander. He was one of my first and most loyal companions, a man I felt I could depend on. My closest friend. He saved my life, and I his... but there was always something rotten inside him. I remember, once..."

"Yes?"

"I found him standing over the body of a woman. She was writhing in pain from a stomach wound, clearly not much longer for this world. He stood there smiling, taking *joy* in her suffering, when our goal was supposed to be to alleviate it. That's when I knew where things were heading."

Valia shivered. "So, you tried to stop him."

Kirin nodded. "By that time, though, the Watchers were more loyal to him than they were to me. They thought I was soft and weak for showing mercy and letting a floramancer escape. When I confronted Leander, he attacked me. We'd fought side by side many times, so I knew just how formidable he was. Others joined him, and I didn't stand a chance. I was beaten near to death. And it was the very floramancer I'd let go, whose escape turned them against me, who saved me and brought me to Avania."

"I..." Valia hesitated. "Before that, how many floramancers did you kill?"

"Seventeen. I swear to you, Valia, each death was a sentence more merciful than they deserved."

"Your token," Valia said softly. "The one you gave me. It said you were an Olanthian Seeker."

"Yes." Kirin nodded slightly. "*The* Olanthian Seeker. There is only one, appointed by the Council of Nine. When I came to Avania, I realized no one knew what it meant, so I kept it in case I should ever need it."

They lay in silence for a few long moments. Valia's thoughts were racing. Kirin had been responsible for creating an organization that sought to kill her and people like her. Yet, it was clear he didn't agree with it, now. Still...

"You can ask me," Kirin said quietly. "What you carry in your mind."

"Just how long ago was all this?"

"Well, my first action in Avania, to be allowed to stay, was finding you."

"Why *did* you save me?" Valia asked. "You could have taken my father's offer to rescue me and then hidden yourself away. I doubt he would have found you. There was no reason for you to fight a draevor to save a floramancer. One who lived in the capital, in the family leading a kingdom of floramancers. And you must have known I was one."

"I did. And I could have... but maybe I wanted to see you weren't some mindless power-drunken killer, corrupted by the Flora. The floramancer who took me here didn't seem to be. Maybe part of me thought *saving* a floramancer in return would undo some of the damage I've done in creating the Watchers. I didn't expect *you*, though, or any of this."

"Me neither," Valia said.

"So, you understand now." Kirin's voice was still low. "Why I couldn't be close with you."

Valia paused and took a deep breath. "When I was eleven cycles old," she said softly, "I played hide and seek with my sisters and some of the noble children on the summer solstice. We'd just had the annual feast, exchanged gifts, and sang all the songs we could think of. It was late for Litia, so she'd already been put to bed. That meant my friend Celia and I were the youngest players. I was determined to help Celia win, since she was feeling down about her grandfather's return to the Flora."

"My sister Daria began to count, and we all ran. Celia spotted a tree with high branches in the garden and asked me to help her up using my powers. She was sure no one would find her up there. I was excited, too, so I used a little floramancy to bring a branch down. She climbed on, and I lifted her up.

"I didn't do a good job, though. I'd never done a spell quite like that before, and I wasn't in control. Not enough. I brought the branch up too sharply and Celia lost her grip and fell. She broke a leg and two fingers falling to the ground.

"I still feel terrible about it. I was young and foolish, and I should have known better. The royal healers healed Celia at my mother's request. Shortly after that, her family left the palace to return to their village. Perhaps they thought it would be safer to be away from me. I'm sure they were right."

"You made a mistake," Kirin said. "You were a child. It isn't as if you hurt your friend on purpose."

"Right. It wasn't my intention to hurt her. And I haven't sworn off friendship, or the Flora, or anything else because of it. Mistakes happen, sometimes for no fault of your own. It's the intention in your heart which truly matters." She paused. "So, is that how you feel about the Watchers?" The name sounded acidic in Valia's mouth.

"Maybe." Kirin was silent for a long moment. "Maybe it should be. I don't regret trying to reduce the damage caused by out-of-control floramancers. Someone needs to. But I do regret what the Watchers have become."

Valia remembered what the Savani had said to Kirin, back on the island. "And if you have to choose..."

"I suppose I'd follow my heart's intention, Valia. I'd choose to do right by you."

"I believe you," Valia said, putting any last doubts about him aside.

They didn't speak again for the rest of the night, and Valia eventually dozed off. The fact that Kirin had hunted her kind should have haunted her dreams, but instead, she felt reassured. She felt safe with him. She understood *how* he came to hunt floramancers, knowing how his parents were killed. She also understood the courage it took to stand up against the Watchers to save a floramancer in their captivity. Kirin had no doubt kept some of the gruesome details from her, but she was more certain than ever that he *was* a good man.

CHAPTER TWENTY-SIX
COALESCE

The next day, they began their climb into the mountains. At first, it was just rolling foothills that Unicorn and Bird climbed with ease, the purple and white mountains drawing ever closer the further they rode. Kirin made them stop just before umbra to look for food and came back with a freshly killed rabbit.

"We haven't had a lot of fresh meat, and you need to replenish your strength. I see that now, after creating that ball of light," he said as he mounted Unicorn again.

"Thank you."

"Of course, Princess. I can't let you fend for yourself with a substandard diet of ferns and berries."

Valia rolled her eyes as Bird fell into step with Unicorn again.

A short while later, the road turned to a narrow path that shrank until it was little more than a rocky scratch up the side of the mountain. Bird slipped on a rock and nearly sent Valia toppling down a short slope.

"Let's camp here for the night," Kirin decided.

"It's not even getting dark yet. My father's army could be close behind." Valia said, but Kirin was already sliding off Unicorn and leading his horse back down the path to a stand of trees they'd passed earlier.

"Unless he sent fewer than three dozen, which I doubt, they'll be much slower than us. We likely have a day or two on them. Better to reach the monastery fresh tomorrow than tired by nightfall. And it's better to rest where the terrain is still compatible with the horses, in case we need it to be."

They made camp in a scrubby stand of trees. Valia did her best to weave the branches into something resembling a protective barrier, but it wasn't easy. The pines and spruces seemed not to have the energy to grow much beyond what they already had, even when Valia pushed all the power she could muster into them.

"Save your strength," Kirin said, laying a hand on her arm. "Tonight, I'll keep watch."

"We can take turns," Valia countered, dropping her hands from her casting position gratefully. "We can't have you exhausted for whatever tomorrow brings."

"Nor you," Kirin pointed out. He gathered a meager pile of sticks and went about lighting a fire. Valia knelt beside him, stretching her fingers. It was chilly enough that her joints felt stiff. It seemed like a bad sign.

"Are you nervous?" Valia asked as Kirin managed to create a spark with his flint, which he pressed to a dry twig.

"No," Kirin told her plainly. "I learned long ago that nerves served no purpose."

Valia laughed softly. "How *evolved* of you. I wish I could turn off my nerves so easily."

"You have nothing to worry about," Kirin told her. He placed the dry twig into a larger nest of sticks, which caught fire. A smoky, sappy scent filled the clearing as the kindling began to burn. "Whatever happens, you'll be alright."

"Hm." Valia wasn't so sure. "What if my brother really did do all this?" She swept her hand across the clearing, but what she meant was all of Avania, her family, and everything terrible that had happened recently.

"Then we'll deal with him," Kirin replied. He sat back and held his hands up to the growing fire.

"I know. I just... I want to imagine that we'll have a joyous reunion and join together to fight the forces that are actually hurting Avania. But I also know that's unlikely."

"Could be. All we can do is prepare, then meet it as we are. And I've seen you, Valia. More than just in our play fights. You're prepared. Your abilities are unlike any I've ever seen, and it doesn't seem to corrupt you. You can handle this."

"Thank you." Valia looked down at the fire. "I've had a good teacher. Kirin... I'm glad you're with me."

"Nowhere I'd rather be." Valia looked up and saw Kirin watching her with those piercing gray eyes. Instead of feeling simply observed, though, she felt *seen*. Kirin saw past her royal posture and mannerisms, her floramantic powers, and saw Valia as she was.

Valia gave a slight smile and held his gaze. After her time with him, she felt she could see past Kirin's hard shell, too. She saw a considerate, caring, funny, virtuous man with a painful past.

"You good?" Kirin asked, and Valia realized that she'd been staring.

"Yes, fine. I was just thinking."

"About how majestic Unicorn looks eating his nettles?" Kirin asked. His eyes crinkled slightly, the only indication that he was teasing.

"No." Valia grinned. "About how you could possibly have thought Unicorn was an actual unicorn, and about how *that's* what the minstrels will actually sing about someday: your unicorn mis-identification, not your heroic deeds."

"I knew it." Kirin tapped his temple. "I can almost hear the song."

"And if you win today's spar, I'll write and sing it myself."

"I will have to save my strength today..." Kirin rolled his arms. "Before that, though, let's practice floramancy again."

"Really? Okay." Valia tugged off her gloves and held out her hands. "What makes you so eager today?"

"I wouldn't call it eager. I'm trying to understand it. How it works. You said you can feel it, but I've felt nothing yet." Kirin enveloped her hands with his own. "Your hands are cold."

"Sorry." Valia shrugged. "It's cold out. I'm not sure how yours are warm." He rubbed her hands between his own for a moment to warm them.

"Alright. Let's begin." This time, a warm orb of light formed between them almost immediately.

"Wow! Look at that. You didn't even use words. You're a quick study." Valia grinned. "Good job. Let's try something else."

"Like what?"

"You decide."

After a moment's hesitation, Kirin looked down at the ground beneath them. A seedling was pushing up from the soil right between their knees.

"Let's make it grow," he suggested. "What do I say?"

"Just try something." Valia shrugged. "I usually reach out to the plant and ask it to seek the sky."

"Seek the sky," Kirin whispered to the plant, gently pressing a drop of Valia's blood to her surge ring. Valia focused intently on the seedling. The plant didn't grow, exactly, but something did happen.

As they watched, the seedling began to change. The stem became thicker and darker green, the leaves grew small spines, and a spike emerged from the top of the plant. Valia met Kirin's wide eyes.

"What is *that*?" he asked.

"I... don't really know. Joint magic like this is unpredictable. Perhaps we weren't in perfect alignment on our goals. Perhaps one of us was distracted by thoughts of the fight tomorrow, which made the plant grow more defenses. Or perhaps the Flora just misunderstood."

Kirin sighed. "Could be anything, then? Just the will of the Flora?"

"I wish we had more time to practice," Valia said.

"I'm still not sure it matters. Last resort or not, I'm not sure it should be a resort at all," Kirin said, looking down at the spiny plant. "Not sure it's worth the risk."

"I see that." Valia sighed. "Only a few pairs of floramancers have been known to cast anything of consequence together. They call it coalescence—the syncing between both of their minds, bodies, and intentions. My handmaiden and I can manage basic spells together, but they're weaker and more exhausting than casting by myself. Some floramancers pair well together, and others... well, others simply don't. Maybe you're right that it's not worth the risk."

Valia felt disappointed not to share such a connection with Kirin. At the same time, she knew it was an unreasonable expectation from a magic-averse Trominite attempting floramancy for the first time. Still, she wished to be closer with him, and grew tired of masking her feelings.

They both stared down at the armored plant for a bit longer, then Kirin released Valia's hands and stood, stretching.

"Okay. Enough of that. One last spar?" he asked.

"Alright." Valia stood. "Just don't step on our creation."

"Never." Kirin grinned slightly. "Look at that, it has your nose."

"And your warm, inviting exterior," Valia fired back. "Defend yourself."

They took up their positions on opposite sides of the clearing, but neither of them moved to attack. Kirin didn't begin to pace as he usually did. Valia could have reached for her powers, shot a blinding ball of light toward Kirin or used the sparse shrubbery to entangle or distract him, but she didn't.

Instead, Valia took a step closer, and Kirin did the same. He grabbed his whip as if to attack, then slowly dropped it to the ground. He looked down at it, then returned his gaze to Valia, barely raising his head. Valia slowly walked forward and stopped right in front of him. She looked him up and down, then met his gaze. She reached up to the tower of a man, pulled him down by the back of his neck, and greeted his lips with her own. Kirin reciprocated, picked her up in a warm embrace, then gently laid her on the ground, their lips never parting.

Valia pushed him off to the side and rolled onto him. She fiercely pressed herself onto him and ran her hands across his body as if she *were* possessed by the Flora.

For a heartbeat, it was too much. Valia pulled away and sat on top of him. Kirin cupped Valia's cheek and ran his thumb across her cheekbone, sending anticipatory shivers down her spine. They'd touched so many times before, almost thoughtlessly, as they'd pulled each other from danger or huddled for warmth or sparred in sunset-lit clearings. He gazed up at her as though she was the only person who mattered in the world. With everything at stake, and everything resting upon her shoulders, perhaps she *was*.

Valia leaned back down and kissed him again, soft and gentle.

For a merciful moment, time stood still, relieving them of their anxieties about what the following day would bring. They embodied each other's essences and met squarely in the middle. Everything seemed to condense into this moment: all the teasing comments, the fleeting glances, the times they'd practiced fighting. All the nights they'd slept close for warmth. All the times they'd turned to each other instinctively when something went wrong. For an instant, Valia relived it all again: the way Kirin had been so aloof when he'd first rescued her, never responding to her cheerful questions. The way it had felt when he'd won a fight and pinned her hands with his warm, solid body pressing against hers. How her heart warmed when his face transformed from a stolid mercenary to a handsome ally with one of his rare, hard-earned smiles. The way he'd lain so still next to her when telling her about the group aiming to kill people like her. How he didn't hesitate to kill the man in the inn to protect her.

Her knees went weak as the kiss increased in intensity. One of Kirin's hands tangled in her hair as the other went around her waist, holding her close. His mouth tasted of the apples Valia had found earlier that day—sweet and crisp—and beneath that, the faint taste of blood. Whether from the scrape of his stubble or a nip too eager, neither of them seemed to notice or care. His roughness only deepened the moment.

New sensations flooded Valia, from the thousands of nerve endings in her lips she never knew existed until now, to a flood of warm desire drifting from each place Kirin's hands touched her, all the way down to her toes. This sensation was, Valia thought with the small fraction of her brain not completely consumed by him, not unlike drawing on the Flora. She felt powerful and warm with magic, but also vulnerable to something outside herself. Something she didn't fully understand.

After what could have been either moments or days, they separated. Kirin still held Valia around the waist, and her hands were still on his shoulders. Breathlessly, she collapsed her entire weight onto him, turning her head to the side and tucking her arms underneath his neck.

Valia knew there was more they should discuss. They should talk about what this meant for them, for the easy comradery they had begun to share, for a way in which a floramantically-inclined Avanian princess and a former Olanthian Watcher could share any kind of a future. But neither of them spoke another word. Tomorrow, they would face Valia's brother—if he really was at the monastery. Even though Kirin had promised he would keep Valia safe, she worried about what they would find.

Valia listened to his heartbeat for a while, still soaking in what had just happened. She and Kirin laid as they had for the last few nights, sharing blankets and warmth, but this time Kirin offered his shoulder as a pillow and Valia wrapped herself on his side.

Kirin already seemed to be fast asleep. Valia wished she could sleep, too. She felt comforted by his steady breathing and strong arm around her but couldn't stop thinking about tomorrow.

"Kirin?" His chest steadily rose and fell, but he didn't answer. She stared out into the darkness, keeping watch while he slept. "I'm scared..." Valia whispered. "I don't want to die, Kirin... I don't want you to die either. I... need you," she quietly confessed to the sleeping man.

Valia eventually fell asleep, exhaustion overcoming her. Whatever tomorrow would bring, she never wanted to change today.

CHAPTER TWENTY-SEVEN
PENANCE

unlight bore down on Valia as she opened her eyes. It was already well into the morning. She felt as if she had been asleep for days. She sat up and scanned her surroundings. She no longer lay with Kirin; he was nowhere to be found.

"Kirin?" Valia called out. A glint of light caught her eye from the hill above. There Kirin stood, reflecting sunlight off his dagger to get her attention and show her where he was. He worked his way down the hill as Valia rubbed her eyes and collected herself.

"What were you doing?" she asked, as he finally arrived.

"Keeping watch, of course." He raised his eyebrow as if that were obvious. "I found it."

"Found what?"

"The Sacred Triant Monastery. It's right between those three peaks. Tri. Three. Right?"

"Oh! Um, I guess so. Where?" Valia rubbed her eyes.

"Just over the next hill, then a short climb. We'll leave the horses here. It's too steep for them."

Part of Valia wanted to talk about the night before. Part of her wanted to grab Kirin and kiss him again. But she needed to focus on what came next.

"Did you sleep well?" She noticed his puffy eyes, as if he had been awake the entire night. Was he keeping watch the whole time she was asleep? Was he awake when she confessed her feelings? She nervously looked at him for an answer—to both her questions, spoken and unspoken.

"I did! Thanks for asking," he said in an unusually upbeat tone. Valia suspected it to be a courteous lie. Or, if he had slept well, it wasn't for long. He'd likely kept watch all night, as he'd previously offered. At least he seemed chipper today, regardless of their imminent danger.

They packed their things, bringing only the essentials, and Valia put a marking spell on Bird and Unicorn to make finding them later easier. Then, they began their climb up the mountain.

After they stopped to fill their waterskins at a narrow stream with water so cold it quickly chilled Valia's fingers, the hissing sound began again. Valia and Kirin exchanged glances as Valia tugged off her gloves and Kirin drew his whip. Whether the hissing creature was warning them of danger or bringing it, they needed to be prepared.

Here, where there was less vegetation than in the forests and fields they'd traveled through, Valia suspected she might finally be able to catch a glimpse of the hissing thing. Sure enough, as they walked, she spotted a long, white snake with bright scales weaving impossibly quickly in and out of the brush. It looked like a normal field snake, but the unnatural hissing sound and its quick movements made Valia certain that it was the source of the noise. She nudged Kirin and nodded to the snake.

"Do you think that's the thing making that noise? It looks so… ordinary."

Valia stopped short in her tracks and the snake slithered to a halt between a pair of rocks away from the trail, still hissing. Its eyes glowed faintly blue as it coiled, seeming to watch them.

"Wait." Valia hesitated. "I know this."

"You know this... snake?"

"I—"

A low, guttural moan from above cut Valia off in the middle of her sentence. She froze before forcing herself to look up to the sky. The creature appeared over the peak of the hill they'd been climbing, its talons extended, its ragged beak open as it moaned again. It was huge, even from a distance. Its wingspan was easily twice as long as she was tall, and each of its sharp silver talons was as long as her forearm. Its feathers were a sickly gray. Kirin cursed under his breath and Valia summoned the power of the Flora as she scanned their surroundings for life.

The creature dove at them, talons racking the air. Valia reached frantically for a tree, a bush, even a tiny seedling she could use to restrain it, but there was nothing green around them. Kirin grabbed her by the arm, pulling them both to the side, and Valia felt its talons whoosh by her ear. This close, it smelled like fetid meat.

"What do we do?" Valia asked. Kirin replied by lashing out with his whip, which raked across the creature's underbelly as it ascended from the dive.

"Its stomach is vulnerable," Kirin said. The creature circled up, moaning, its talons extending and retracting, and Kirin took the momentary respite to switch his dagger to his right hand and the whip to his left. Valia pricked her finger and pressed a drop of blood to her lumen ring. She held up her hand so Kirin could see what she was doing, and he nodded slightly.

The creature circled above them, its matted gray feathers catching in the sunlight, then dove again, swift and sure as any other bird of prey. Valia whispered a prayer to the Flora and light erupted in front of the creature's eyes, momentarily blinding it. She and Kirin dove out of its path as it landed and slid across the ground behind them.

Kirin flicked his whip, catching the creature around one leg and yanked. Moaning eerily, the creature jerked against the whip as Kirin pulled.

Valia could feel its heart pulsing and remembered the water she'd warmed while riding the day before. Valia had been hesitant to use it but now, with Kirin's life in danger, it was worth it to try. Taking a deep breath, she imagined the blood freezing in the creature's veins as she pressed a finger to her flux ring. Its movements slowed and relief warred with nausea in Valia's stomach.

Kirin still had the creature's leg in his whip. It flailed its wings erratically, struggling to move as its blood cooled. He dropped his whip and ran toward it with his dagger. Its talons raked wildly against the air and its wings beat frantically as Kirin stabbed and slashed at it. Finally, with one last great jerk, the creature toppled onto the ground and splayed in front of them, its wings unfurling as it convulsed. The fetid meat smell was stronger now.

Kirin and Valia stepped back to a safe distance as the creature finally stopped moving. Kirin's hands were covered in the creature's dark blood.

"What is that thing? I've never seen a bird like that." Valia asked. Kirin tugged his whip free of the creature's leg and stepped back, wiping the tip of the whip and his dagger against a clean part of his trousers in turn.

"It's called a fetterbeak. I know them well. They're native to Tromin. See the hole through its beak? That's how a rider restrains them."

Valia wiped sweat from her brow. "I don't like flying creatures."

"Neither do I. But this was a good thing."

"How, exactly?" Valia raised her eyebrows.

"Now I know who's pulling the strings. Remember that former friend I told you about?"

"Leander? Wait, you think—"

"He's here. If your brother is with Leander, he's more dangerous than we thought." Kirin looked toward the monastery.

"I still don't know what my brother is even capable of," Valia said as she stumbled toward Kirin. She began to feel faint and sat on the ground.

"Valia? Are you alright?" Kirin asked. She looked down at her body, checking for injuries.

"I think so. But... I don't... feel right." Kirin moved brisky toward her and caught her just as she fell to her side.

"Valia! You're burning up!" Kirin struggled to hold her as her skin scorched his arms.

"The water. Kirin... put me in... the water," Valia said through strained breaths.

Kirin swiftly picked Valia up and ran back to the stream where they had filled their waterskins. Steam rose from Valia's skin into the crisp air. Kirin quickly laid Valia in the stream with her body immersed in the water and her head on the bank. Valia rolled herself all the way in.

Through the water, Valia could see Kirin's concerned face above hers. She could hear him talking to her but couldn't make out the words. He reached a hand in to pull her head out, and she returned hers toward him as a signal to stop. He held her hand in his.

After a moment, Valia's mind returned, and she began to feel cool again. She popped up out of the water, taking a large breath.

"Valia?!" Kirin pulled her the rest of the way out of the water and wrapped his cloak around her. "Now you're cold again. What was that? What did you do?"

"I froze its blood."

"You froze its blood?! So, Flora decided to boil yours?"

"Not decided. That's just how it works, I think. I've never tried it before. Not like that." She pulled Kirin's cloak tight around herself and hugged her knees. Perhaps she'd stayed too long in the icy water.

"And what would have happened if we hadn't been near the water?"

"Luckily, we won't have to find out. I think I'm supposed to transfer the heat somewhere else when I use a spell like that. Lesson learned." She smiled at Kirin cheerfully and giggled. She was surprised with how calm she was after narrowly avoiding being boiled from the inside. Perhaps it was the only way for her to feel okay enough to push forward toward the monastery. Kirin let out an annoyed yet relieved sigh.

"This is why your powers concern me. It's reckless and un-predictable. I had the creature under control."

"We're so close to the monastery. I couldn't risk letting anything happen to you before we got there."

"And you almost sacrificed yourself to prevent that?"

"'Almost' doesn't mean anything. I'm not sacrificed. I'm still here. It's fine, and I've learned a valuable lesson. Like you said, this was a good thing. Kirin, listen. That creature. The hissing one."

"The snake?" Kirin narrowed his eyes.

"Right. The snake. Yes, I think I know it." Valia bit her lip. "This might sound silly, but my mother loved snakes. She thought they had a bad reputation that they didn't deserve. I think, maybe, somehow, my mother sent this snake to protect me."

"Valia." Kirin's expression was both sympathetic and skeptical. "You think your mother sent a *snake* to protect you?"

"I don't know." Valia bit her lip harder. "I know it doesn't make sense, but I have a feeling. Maybe, in her last moments, she was able to summon a power she didn't know she had. Or, maybe she did it before that day. I don't know."

"I suppose that's one explanation." Kirin nodded, but Valia was sure he still doubted that her mother could have sent the snake. It didn't matter. It comforted Valia to think that her mother had tried to protect her, even if it seemed far-fetched.

Kirin washed his hands in the water and stood. The giant bird's bloodstains were barely visible against the dark material of his shirt.

"So, is this why you wear black?" Valia asked, straightening up.

"What?" She pointed at his chest, and he looked at the blood. "Oh. Not really. More to... blend into the shadows." Kirin smirked at Valia, and she rolled her eyes. His expression turned somber as his gaze shifted to the mountains. They were well up the mountainside now, but the peaks still towered over them. The view might have been beautiful if it wasn't so stark. "Feeling better now?"

"Yes, I'm fine. This cloak of yours is quite heavy and warm."

A distant horn broke through the air in the foothills below them. Kirin's head quickly turned toward it. His eyes looked sharp like a hawk's looking for its source. He pointed down as Valia stood and looked with him.

"There. Looks like a hundred, maybe two. Your father's troops move quicker than I thought. They're not far behind." Valia grabbed Kirin's hand and pulled as she moved up the mountain.

"No, it's too soon. Come on, Kirin! We have to go. We don't have much time. We have to—"

"Valia, they're not far behind. They'll reach us by umbra. You've barely had time to rest after using your powers."

"I'm fine, Kirin. We're so close. We still have time." Valia tugged Kirin's hand again and he followed. "Hurry!"

Valia grabbed Kirin's hand, squeezing a little too hard, as they sprinted headlong up the mountain. Her heart raced and her mind spun. She had come so far to find her brother. Now, though, she would only have a short time to reach him before the Avanian forces arrived.

They ran so quickly that Valia was panting for breath before long. Even Kirin slowed a little as they passed scrubby coniferous trees and climbed steep, rocky sections. Valia's muscles screamed for her to pause, but she couldn't. Beside her, Kirin looked just as focused.

She wanted a moment with him. A moment to reflect on everything they'd overcome, to talk through the plan one more time, even to kiss him again... but there was no time for any of that now. Their few days of sparring, conversation, and last night's kiss would have to be enough.

Just as Valia's heart threatened to give out and her lungs could barely draw in enough air anymore, the path flattened out. They both stumbled to a stop as they scanned the clearing.

In the late morning light, the monastery looked barren. Wind whistled through the three modest stone buildings. A garden of overgrown vegetables stood on one side of the main temple. Tattered flags of threadbare fabric hung between the buildings. The ground was rocky and hard with little foliage nearby.

As Valia scanned her surroundings, she noticed one of the flags on the ground by her feet. She bent to pick it up.

"Free me from my sins," she read quietly. "Kirin, this place doesn't seem right."

"Looks abandoned." Kirin's expression was grim.

There were no signs of life between the dilapidated buildings. Even the vegetable garden, upon closer inspection, was comprised of overlarge green pumpkins tangled in sprawling, unkempt vines and heads of withered cabbage. It was possible no one had tended the garden in seasons—perhaps longer. There were no sounds of life, either.

Panic surged in Valia's chest.

"What if he isn't even here anymore?" she asked, her breath coming in quick gasps. "What if we came to the wrong place? What if he's already gone?"

"No, he's here." Kirin stared straight ahead at the building in front of them. "The snake."

Valia followed his gaze and saw the white snake slither into view in front of them and let out another low hiss. Kirin gave Valia a warning look and she nodded, tugging off her gloves and tucking them away as she walked. Wordlessly, they both understood that the snake was warning them of danger, and what greater danger could there be than Valia's brother and Kirin's friend-turned-enemy?

The temple was large and foreboding, with dark walls and a closed door. Taking a deep breath, Valia pushed open the door and stepped inside. It took a moment for her eyes to adjust to the relative darkness, but when she did, she let out a soft gasp. Behind her, Kirin reached protectively for her waist.

Inside the temple stood two men. One was tall and fair, with sand-colored hair and gray eyes that looked eerily reminiscent of Kirin's. He sat atop the altar at the front of the temple and reclined against the wall as he used a small, curved blade to cut and eat an apple. A wicked sword rested beside him, unsheathed and gleaming in the soft light from the windows high above. *This must be Leander*, Valia thought.

The other man stood behind him. Valia had never seen him before, but she would have recognized him anywhere. His hair was wavy and raven-dark, the same as her own. He had her blue eyes, though his had darkened to a deep, almost glowing color. Unlike the sandy-haired man, he was unarmed except for a long staff in his right hand. The staff appeared to be made of a polished gray stone.

This was Valia's brother, her twin, the remaining star on her family tree.

"Welcome!" Leander straightened himself, tossed the apple over his shoulder, and swept his arms wide in the gesture of a king inviting honored guests to his court. "We've been expecting you."

"Leander," Kirin said. His tone was low and calm, but Valia sensed something else bubbling beneath the surface.

"How nice that you've brought Kirin with you," Leander said. He sounded truly pleased, as though they were holding a wedding breakfast and Valia had invited an old friend as a surprise. "How have you been, old friend? How's your leg?"

"Friend?" Kirin growled. "Perhaps you've forgotten you tried to kill me?"

"Well, friends fight." Leander smiled, a white-toothed, too-wide smile. "Princess Valia Martev, perhaps you'd like to meet your brother. You've come all this way, after all. This is Niko. My right hand. My most trusted. He's been helping restore balance to this backward kingdom for quite some time." Leander gestured to the man who Valia knew to be her twin. Niko still hadn't moved from his standing position behind the altar. His face was impassive, expressionless. "I suppose he would normally be a Martev, but since he was abandoned at birth..." Leander shrugged and raised his eyebrows expressively. "Given away to this very place, if I'm correct. Oh, and Kirin, you've already met."

"Niko... the boy from Norhglenn?" Kirin looked at Valia with a confused face and shook his head.

"Niko?" Valia took a step forward. "I'm sorry we're only meeting like this, but I am glad to meet you. If you'll just let me explain..." Her voice shook. She was scared to meet this man, a stranger with her eyes who'd caused unknown pain and suffering.

"Pretty words. But they're just words, aren't they, Niko?" Leander stepped closer to Valia and Kirin. Kirin gently nudged Valia back with his hand at her waist. "Niko, this is your sister, Princess

Valia Martev. She grew up in the palace, surrounded by loving family, her powers nurtured and celebrated from a young age, her destiny always clear. Never caring who she hurt." Every moment Leander continued his speech was another moment the Avanians marched closer. They were running out of time.

"Niko—" Valia began again, but Leander held up a hand.

"Floramancers. They're all the same. Kirin would have said the same not long ago, but I see he's fallen under the Flora's spell at the first sight of a pretty girl. A pity, truly. We could have accomplished so much together."

"Leander, you always did enjoy the sound of your own voice." Kirin's words were sharp. "We're here to speak with him, not you."

"Oh, I'm sure. You'd like to get him alone, whisper some insidious lies into his ear, perhaps? I'm sorry, but I'm the closest thing this poor boy has to family, and I won't leave him defenseless."

"How did you even know we were coming here?" Valia asked. Her eyes remained on Niko, who stood motionless behind Leander.

"Oh, I'm glad you asked. It wasn't hard. I understand you've been using blood magic to track Niko. Easy enough to block, once we knew to watch for it. And even easier to get you to leave the safety of Avania by letting you get a glimpse of him here, once everything was in place. Perhaps you forgot that Niko is also your brother, and your Flora runs through him too, to say the least. Now, the most interesting part is that he was able to track Kirin, too, once you were closer. Isn't that strange, Kirin? What exactly have you been up to, old friend?"

"Niko, please." Valia stepped closer again. "Let me talk to you. I know that the way our family, our kingdom, has treated you is unforgivable, but this doesn't have to be the end of our story. Let's just talk. Just us. We're family."

"Leander," Niko said in a low voice. Valia was almost startled to hear him speak, after his silence. "What if—"

"Niko, my boy." Leander turned toward him. "What can this woman, connected to you by little more than your unclean blood, have to say that I haven't already—"

In that moment, Kirin struck while Leander was turned. He threw his dagger, quick and true, directly at him. Valia saw Niko's deep blue eyes widen and his grip tighten on his staff. The dagger shattered in midair with a cascade of green sparks. Shards fell to the ground at Leander's feet before melting into the stone floor. Valia's stomach dropped. If there had ever been a chance to talk, it was gone now.

"A dagger from home, Kirin? How special. Do you see, Niko?" Leander said, turning slowly back toward Valia and Kirin. "They would rather kill us than talk. And even if Valia here *does* want to speak to you, it's only because she has one question to ask. She wants to know if you killed her mother and sisters. Isn't that right, Valia?"

Valia didn't reply. Whatever she said would just be spun by this silver-tongued man into something completely different from what she intended.

"Well, let me clear things up for you. We aren't the only ones in the world who have woken up to the dangers of your family. Unfortunately, we didn't have the pleasure of eliminating them ourselves, but we're glad they're gone. Niko knows better than anyone the curse your family has put on the land by inviting your 'Flora.' And he knows the rest of your family needs to be stopped before you curse the whole world."

Valia raised her hands, fingers spread. She pressed a bloodied finger to her link ring, and sent a single word, *listen*, toward her brother, but it was as though she encountered a stinging wall of ice that rejected the message. She couldn't get through to him, but she couldn't give up, either. No matter what he'd done, he was her brother. He deserved the chance to hear the truth and to speak his own. Especially knowing he didn't have a hand in killing their family, at least directly.

"Well, time's up. Niko, you know what must be done." With that, Leander stepped back into the shadows and Niko prowled forward, his eyes locked on Valia. Beside her, Kirin unfurled his whip behind them.

"Don't," Valia hissed. "He's like the bear. He doesn't know any different."

"I know more than you! And I wish I didn't share your blood." His emotionless face turned into one displaying such malice and hatred toward Valia that her breath caught in her throat. "Leander told me everything. You knew I existed. You and... *your* family have tried to have me killed, ever since I discovered I was in control of what's in me."

"No!" Valia shook her head. "I swear it. I didn't know you *existed* until just before coming here. To talk to you. I've never sent anything or anyone to kill you."

"Then you are naive, twin sister, and even more the threat for it." Niko paced along the floor in front of them. "Leander showed me. He proved it by forcing those men to tell the truth after all their lies. Those *Avanians*, sent by the king himself. Leander protected me and gave me a family. He came for me when no one else did. When I was the only one left."

"What do you mean, the only one left?" Valia asked.

"Enough talking!" Leander snapped, despite having done most of it. "There's only one way this ends."

With that, Niko brought his staff down against the floor. There was a crackle of energy and a spark of green light as the bottom of the staff struck, then the stone floor cracked and rippled, knocking Valia and Kirin down. Valia fell hard onto her back, then scrambled to her feet and raised her hands, fingers still spread. Kirin rolled to his feet beside her, whip in hand, but he still didn't attack Niko. Leander had used the opportunity to disappear; he was no longer standing beside Niko.

"Niko, please! Let's talk."

"We have nothing to talk about."

"Please, Niko!"

Niko raised his staff. Kirin stepped forward and shifted his whip to his right hand.

"I'm sorry, Valia. I can't let this happen." He struck with his whip at Niko, who lunged away from the strike and threw a bolt of crackling green energy toward Kirin from his staff.

Kirin rolled out of the way as Valia brought her hands into a casting position behind her back, tears filling her eyes. It had all come to this. Clearly, her brother was no more than a puppet to Leander, but she couldn't let him kill Kirin. And even if Niko was a puppet, his power had undoubtedly hurt people. She needed to subdue him, or she'd never get a chance to talk to him.

The temple doors slammed shut behind them. Leander crept through the building, preventing their movements and possibility of escape.

Niko struck with another bolt, this time at Valia, who redirected it with a push of force. She reached for the garden outside, where the thick tangle of vines and pumpkins grew, and pulled on her power. Two vines burst through the stone wall of the temple, showering rocks across the room, and struck at Niko with the speed and precision of vipers. Niko whirled his staff at the vines, green energy sparking, and they withered in each place the staff touched, flinching back like hands from a hot stove.

Kirin took advantage of Niko's distraction to strike. His whip wrapped around the tip of Niko's staff and pulled him off balance, but Niko caught himself and sent a crackling burst of energy down the length of the whip. Kirin let go of the handle as the energy discharged in front of him, then caught the whip with the other hand. In a less dire situation, Valia might have had the capacity to be impressed. This clearly wasn't the first time Kirin had fought a metemancer.

Kirin retracted the whip and struck again as Valia wound the vines around Niko's feet. For a moment, it seemed they had the advantage, but Niko freed himself of the whip and the vines and taken a huge leap toward her, his staff raised. Valia dove out of the way, her knees scraping painfully against the stone floor.

Leander finally made his move from the shadows. His sword came slashing through the air, straight toward Kirin. Kirin dodged to the side and kicked Leander's knee, causing him to drop halfway to the floor. Kirin grabbed him by the neck, slamming him the rest of the way down onto his back. Kirin quickly wrapped his whip around Leander's neck, pinning him down with the weight of his knee.

Niko blasted a large rock at Kirin—one of the ones that had broken from the wall when the vines punched through. Smaller stones and pebbles struck Kirin, knocking him down beside Leander. Leander seized the opportunity to roll away and pick up his blade.

Valia reached for her vines again, but they had become charred and lifeless. Her head pounded and her body ached. Her energy was nearly depleted.

Kirin stood up, bruised and bloody, and placed himself in front of Valia. He steadied himself and stared them down, slowly repositioning himself and Valia as Leander slowly moved around their side.

It had all been a trap. Valia saw that now. They'd seen her coming, and Leander had recognized an opportunity to finally dispatch both Valia and Kirin in one fell swoop. There was no reasoning with this man, and Niko was too far under his spell. As long as things were like this, Niko could never hear her.

Valia couldn't help Niko. She couldn't save him, not with Leander whispering in his ear. But maybe if Leander were gone, she and Kirin could get through to him. Tears formed in her eyes as she spun her rings and searched for a spell—the kind to end a life. Leander was a bad man. He'd hurt Kirin. He'd manipulated Niko. He'd been a part of her family's deaths, directly or not. But still, Valia didn't want to take his life. If she believed Niko could be redeemed—and if *Kirin* could be redeemed—surely Leander could be too. But she saw no other way.

Just as she was gathering the power of the Flora to herself, choking on the words of a spell she never wanted to utter, a sound rang out: the long, mournful call of a horn, followed by the light from the windows above fading away. Umbra had set in, and with it, came the Avanian army. Everyone in the temple froze.

They were out of time.

Leander seemed to realize that, too. He stepped back, sheathed his sword, and dusted off his trousers.

"It was a pleasure meeting you both. I can't imagine we'll have another opportunity. Niko, enough toying around. Kill them all and return to Grenhold. Give me a hundred paces or so before you..." he gestured strangely and nodded his head.

Leander turned on his heel and hurried out the back entrance as though he were late for an important ball rather than fleeing combat. Valia's mouth dropped open, the remnants of the spell she'd been gathering fading and dispersing in the air. Her eyes lifted to Niko's. He stared at her, then glanced over his shoulder.

This was their chance. Niko might listen to her now, with his puppeteer gone. Even if they had only a moment, she could use it.

"Niko," Valia said. She raised her hands, clasped into fists to show that she wasn't going to cast anything. "Let's run. Away from father's army. I won't let them hurt you. I'll protect you from them."

"They can't hurt me," Niko said, expressionless.

"Valia." Kirin moved back toward her, his eyes never leaving Niko. "They're already here. As soon as umbra breaks, they'll move in."

He was right. From behind them came the rumble of the army's drum and, in the distance, the sound of voices. They had only moments before the army was here—and those soldiers weren't going to want to talk. They would find the metemancer suspected of killing the queen and princesses, and they would kill him or die trying.

"Niko, I'm so sorry," Valia said, her words choking in her throat. "I can't undo what happened to you. I wish I could."

Niko stood in front of them, his staff in his hand. "I'm sorry too, sister. But it's not about that. You have to die. If only we were exiled together, we might have had a chance to know one another." He stared into Valia's eyes, pausing for a moment as if committing her image into his memory. A hint of sadness appeared on his face as he looked more like a lost child than a fearsome metemancer. For a moment, it was all too easy to imagine him as a boy of eight, as he'd been in Valia's dream. "Leander gave me clarity. He needs me to kill you and everyone else infected by the Flora." He raised his staff, and it began to glow with a faint green light across its entire surface.

"Leander left you, boy!" Kirin snapped. "What do *you* need? Not Leander. *You!*" He turned to Valia, his tone turning gentler. "Call on the Flora. Whatever you have to do. I wish I could undo what's been done to him too, but right now it's him or us. It's time for *you* to choose, Valia."

"I..." Valia twisted her rings, but her hands were shaking, and her stomach hurt. She tried to gather a spell, but when she reached for the Flora, a hard, metallic-tasting wave of sickness pushed her back. Whether she had overreached when she'd tried to kill Leander or she was simply exhausted, she wasn't sure. "I don't know if I can."

"You can." Kirin's voice was steady. "We can. Together. No other options." He held out his hands, and Valia's heart almost broke at the way he was so willing to use floramancy in this moment, even though he hated it, even though it was probably too late. If they still lived after today, she would never forget his trust.

They clasped their hands and Valia lifted her head toward the temple's high windows, still covered in darkness. *Please,* she begged silently. *I don't want him to die. We need more time. We need to know if he can be saved. We need to know his past, his life, everything that led up to this point. We need to know what he's done. We need to understand him.* The green glow increased in intensity, fully illuminating the temple through the darkness of umbra.

Even though Valia hadn't pricked her finger, power began to gather around them. It was gentle, at first, like ocean waves lapping along the shore. Then the power built inside Valia until she was almost trembling from its weight. She met Kirin's eyes, still holding his hands like a lifeline, and saw that he was shaking, too. Valia's throat burned, and she felt on the verge of losing consciousness. Still, the power gathered, stronger than any spell Valia had ever cast. It was no longer a gentle ocean. It was a raging tsunami.

And then Niko cried out. Valia managed to turn her head toward him, though it was like moving through chilled sap, and saw that he'd fallen to his knees on the hard stone floor, his staff lying next to him. He shook uncontrollably, and when he looked up at her, his eyes were wide with fear. He was... changing.

It was then that Valia realized her mistake. She'd cast something beyond her knowledge in a time when she was emotional and unclear about her intentions. Worse than that, Kirin was involved, and intentions would be harder to align between two casters.

"Stop!" she tried to shout, but her throat burned so much that she could barely get the word out. She tried to pull her hands from

Kirin's, but he held her firmly. Kirin's eyes began to glow, and Valia was horrified to see that a peaceful smile had replaced his earlier intensity. Something was flowing into him. Something intangible, like sunlight in another form.

"Stop!" she tried again, but she couldn't. A loud whistling built in her ears as power surged through her, as Niko convulsed, as Kirin smiled. There was no stopping this now.

And then, with a great whoosh of power, the Flora left. Kirin slumped to the side, and Valia quickly softened his fall. Light returned through windows above. Umbra had passed, and the Avanians would soon be upon them.

"Kirin?" Her throat burned, and his name came out raspy. She turned him onto his back. "Kirin?"

"I'm... free..." His eyes fluttered open, and he smiled warmly at her. He lifted one hand to Valia's cheek. "It's okay, Valia. This is my penance, for all I've done."

"Penance? What are you talking about?" Tears threatened to fall again. "Kirin?!"

"Hello?" a soft voice called out. Valia turned toward the sound, and her breath hitched when she saw... *Niko?* In his place sat an adolescent boy with the same wavy dark hair. His eyes were blue, too, but they were lighter—more like Valia's. His face was streaked with something that looked like ash, and his hair was mussed, but he looked unhurt. The staff rested on the ground beside him, broken in two.

The man they'd been fighting, her twin, was just a boy now.

"N... Niko?" Valia asked. The boy rubbed his eyes as he nodded.

"Who are you?" he asked.

Just then, with a loud crash, the door of the temple flung open. Sunlight spilled in through the temple doors as the first Avanian soldiers poured in.

CHAPTER TWENTY-EIGHT
PEACE

ithin moments, the temple was filled with soldiers. They fanned out to the sides, gazes sweeping across the rubble and debris. Most held swords at the ready, while a couple raised their hands, ready to call on the Flora.

"Princess?"

Valia tore her gaze away from the little boy who must be Niko to see Lord Captain Poriev standing over her. He looked tired and worn from the long march here, but he stood as tall and imposing as ever. Seeing him in this strange place, so far from home, made her head spin. Or perhaps that was still the aftereffects of the spell.

"Lord Captain Poriev?" Valia managed to push herself onto her feet, though she swayed dangerously. Poriev steadied her with a hand on her elbow, as he had so many times.

"Princess Valia! Are you hurt?" he asked.

"No. I'm happy to see you, Poriev. It makes sense father would send you. And no wonder you all arrived so quickly—you've been here before." Poriev looked at Valia with a mix of guilt and sympathy, realizing she knew he had brought the newborn Niko here.

Another soldier pulled Kirin roughly to his feet, and Valia went to him. If she was this drained, Kirin must be feeling twice as badly.

"Let him go," she said, already reaching for her power to compel the soldier. Instead of the warm rush of the Flora, though, a sharp pain shot through her head, and she let go of the attempted spell. "He's been protecting me. He's the only reason I've survived this long."

Poriev gestured to the guard who'd been holding Kirin's arm, and the guard let him go. Valia rushed to his side, sure that he would be feeling as woozy and achy as she was—or worse, after such a major spell—but he stood steadily. Instead, it was her who fell into his side, and him who held her up. Valia looked up at him in search of reassurance, and he smiled at her with a warm confidence she'd never seen before. Despite the ruined temple packed with Avanian soldiers and the mess of the spell they'd just cast, he looked... at peace. Valia pulled her gaze away, more concerned than comforted.

"And who is this?" a soldier carrying floramantic amulets asked as he helped Niko to his feet. The young boy looked bewildered and near tears. Valia's heart went out to him; he'd genuinely seemed not to recognize her. It seemed the spell they'd cast had not only put Niko in the body of a child but turned his mind to a child's as well.

Kirin's steady gaze swept from the soldier to Poriev and back. "He's an orphan, a farmer's son, perhaps, who happened to be in the wrong place at the wrong time."

It didn't seem plausible at all, but the soldier who'd helped Niko to his feet just shrugged and turned to continue searching the temple. Valia's brow furrowed.

"Where's the... where is he?" Poriev asked. When he turned back toward Valia, she could see pain behind his eyes.

"He's gone. He's dead," Valia said. Her voice shook from the force of the spell, but she didn't hesitate in her lie. "We killed him."

"You killed him? Here? Where's the body?" the captain asked, his eyes narrowing.

"He had an accomplice," Kirin filled in. "A man named Leander. He took the body."

The story was shaky, and they both knew it. Poriev must have wanted to believe it, because as Kirin spoke, he nodded and the tension around his eyes relaxed.

"Very well," he said. "I will inform the king at once."

Just then, another soldier flew in. She looked young and scared, her blonde hair plastered to her forehead, and her uniform a little too large.

"Kanaleans, in the peaks!" she panted, her breath uneven. "They're surrounding us."

Poriev swore under his breath and turned to Valia.

"Princess, you must return to Wyra. I'll send a squadron with you—"

"No." Valia shook her head. "You need all your men to face the Kanaleans, and Kirin has protected me all this time. We can slip out, quietly, just the three of us."

"The three of you?"

"Yes. We'll take the boy, too," Valia said. "We'll try to… reunite him with family."

Poriev looked deeply skeptical. "You'd travel faster without the boy…"

"The boy is not safe here. He's an Avanian. All will be well," Kirin said.

Poriev nodded. "You're right, of course."

Valia's brow furrowed again. Poriev seemed skeptical when she spoke, but the moment Kirin opened his mouth, he agreed. It was strange. Kirin had never been this convincing before, especially toward a man like Poriev, but there was no time to question it. They could already hear a faint whistling sound coming from outside. Whistles were the preferred communication method of Kanalean forces, who often fought in forests and on mountainsides where visibility wasn't good and covert communication was key.

"Then go." Poriev turned to Kirin. "Keep her safe."

"I will." Kirin turned to Niko. "Come on."

Still looking uncertain, the boy crossed to them. Valia took Niko's hand, and Kirin led the way to the door.

"Wait!" Valia stopped and bent down with some difficulty to pick up Kirin's whip, which was still lying on the ground near where he'd slumped after the spell. "Don't you need this?" She held it out to him, her hand shaking from the effort.

"Not anymore," Kirin said, and he smiled.

"What..." Valia cut herself off. Something wasn't right with him, but arguing about it in front of Poriev and the Avanian forces while the Kanaleans closed in was unwise.

Valia let the whip fall and followed Kirin out into the cool mountain air. Avanian troops stood in a square formation in the flat area in front of the monastery, their eyes trained on the mountain-tops, their hands resting on their weapons. Valia and Kirin hurried past them, Valia still holding Niko's hand. She couldn't quite process the fact that she was holding hands with her twin and that he was now a child. She didn't even know how she and Kirin had done this. In her mind, she kept waiting to wake up and realize it had all been a vivid dream, but no such awakening came for her.

"Not the path," Kirin said. "They'll be watching."

"Where do we go, then?" Panic surged in Valia, tightening her chest. The area around the path was rocky and barren, and they would be easy to spot anywhere from the peaks above.

"There. Up." Kirin turned and scanned the nearest slope. Above them was a grove of trees, and Kirin began to climb toward it. His strides were long and athletic, as though he'd just awoken from a long and restful sleep instead of fighting two men and passing out while casting a floramantic spell.

"Up," Valia repeated. "Where the Kanaleans are? Kirin, that's a terrible idea."

But he was already halfway up the slope, so Valia had no choice but to follow. She gently tugged Niko's hand and led him after Kirin.

"Where are we going?" Niko asked. His small voice broke as he looked up at her plaintively with his big blue eyes. They were bright now, the same color as Valia's own, instead of the dark blue of magic. "Who are you? Where's Father Rhyse?"

Valia stopped and dropped to her knees beside him. "I'm your sister," she said. "We're family. I'm taking you home. Will you follow me?"

"My sister?" Niko nodded bravely. "Okay."

They began to climb again. Kirin was the first into the trees, but he stopped and turned back to make sure they made it safely. He led them along the tree line. The ground began to slope downward, and, for a short while, everything was quiet. Valia could almost hear her heart racing.

Then, a loud whistle cut through the air. It was matched by another whistle from somewhere behind them, then a third from downslope. Valia's blood froze in her veins, and she let go of Niko's hand to spin her rings around her fingers. Despite her exhaustion, despite the fear of the Flora that had been growing within her since the out-of-control spell, Valia needed to stop these men. Kirin was unarmed and delirious, and Niko was just a child. She was the only one who could save them. If she had any power left, she needed to find it now.

The whistling grew louder, then men stepped out of the trees around them, wearing masks and wrapped in heavy fur cloaks. There were... Valia counted quickly, her chest tight... eight of them. Too many for her to fight on her own.

Was this it? Truly? After all they'd been through, after finding Niko, were they really going to be captured or killed by Kanalean forces?

No. Valia lifted her hands. She would fight until the end. Taking a deep breath, she sought out Kirin, hoping for one last moment for their eyes to meet so she could silently thank him for all he'd done for her.

When she met Kirin's eyes, though, he didn't look determined or scared or any other way she might have expected. He reached for her hand, and his touch was as warm and reassuring as always.

"Come," he said. He led them through the Kanaleans as if they weren't even there. Valia's eyes darted back and forth between them, anticipating them to strike at any moment. Instead, they stood like pale-faced statues. Statues, if not for their eyes following them as they passed.

She shook her head. "Kirin? What was that?" She picked up her pace to put more distance between them and the Kanaleans. "Do you know them?"

"In some sense." Kirin turned to Niko, who was standing with his mouth open and fear written all over his young face. "We're safe. Niko, I'm sure we can find you some blueberry ranoli once we get back to Wyra. That would be nice, wouldn't it?"

"Blueberry ranoli?" Niko's eyes lit up at the mention of the sticky-sweet fruit candy, his fear seemingly forgotten. "That's my favorite."

"Yes." Kirin smiled again. He released Valia's hand and led a path out of the clearing. Niko followed, clearly excited for his ranoli, and

Valia took up the last position. Her heart was still hammering and her chest still felt tight.

They raced down the mountain, sticking to areas with trees and foliage. To Valia's relief, they didn't meet any more Kanaleans, but it was a narrow comfort. There was still too much unknown. Niko stumbled a few times on the roots and rocks, but Valia held his hand and whispered encouragement to him, and he kept going.

Soon, they reached the horses. They had wandered a bit from where they left them, but Kirin had easily found them. Unicorn and Bird were grazing on scrubby grasses, looking as relaxed as though they were standing in the palace stables. Niko excitedly requested to ride Unicorn, never having seen a horse so large before. Kirin helped Niko onto Unicorn's back, but before he could mount, Valia grabbed his hand.

"Kirin," she said, and he looked back at her. Were there flecks of blue in his steely gray eyes now? Valia blinked and looked again, and confirmed his eyes were still as gray as ever.

"It's okay, Valia," Kirin said softly. He led her away from the horses and Niko, who was currently stroking Unicorn's mane.

"What happened?" she asked, her voice catching in her throat, unsure exactly how to ask all the questions she now had.

"We asked for more time," Kirin said, "and we got it." He nodded to Niko. "He's a boy again. He has a chance to grow up again, differently this time. He has no memory of what happened or what he did. We have a chance to give him the life he should have had. And we can give your father a chance to make a better choice."

"I understand that," Valia said, with a hint of exasperation now. "Somehow, maybe because we were thinking about buying more time or erasing what had happened or about how Niko was as a child, we turned back time for him. But did something happen to you?"

"He doesn't remember anything anymore," Kirin repeated,

looking past Valia at the young boy. "Because I do. I remember it for him. I have all his memories, the ones he's lost. All his pain, all his suffering. Everything he's done to others. He gets to start over, and I'll carry these things for him."

Valia's jaw dropped. That was why Kirin had been acting so strangely, why he'd spoken of penance and why he seemed so calm: he had taken on Niko's burdens.

"No. What?" Valia shook his head and reached for his hands. "You can't. That's too much. Kirin, am I dreaming?"

"No," Kirin echoed. He smiled at her with that confident, peaceful smile he'd worn as Niko's memories flowed into him. "It isn't too much. My own burdens are not so different. This is a penance for me. A way to make up for what I've done wrong. It's going to be okay."

Then he leaned forward and kissed Valia. His lips brushed hers for only a few heartbeats, but warmth spread from Valia's lips through her limbs and down into her toes. Peace settled over her. Kirin was right. As long as they were together, everything would be okay. Even if Kirin had Niko's memories, he was still himself. They were all alive, and that was all that mattered.

Her worries floated away like dead leaves in a strong wind as Kirin smiled down at her.

CHAPTER TWENTY-NINE
RETURN

he journey back to Wyra was long but uneventful. Whether by luck or by peace returning to Avania, Valia even considered it a pleasant journey, with the people along the way being unusually kind and friendly. The trio rode all day and slept at inns now that Kirin was no longer concerned about potential threats. They bought blueberry ranoli for Niko. They told him a little about the kingdom, enough that he wouldn't be confused when they returned to the palace, but they didn't tell him anything of what happened.

At night, after Niko was asleep, Kirin and Valia would sit in the inn's common hall to talk, or outside to watch the stars. There was something different about Kirin now that he was carrying Niko's memories, but he was still the same man whose arms Valia had fallen asleep in, who'd saved her when no one else could, and who'd laughed with her until their stomachs hurt.

One evening, when Valia took her turn to bathe, she didn't put her rings back on after getting out of the water. Instead, she slipped them into a small pouch and tucked them away in a pocket of her saddle bag. She didn't know if she could trust the Flora again. Not yet. Not now. What had always been a comforting presence in her life now felt strange, and she wasn't ready to face that yet. Maybe, eventually, she would come to terms with the way the Flora interpreted her spell, but for now, she would take a step back. There was no way to take the Flora out of her veins, but she could avoid calling on it for now.

Kirin noticed that she wasn't wearing her rings, but he didn't say anything. He just pressed a kiss to her bare knuckles and gently said, "Have no fear. All will be well."

After days of riding, Valia started to recognize the landmarks of Wyra again. There were the same large farms of corn or wheat. The crops looked healthier, now, though perhaps she was imagining things. Soon, the buildings grew closer together, and the palace came into view. Valia was tempted to stop and fix her hair, perhaps find a dress to wear, but she shook off the urge. She would arrive in the palace as herself, both a princess and a warrior.

They rode straight in through the palace gates. One young guard almost tried to stop them, but when Valia smiled down at him, his eyes widened, and he stepped aside. This time, the king didn't come down to greet them, as he had when Valia was rescued from the draevori. Instead, Valia climbed the stairs to his chancery, accompanied by Kirin on one side and Niko on the other.

"You're back, I see." King Aran's voice cracked slightly as he stood, circled the desk, and came to Valia. This time, he didn't hug her. Things were different between them, and Valia felt more like a princess addressing a king than a young girl addressing her father. "You're well."

"I am," Valia said.

"Poriev sent word by wing that you were successful but surrounded by Kanaleans." King Aran cleared his throat. "His reports have gone silent since then, so..." He finally tore his eyes away from Valia and turned to Kirin. "I suppose I have you to thank for saving my daughter, yet again."

Kirin shook his head. "We saved each other, Your Majesty."

"Well, I am... grateful." It sounded as though the last word were difficult to speak. King Aran's gaze was fixed on Kirin, and there was something in his expression that Valia couldn't place. It wasn't the same distrust as before, but it wasn't gratitude, either. "I owe you a great debt. Coin or land? What shall it be?"

Valia and Kirin had talked about this, during those long nights while Niko slept, and Kirin answered as they'd planned.

"I'd like to stay here and offer my services to the palace," Kirin said. "I believe I may still be needed."

King Aran paused to consider and looked at Kirin suspiciously. Then, his face softened, and he nodded slowly. "Perhaps it is better to keep you close. Very well. You've kept my daughter alive on more than one occasion. I grant you the position of personal guard to the princess. You may choose your own quarters. I expect full co-operation with Poriev once he returns as you get acquainted with our ways."

"Thank you, Your Majesty. It's an honor to be joining Palace Annulus." Kirin made a polite facsimile of a bow, which looked very out of place on him, then stepped back behind Valia's right shoulder. Finally, Aran turned to Niko, who had been looking at the floor and tossing a small gray stone back and forth between his hands.

"And... who is the boy?" he asked.

Valia placed a hand on Niko's shoulder. She'd grown protective of him during their days of travel, and her chest was tight at the thought of what might come next.

"Father, meet Niko Martev," she said. "Your son."

King Aran sat back, and for a long moment, he didn't speak. His brow was narrowed, his hands steepled. He didn't look particularly surprised or concerned.

"Valia," he said at last. "What cruel joke is this? I received word he was..." Aran trailed off, reserving his words as to not upset the child. "He would be the same age as you, dearest, not a child. You must be mistaken." His tone was kind but condescending, the same as it had been when a young Valia had worried that a fallow might be lurking beneath her bed.

Valia squeezed Niko's shoulders reassuringly. "Father, look at him. Just look at him."

"I have no need—" King Aran began, but Kirin cleared his throat.

"Take a look, Your Majesty," Kirin said. "This child is not the one you feared. He knows nothing. He is a second chance."

Without further hesitation, King Aran leaned forward and swept his gaze over Niko. Valia knew what he was seeing: a boy with pale skin, bright blue eyes, wavy, dark hair, and long, slim limbs. The spitting image of Valia's paintings from her adolescence, just with shorter hair.

King Aran drew in a long, slow breath. Then, to Valia's shock, a tear spilled down one of his cheeks. She had never seen her father cry before. It was like umbra coming at the wrong time or water flowing backward. Her father stood and walked around the desk. He came to kneel in front of Niko.

"My son?" Aran put his hands on Niko's shoulders and looked in his eyes.

"Yes," Valia said.

"Hello, Niko," King Aran said to the small boy. His voice came out as a croak. "I don't understand it. But I know it's true."

Niko looked up, his eyes wide. He knew he was meeting his father—Valia had told him that much—and he seemed nervous. "Hello, Your Majesty," he said, imitating Kirin's mannerisms.

King Aran drew another deep breath and stood. He turned his gaze to Valia.

"The... man... who killed your sisters and mother..."

Valia understood what he was trying to say. He was posing the question that had rattled around Valia's mind at first, too. The question of how to accept the man who'd killed their family into their home, even though Niko was only a remnant of that man. Even though Niko was a child with no memory of what his older self had done. Even though this child was innocent, far more innocent than Valia.

She met her father's eyes and shook her head. "This boy knows nothing of that."

"Yes. Yes." King Aran rubbed at his brow.

"You can't change what happened to them," Valia said. "But you can have a second chance with your son. A chance to do things better. A chance to teach him to be a good man."

"We have much to discuss, Valia. No... all of us, together. No more secrets. Oh, what will we tell the people?"

Aran looked back at the portrait of Queen Ellara that hung behind his desk. In it, she smiled back at him with that serene smile of hers, frozen forever in time. Her necklace shone from the hollow of her collarbone and her painted eyes were watchful.

"Oh..." He took a sharp breath. "If only she were here now. She wished for this. To have him back," the king said. Then he looked back down at Niko. "Welcome to Wyra, Prince Niko. You're home now."

The little boy looked up at him, his brow furrowed, as though he hadn't quite followed the conversation that had led to this point. Valia couldn't blame him. Neither she nor Kirin had been able to bring themselves to tell him of his past, so he still didn't know what he had done. Or what a *version* of himself had done. He only knew that his father was a king. A king who was now welcoming him home.

"Thank you," Niko said in a small voice.

"Crown Princess Valia," Aran said. "Kirin Adante. You have both done well. I honor you for your service to the kingdom of Avania. Thank you. You may go, for now. I would like to get to know the young prince."

Kirin made for the door, but Valia hesitated. It felt strange to leave her brother now. After all, her father had already banished the boy once when he was only an infant. What if her father didn't believe Niko was innocent or that he remembered nothing? But nothing about this situation was normal. It was still strange to know she had a brother at all. She would have to learn to navigate it all.

Kirin took her hand, giving it a gentle squeeze. "All is well, Valia."

So, taking a deep breath, Valia left the king and prince of Avania alone and followed Kirin out of the room.

are to give me a tour of the palace?" Kirin suggested. "I suppose this is my home now, too." His tone had changed from the comforting one into his usual brisk but kind tone. "You can tell me all about how a princess grows up in a place like this."

Valia managed a smile. At least he was talking normally again. "The minstrels will sing songs about my palace upbringing, I'm sure. There was one thing I wanted to show you, though. Follow me."

She took the lead now, bringing Kirin down a flight of stone steps and along a chill hallway to the royal receiving room. The room was dimly lit and smelled faintly of old stone and wood. A little late-day sunlight streamed through the windows, casting long shadows from the thrones at the end of the hallway. Valia instinctively reached to prick her finger to light the candles along the walls but aborted the movement in the middle. She didn't wear her rings anymore, so if she wanted light, she'd have to do it herself.

Valia took a torch from the wall and led Kirin along the side of the hall. This was where portraits of all Avania's rulers hung, from the First King to Valia's family. The very last portrait showed Valia, her sisters, and her parents standing together when Valia had been a girl of ten cycles with a gap in her teeth and unruly curls. It was a magically enhanced painting and so realistic that Valia almost felt she could reach back through time and touch her mother's cheek once more.

"See?" she said, pushing through the pang of loss that jutted into her heart at the sight of her family all together, unaware of what was to come. "Look at my mother."

Kirin came closer, and Valia held up the torch so he could see. Then he nodded.

"The necklace, right? And the snake."

"Exactly."

Queen Ellara wore her favorite necklace, the one she had in every painting, which was set with a dark stone. Twined around her feet was a small white snake, much like the one Valia had seen at the monastery.

"Did she really pose for a family portrait with a snake?" Kirin asked.

"I don't know." Valia smiled. "I don't think so. But she did like them. I'd often find her in the garden with a snake in her lap, petting it. And that necklace... it looks almost like metemantic stone, doesn't it?"

"Maybe you're right," Kirin said. He smiled at her. "I suppose we can ask her."

"Ask her?" Valia's stomach clenched, and tears pricked at her eyes. "Kirin, don't you remember? She's... dead. She and my sisters."

"I remember." Kirin looked away. "I must have been mistaken. There are so many memories in my head now. Mine, Niko's... they all blur together."

"I suppose so." Valia looked down, away from her mother's smiling face. The mysteries of the snake and her mother's necklace remained, but they weren't important now. "What's it like, carrying Niko's memories?"

"That's a difficult question." Kirin took her hand and led her to the door at the back of the room. It opened onto the gardens, though Valia wasn't sure how he'd known that. It wouldn't have been part of either his or Niko's memories, though perhaps he'd just spotted it from across the room and guessed. The door had been built as an escape route for the royal family, should trouble find them here. They stepped out into the chill evening air, leaving the torch on a sconce inside, and Kirin took a deep breath.

"Well, try to answer," Valia prodded. She smiled. "It's been a long time since I pushed you to talk."

Kirin smiled back down at her. "I suppose it has." They crossed the garden and sat on a low stone bench. In the summer, roses bloomed on a trellis overhead, but now, at the end of autumn, the trellis was bare. Darkness was setting in, the sky already fading to a deep purple, and a shiver ran through Valia. Kirin put his arm around her and drew her closer to share his warmth.

"The memories, his memories, don't feel the same as my own," Kirin said after a while. "They're almost like a dream. They feel real, but not real at the same time. I know how he felt, how scared and lonely he often was, but they're shadows of feelings, like trying to remember a nightmare after you wake up."

"Scared and lonely." Valia took a breath and let it out. "I don't like to imagine him feeling that way. And I don't like to think of you having to carry that either." Her heart twisted, and she wondered, not for the first time, why the Flora had given Niko's memories to Kirin. Had she been too weak to take them? Had Kirin asked to be the one to make the sacrifice? She wondered, too, if the memories really were the whole price of what they'd done. It had been an enormous spell; it would be considered a leaf spell by the court's floramancers, no doubt. Taking the burden of Niko's memories, while certainly difficult, didn't seem like a high enough sacrifice. Especially for someone like Kirin.

"Niko made some terrible decisions, too," Kirin continued. "He was misled, manipulated, and hurt by Leander, but he also hurt people. He was angry. He tried to kill your family, and you, more than once."

"I know," Valia breathed. She leaned her head against Kirin's shoulder and drew strength from his warmth and steadiness. "I'm sorry you have to live with that."

"It's okay," Kirin said. "I can see it now. It's as though I saw through a looking glass before, only able to make out a few far-away details. Now, I can see the whole world. It's as if I'm seeing color for the first time."

Valia's brow furrowed, and she sat up so that she could look at Kirin. He had that peaceful smile on again, and he was looking far beyond her at the trellis of roses above. Valia blinked. A moment ago, they'd been dead, but now a few small buds were filling the air with a soft floral scent. *How strange.* Valia blinked and looked away, turning her focus back to Kirin.

"What do you mean?" she asked. "Niko's memories can't have changed that much for you." *There's something more,* a soft voice told her. *Something isn't right.*

"It's not about the memories." Kirin turned toward her and took her hands. "I feel it now, Valia."

"Feel what?" But already, realization was dawning. She remembered the Kanalean soldiers frozen still in the forest. The way everyone believed and followed Kirin now without thinking twice. The roses blooming overhead in the seventh season nearby. How could she have been so blind? How could she not have seen it?

"The Flora," Kirin said. He smiled that peaceful smile at her. "I didn't feel it when we first casted together, but I do now. I understand what you said about how the Flora is all around us, how the Flora is a force for good." He tilted his head back.

"But Kirin." Valia almost choked on the words. "I'm not so sure the Flora is a force for good anymore. You were the one who made me doubt it."

"I was." That peaceful smile grew again. "But I was wrong, Valia."

"No, I think maybe you were right." Her heart was racing now. "I took off my rings, Kirin." She lifted her hands from his to show her bare fingers. "I listened to you. Now, you need to listen to me."

"I will, Valia." He looked down at her, seeming a little confused by her concern. "I will always listen to you."

"Then listen right now. Is the Flora what let you walk through those Kanalean soldiers so easily?"

"Yes. Don't you see? The Flora saved us time and time again. Perhaps it knew you were turning away, so that's why it awakened in me." He smiled again, and Valia felt sick to her stomach.

"But it was *you* who turned me from it! Kirin, I need to ask. Have you been... manipulating people?" Her heart skipped a beat, and her hands began to shake. She couldn't bring herself to ask if he'd been manipulating her, too, and if that was the reason she hadn't seen this more clearly before when it was right in front of her.

"No," Kirin said firmly. Then a flicker of hesitation broke into his tone. "I don't... no. I haven't. I wouldn't."

But Valia wasn't so sure. Maybe the Flora was compelling people through him, even if he didn't know it. Perhaps it was manipulating *him*. Everything was spiraling out of control. She'd freed herself from the Flora's manipulations, but it was everywhere. Perhaps it had chosen Kirin now, and Valia had reached the end of her usefulness to it. Perhaps he was right, and it had given him the powers she'd given up.

"*Please*, Kirin." Valia's voice almost broke. "I know how it feels to be close to the Flora. I know how wonderful it is to be chosen, to feel that powerful. I *know*. But you must be careful."

"You don't understand... I don't have to be careful anymore." Kirin's brow pinched. "Valia, don't be scared. I'm still me."

"I know." But her chest was still tight. He seemed to be casting without rings, amulets, or any other materials, and she didn't know how. He didn't speak incantations, yet he affected his surroundings floramantically. And he didn't seem worried about that at all.

Kirin stood and pulled her into a tight embrace. Valia softened against him as she heard the now-familiar rhythm of his heartbeat and smelled that forest scent of his. This *was* Kirin. Just Kirin. The man who'd saved her. The man she'd saved. The man she thought she might someday love. She felt herself relaxing, the frenetic fear draining away.

She pulled away from the hug after a few moments and looked up at Kirin.

"The Flora is strong and unpredictable. I see that now, and it's seemed to have chosen you for something. You were right before, Kirin. You can't control anyone. It's wrong. You might not even know you're doing it."

"I understand," Kirin said, squeezing her hands.

"And let me guide you." Even if he was full of floramantic power, Valia could help him. She could get him through this. She could train him to wield the Flora in the right way. And if that failed, she could convince him to give up his power, as she had.

"I will." Kirin smiled at her. "It's okay, Valia. All is as it should be."

"Okay." Valia forced herself to take a deep breath and return his smile. "I trust you." *I just don't trust the Flora anymore*, she thought.

"Soon, the minstrels will sing songs about how we saved the kingdom." Kirin winked and, despite herself, despite the fear that still lurked in her chest, Valia laughed.

"I'll write it myself."

"I'll help." Kirin tucked her hand into the crook of his elbow, and they strolled back toward the palace. Despite the unease in her heart, Valia relaxed into his touch.

Not long ago, she would have been overjoyed that he was a floramancer now, too. She would have imagined all they could do together. Only now, because she'd seen the more dangerous and unpredictable side of the Flora's manipulations, she worried.

"Oh, Valia the Brave," Kirin sang under his breath. "Oh, Kirin the Strong. They journeyed faaaaaaar. They journeyed looooooong."

Valia began to laugh at his terrible singing voice. She was so relieved to see him acting like himself that she wanted to kiss him in that moment. She looked up at him and, distracted, managed to trip over a loose paving stone. Kirin caught her easily and helped her back to her feet.

"Careful, the minstrels won't sing about you if you die on a walking path in the heart of the palace," he joked.

"I suppose not. But they also won't sing about you if you protected me from draevori and bears and bounty hunters but let me die by tripping."

Kirin chuckled. "I suppose not. I'd better get you some light."

"We left the torch inside," Valia reminded him.

"That's alright." He lifted a single finger, and bright white light flickered at the top, shedding light across the garden.

Valia gasped.

"This is just your light spell," Kirin said. "The only difference is that I don't need rings to do it."

"It's not that." Valia's chest tightened. She wanted to grab Kirin by the hand and run as hard and as far as she could. The only reason she didn't was that she knew it wouldn't help.

Look in the sky and look in the sea.

The Flora is anywhere you can be.

"It's... your eyes," Valia said.

"My eyes?" Kirin turned to her, and in the flickering light of the flame, it was clearer than ever.

"They're blue," Valia said. "Deep blue." The deep dark blue of someone so corrupted by magic that there was no turning back. Kirin wasn't just a powerful floramancer now. The Flora was *inside* him, twisted within his very being like a viny, insidious liana. This was the true price for bringing Niko back to before he was corrupted. Kirin belonged to the Flora now.

"Hm." Kirin lifted his hand to his cheek as though hoping to confirm what she'd said. "I suppose they are."

Wearing that peaceful smile, he led her toward the palace as though nothing had happened. As though all was well. As though the Flora wasn't lurking within him, corrupting him, ready to whisper its enigmatic will at any moment.

THANK YOU

You made it all the way to the end! I'm truly honored you spent your time reading my story. This is just the first book in my *Whispers of the Flora* series, and there's so much more coming in the following books. I'm pressing a circle hoping you enjoyed this one at least as much as I enjoyed writing it. It was so much fun to create for you.

If you've got a spare minute or two, would you mind sharing a review? It's one of the very best ways to support authors like me and help others find my work. You can leave one wherever you purchased the book, or at my publisher's website below. Sincerely, THANK YOU!

https://hylosis.pub

ABOUT THE AUTHOR

https://hylosis.pub/pages/author-haley-gallant

Haley Gallant is a writer and English teacher. She lives in Prague with her husband, where she spends her free time reading, running, cooking, and dreaming up new stories while wandering the streets of the old town. Originally from Portland, Oregon, she loves incorporating mystery, romance, and nature into her stories.

Haley has ghostwritten numerous romance and psychology books, as well as several YA novels under the pen name Emily Winters.

ALSO BY HALEY GALLANT

Find the next books in the Whispers of the Flora series soon at Hylosis Publishing or your favorite retailer.

ABOUT THE PUBLISHER

https://hylosis.pub/pages/publishing

Hylosis Publishing is an independent publisher located in Chandler, Arizona. We firmly believe everyone has a story to tell or a unique perspective to share. We are always on the lookout for talented thinkers and storytellers.

Interested in getting published? Apply using the link above.